BLENDING IN

A Magical Romantic Comedy (with a body count)

RJ BLAIN

BLENDING IN
A MAGICAL ROMANTIC COMEDY (WITH A BODY COUNT)
BY R.J. BLAIN

Thanks to a jealous divine, whenever Chase Butler comes anywhere near Miriah, she turns into a chameleon. While her hopes of having a happily ever with Mr. Right are dashed, she's determined to have the next best thing: a perfect Christmas.

Finding a puppy for her son, dodging the unwanted attention of her divine fling of an ex, and keeping on top of a holiday charity drive for local pet shelters sure is complicated when prone to transforming into a twelve-inch lizard with a severe allergy to snowbanks.

Since blending in has gotten her nowhere fast, she's going to have to pull out all the stops to get what she wants, even if it lands her on Santa's naughty list.

Warning: This holiday story contains excessive humor, action, excitement, adventure, magic, romance, and bodies. Proceed with caution.

ONE

To get my son the puppy
he wanted for Christmas,
I needed to keep my job.

As always, when Chase Butler visited Price Financial Industry Solutions, I transformed into a twelve inch long chameleon, which made preparing the afternoon spreadsheets difficult at best. I gave it a week before I lost my job thanks to the CEO of our competitor visiting so often. Scrambling onto my desk, I nosed my trackpad closer to my keyboard. Come hell or high water, I'd finish my work on time.

To get my son the puppy he wanted for Christmas, I needed to keep my job. To keep my job, I needed to get my head out of my rear end and find every last one of Chase Butler's faults so I'd stop my headlong tumble into unrequited love.

If I murdered Gavin, a week-long fling, a divine, and father of my child, would his curse break? How the heck was I supposed to find a man who could love me better than a frisky divine with bed-hopping tendencies when I turned into a blasted chameleon whenever a man I liked came too close?

Chase Butler needed to stop being a handsome, generous man who liked animals immediately if not sooner. Also, he needed to stop challenging my boss and coordinating competitive charity drives. If he gave up his goody-goody tendencies, maybe I'd be able to rein in my admiration.

As usual, my traitor heart refused to listen to me.

I needed to have a long talk with Gavin about his danged curse. A during-work-hours exemption would make my life a lot easier.

Flicking my tongue and using my tail to control the trackpad, I plugged data into my spreadsheet. Whatever made me able to operate touch devices had saved my bacon more than once; had I been more like a natural chameleon, I would've been sunk weeks ago.

My efforts worked well enough, and I enjoyed blending in with my desk, able to work without casual observers noticing me. Unfortunately, everyone in the open workspace knew I had a few quirks and a shapeshifting problem.

My desk neighbor, best friend, sometimes babysitter, and general gossip rolled her chair towards my desk. "You're so damned lucky Alex likes your work, Miriah. Must you do this every damned charity drive?"

Charity drives always landed me in trouble. Without fail, I'd find some man who checked off every one of my boxes for a husband and father of my son. Every year, the story ended the same way.

None of the men I liked could ever see past the chameleon to the woman beneath. Most of them hadn't even noticed my existence.

I tapped on the trackpad, opened a note file, and suggested Tiana should go suck on some goose eggs before I returned to work.

"While I understand Mr. Butler has an ass to kill for, you might be taking this a little too far."

I checked if any of our co-workers were listening in. Fortunately, her comment went unnoticed.

Why couldn't my tactic of ignoring Tiana work for a change? It hadn't done me any good the ten other times the past week Chase had needed something from Alex. In person. I did my best to pretend she didn't exist, working on calculating the charity drive results for the week and the projections for the rest of the event.

Five pet shelters and six homeless shelters running out of supplies and funding had spurred the latest charity blitz, and the holidays helped convince the company's clients to give their brands an ethical boost. When all was said and done, I'd join in the festivities, bringing Caleb home a puppy for Christmas.

Despite my hopeless crush on Chase Butler, my son would get his puppy, and that meant working my reptilian, color-changing butt off to finish my report within the next two hours without the benefit of human hands.

"It's hopeless," Tiana informed me before rolling back to her desk. "Good luck. You're going to need it."

After I returned to human, I'd make a special trip to the salon, get conditioner for dry hair like she usually used, add extra oil, and to be even more helpful, add even more oil of the coconut variety so she smelled delicious, all so I could teach my fro-haired friend an oily lesson. Maybe if she needed to figure out how to get the excess oil out of her uncooperative mane, she'd leave my failed love life alone for a while.

With my luck, I'd actually unlock the secrets of fro hair care.

WITH SEVEN MINUTES TO SPARE, I sent the weekly report to my boss. As Chase seemed determined to stay in the building, I hid under my desk to ride out Gavin's curse.

I wished Tiana would stop laughing at me.

"Where's Miss Cox?" my boss demanded.

My best friend about to turn arch enemy giggled. "She's hanging out under her desk, Alex."

"Again?"

"Did you know chameleons can use a computer surprisingly well?"

"She did the report while shifted, didn't she?"

"She sure did."

My boss sighed. "Fetch her scaly rump and bring her to my office. Mr. Butler wishes to speak to her."

Life ended for everyone, and my cause of death would be embarrassment. Before I could escape, Tiana grabbed me around the middle and carried me to my doom. If I blended in with her dark skin, would Chase notice me?

Probably.

I camouflaged despite the futility and wrapped myself around Tiana's wrist.

"That's not going to work, Miriah."

Nipping her earned my nose a light swat. I hissed and nipped her again.

"I'll rip your tail off, asshole. Go ahead. Try me."

As I needed my tail to work, I kept my teeth to myself.

"You're so damned lucky I pay attention and know how to read your damned spreadsheets, girl. I own you for at least a week for this."

Tomorrow, I'd be grateful for my kind-hearted friend, who always stood ready to jump in and keep me from losing my job yet again. In the meantime, I considered taking leave of my solemn vow not to curse up a storm. I kept close watch over my mouth to keep Caleb from learning bad habits from me, but he was twelve. He could handle his mother dropping a few foul words now and then.

Instead of modifying her conditioner, I'd buy her the flattening iron she kept drooling over and a bottle of tequila for saving my rump again. As Caleb, too wise for his twelve years, would snitch to his father if I had a single sip, I'd watch her drink and dream of the day my son turned eighteen so I could earn the worst hangover of my life.

Gavin loved trying to get me to drink something to unwind, I enjoyed telling him no, and my son took after his father too much for my comfort. Gavin never had understood my poor relationship with alcohol.

I didn't like who I became when drunk, and that was that.

Our boss beat us to his office, held the door open until Tiana stepped through, and closed it behind her. Closed door meetings meant trouble.

A closed door meeting with Chase Butler would test my patience and sanity. With my luck, he'd open his mouth and say something irresistibly glorious, further entrenching himself in my traitor heart.

"I thought Miss Harting was your top marketing guru," Chase Butler stated from his perch on my boss's desk.

He wore a black suit with bright purple tie offset by a cream dress shirt.

"Miss Harting is my top marketing guru," Alex replied, circling his desk and plopping into his oversized leather chair. "Miss Cox is her bracelet. I've found these two ladies work quite well together, so it's been to my company's benefit to encourage their partnership."

Tiana lifted her hand to show me off. "She mouthed off to a divine."

My best friend hated me, and I pondered locating the nearest snowbank. I estimated I'd freeze to death within five minutes. Gavin might be capable of caring for Caleb if I left him a manual before putting myself out of my misery.

"That takes guts," my crush replied. "And how long has Miss Cox been a lizard?"

"A karma chameleon," Tiana chirped.

I gave up trying to be a good example for my son. For the next few weeks, I'd make a point about saying unfavorable things about my best friend, and I wouldn't swallow my words around him. What a bitch.

That would teach her.

Alex choked on his laughter. With a smile I wanted to photograph and immortalize, Chase gave Tiana his full attention. "I appreciate the warning and will endeavor to avoid mouthing off to a divine. May I ask which one?"

"Dunno. She calls her baby daddy Gavin; he won't fess up to his portfolio. For the record, he earned a tongue lashing, and I don't mean the nice kind. He's the baby daddy of six kids, and after making the rounds, he thought he could come back and marry Miriah. Her hell no included a healthy dose of mouthing off. So here we are. She's on job fifty-six due to unintentional shapeshifting and has been a chameleon for maybe two hours so far today."

My boss blinked. "She really did the entire report while shifted?"

"She sure did."

I couldn't tell if Tiana meant to save or lose me my job.

"I'll be damned. All right. Since keyboard use isn't out of the question, we have a few questions about the report."

"I might be able to answer them for you, sir. She's explained how her spreadsheets work before. I often use her data and metrics to monitor campaign performance."

"Good. Set her down. We were wondering about the projection columns. How is she figuring it out so accurately?"

"Math, sir. It's like black magic but worse. Be grateful she can't talk. She might math you to death. Essentially, we run these campaigns the same way every drive. She accounts for current market conditions, the health of the companies contributing, and the current public economic conditions, and then she compares these figures to the past performance of similar campaigns. She then creates the projections from that data."

"Could she do that work for Mr. Butler's company?"

"Any analyst worth their paycheck can."

"Good. Someone in his company has sabotaged his data, and he asked me to loan him a trusted employee to jump fences for a while. I suggested he could borrow Miss Cox for the holidays."

I needed to make a date with the nearest snowbank immediately.

"That's going to be a problem," Tiana whispered.

If she told anyone Chase triggered my transformation, I wouldn't need to find a snowbank. I'd fall over dead from horror.

"If she can do this caliber of work while a chameleon, I see no problems," Chase replied. "I can set up a touchscreen system and anything else she needs to do her work in either form. It's her brains I'm after, not her body. I don't care what shape she is. She can do the work. That's what I need."

He needed to stop saying nice things about me before my heart finished breaking under the strain of my hopeless crush.

"Looks like it's your lucky day, Miriah. You get to work for our competitor for Christmas."

"If you can send me an email with everything you need, I'll have it ready for you by tomorrow morning." Chase pulled out a business card from his wallet and handed it to Tiana. "I'll see you at nine, Miss Cox."

Following a flicked salute to my boss, Chase left.

How the hell was I supposed to work through a curse, especially when the subject of my infatuation refused to act like a jackass?

I was so screwed.

IT TOOK an hour after Chase left for me to return to my human form. It hurt, and had I possessed the right magic, I would've cursed Gavin back in some horrific fashion. While guilty of mouthing off to Gavin, if he hadn't worked me and five other women at the same time, I might've been a little gentler about my hell no.

The divine thought the world of himself.

I'd recognized from the start he was too in love with himself to love me or Caleb like we deserved. On one front, he did well; Gavin didn't show up often, but when he did, he gave Caleb his undivided attention.

When the jackass made his appearance, I bailed so I wouldn't attempt murder.

Each and every time, Gavin insisted on leaving presents and a note begging me to reconsider his proposal. I bet the dead heard my infuriated refusals.

I considered remaining huddled under my desk and hiding for all eternity.

"There's a pop when you shift, Miriah. You can come out." Tiana rolled her chair over. "On a scale of one to ten, you're fucked, babe."

"I'm going to need someone to take me to and from his office," I whispered, hating I wouldn't be able to handle the basics on my own.

I really would die if I made friends with a snowbank.

"I'm on it, girlfriend. I'll get Alex to waive my late penalties and blame him. I'll tell him you're bad off over the holidays. Total truth, too."

"Caleb wants a puppy. I'm going to be eaten by my son's puppy. Or I'll die in a snowbank. That's how my life is going to end, Tiana."

"That's morbid."

"But true."

"It's not like you're usually scaly at home. It'll be fine.

Anyway, Caleb's aces at taking care of you when needed. He's not going to let his puppy eat you."

"On purpose," I corrected.

"It's only for a few weeks. You know how Alex gets. He prefers a challenge, and having you batting for Mr. Butler's team makes it a challenge. The faster you figure out what's going on with his company, the faster you're back to work here. It'll be fine. I'm sure he'll prove he's an insufferable ass within a week. No infatuation, no curse."

"Did you really have to tell them about Gavin?"

"Of course. Alex hates bullies, and he now knows a divine is being a jerk to you while you're doing the single mom thing. It's called job security. I just landed you a lot of it. Merry Christmas. Keep doing your best and he'll keep you. He can be a jerk, but he's not a jerk like that."

"If you tell him why, I really might kill you," I warned.

"While true, you'd miss me. Don't you worry about a thing. Just email the love of your life the list, tell him the curse is always really active this time of year, and enjoy the view—and don't even try to tell me that view didn't start this whole mess."

"Hot and nice needs to be illegal."

"Hot, nice, and rich is just wrong. He probably sucks in the sack."

"Hot, nice, rich, and great in bed is impossible. Just impossible," I confirmed.

"Did Gavin suck in the sack?"

"I refuse to answer that question, but I'll say this much: he wasn't good enough to marry just for the sex."

"Good to know. And Miriah?"

"What?"

"Next time, remember birth control isn't effective when dating divines."

"We weren't dating. We were exploring mutual interests in bed."

"At least you're honest about it."

I rolled my eyes. "My tramp stamp's a fire-breathing dragon, Tiana. No man's seen it, especially not Gavin."

"Go bed a few men you hate. Just confirm they're not divines first. You have a hard enough time handling one boy. You don't need another right now."

"One divine is one divine too many. It's not like there are a lot of them around waiting for a chance to admire my tramp stamp."

"It's not a tramp stamp if you're a goody-goody, babe. Go forth and tramp!"

I sighed and crawled out from beneath my desk. "You're ridiculous."

"I'm more fun than a basket of ferrets. Go home, Miriah. I'll pick you up early, and I'll even make sure Caleb makes it to school."

I'd need to find extra presents to repay Tiana. "Thank you. I owe you one."

"You sure do, but I'll accept juicy gossip about your quest to validate your tramp stamp in exchange."

"I'm swiping left on your generous offer."

"Live a little! That divine didn't bar you from all of life's pleasures. Look on the bright side. Any man who gets past that curse ain't kidding around. No doubt, right?'

"I don't find that comforting right now."

"It's only a few weeks. How bad can it be?"

TWO

Chaos greeted me when I
stepped through the door.

EXPECTING to spend most of December as a chameleon, I headed home to make plans. I couldn't disappoint Caleb; last Christmas, his divine and time-impaired father forgot to visit, and while my son did his best to hide the hurt, I'd caught him crying.

Caleb loved Gavin far more than he deserved, which made the damned curse even harder to swallow.

I tried, but I couldn't be my son's mother and father. Unfortunately, the curse made it difficult to find a step-father for Caleb and did a good job of ensuring I played both roles when Gavin wasn't around, which was most of the time.

Chaos greeted me when I stepped through the door. Despite the two-week rule for Christmas decorations, someone named Caleb was sorting through my ornaments, a tinsel explosion ravaged most of the living room, and a mountain of shining lights overwhelmed my coffee table.

As far as child-created disasters went, I could deal with a holiday-themed mess without losing my temper. My son didn't create messes without a good reason, and nature would run its course within a few hours. His father's divine influence would take hold and manifest as some form of OCD.

If my son couldn't restore the apartment to rights within three or four hours, I'd have an epic temper tantrum and general meltdown on my hands, the kind I'd only resolve through helping him with copious amounts of cleaning and decorating.

It wasn't Caleb's fault he carried a god's genes and tendencies, and despite Gavin's best efforts, everything had a place and purpose, and when something fell out of place, he needed to fix it.

I closed the door behind me, fighting my initial urge to snap at Caleb for breaking the rules. For a twelve-year-old, he rarely broke my rules, and when he did, there was usually a reason for it.

Sometimes, that reason involved him being his father's son.

All I needed to do was rein in my temper long enough to figure out why my son had taken leave of his senses and broke our tradition of decorating the tree two weeks before Christmas.

It took me thinking through the situation twice to find the silver lining: I wouldn't have to test all the damned little LED lights to make sure they met my son's standards, which meant perfection. If one was even slightly too dim, I'd have to replace the entire string. No matter how many times I argued to replace just the one light, he wouldn't hear anything of it.

The entire string would have to go, replaced with a new, perfect one.

The lights needed to be perfect.

Christmas needed to be perfect.

Maybe it would do me a little good to lift my standards to his and care less about how much money I spent satisfying him.

No, I would not allow my frustrations to hurt Caleb. I drew in a breath, held it, and waited until my annoyance bled away to nothing. I exhaled. "Thank you for testing the Christmas lights. What's going on?"

Caleb flashed me a brilliant smile. "Dad's bringing a tree tonight. He felt bad about last year and called asking if we had a tree yet. I told him about your two-week rule because you're worried about live trees catching fire. He promised he'd bring a good tree over tonight, and it won't be a fire risk! He *promised.*"

Every time Gavin came around, my temper flared, boiling beneath my skin and threatening to erupt. Every time I thought we'd settled in his long absences, he showed up and renewed our son's excitement, which made for a difficult few months while Caleb hoped his father would stick around for just a little longer.

Gavin couldn't leave my little family alone, could he? He pulled the same crap with the other mothers and the children he'd created on his spree thirteen years ago, I bet.

"No, I don't," the deep voice of Caleb's father announced behind me.

As was his way, the bastard had managed to open the door without me noticing.

"I should be yelling at you about fire risks for putting the tree up too early, but it seems you've informed our son you have found a magical fire-resistant pine tree."

"Magic, dear Miriah. It won't dry out or catch fire. I know how much trees worry you, so I wouldn't bring a fire hazard into your apartment. Have you given any thought into moving into a house? There's a nice one I've got in mind for you."

Alarm bells went off, and I turned to face the father of our son, planting my hands on my hips. Any other day, I would've been exchanging basic courtesies and running away so they could visit without my bad mood getting in the way.

When Gavin normally mentioned houses, he was the primary part of the picture. It was his house I was moving into, and he always phrased his question in such a way it was clear we knew he hadn't given up on his quest to marry me.

"No, Gavin. I'm sorry my apartment offends you. I'll allow the tree, but I'm going to my bedroom while you two handle it. I've been transferred today, and I need to email my new boss."

Caleb sighed. "Fired again, Mom?"

His assumption stung despite it being justified. "No. Transferred until after Christmas. My boss is helping someone he knows with a business problem. I'm qualified to do the work, so I'm being loaned out. I wasn't fired."

Yet.

"Wow. Good job, Mom!"

Gavin's brows rose. "What he said. I'm impressed, Miriah. It's a new record. Given a few weeks, you'll have held the same job for six entire months."

Why couldn't I smack the smug look off the divine's face? Oh, right. He'd find some way to worsen the curse. To add insult to injury, my son expected me to be fired despite having found some stability at my current job. "No thanks to you, Gavin."

"Maybe if better men interested you, you wouldn't be in your position right now."

"Dad," Caleb protested. "Mom's been doing really well lately. Be nice."

"Why? She won't marry me."

Our son rolled his eyes. "Duh. You're inconsistent. Mom hates that. You'd kill each other within a month. I love you Dad, but you're not good for Mom."

Elation surged through me. "Thank you, Cal. Now, I do have some work to do. You two have fun with the tree. No fires, and make sure you get rid of the strings of old lights that run hot like you promised."

"I boxed them to be thrown out," my son replied.

I smiled, detoured on my way to my bedroom long enough to kiss my son's cheek, and retreated to safety. "Try not to cry over your loss, Gavin."

"You haven't won this yet, Miriah."

Like hell I hadn't. "Whatever you say, Mr. Divine."

"You don't need to be mean," my son's father complained.

"Stop whining, Dad. If Mom was being mean, she'd yell at you to leave. She even stayed home this time. She's being nice."

There really was no hiding anything from my son, was there?

I EMAILED Chase with a list of everything I needed to play corporate spy, and I giggled over my addition of a chameleon-compatible harness with a camera attached. I informed him about the realities of corrupted or modified data; unless the source remained clean of tampering, his numbers might never add up. As I wanted to regain control of my life as quickly as possible, I detailed what sort of information I needed, how I'd use it, and at what points industrious saboteurs might modify the data.

As part of my job, I'd hunt for discrepancies, but I could only do so much unless he provided me with complete financial information and permitted me to do a full evaluation of his business.

To make it clear how much work needed to be done, I wrote up an example spreadsheet, explained the finer points of creating an accurate projection, and left a list of potential candidates behind the discrepancies. At the top of my list was someone within his marketing department, who had the most to lose for poor performance.

I worried tomorrow would test my patience, skills, and luck.

The email ate three hours of time, and the murmur of conversation in the living room warned me that Gavin lingered. I figured his magic warned him whenever his curse activated, and I'd spent an enormous amount of time as a chameleon lately and would continue to do so for the fore-seeable future.

It was only a matter of time before he poked his nose in my business again.

I steeled myself for exposure to the jealous divine and marched into the other room. A tinsel disaster, a half-decorated tree, and a bucket of fried chicken from my favorite waited for me.

If the pair hadn't saved me any, I'd find out if I could strangle an annoying divine.

"Having fun?"

My son ignored me as expected, lost in his work. Every ornament would be hung just right, and he had his ruler out to ensure perfect placement. On a bad day, he cleaned the apartment, measured everything five times, and otherwise drove me to the brink of insanity because nothing ever met his standards. On a good day, like today, he focused his effort on decorating a tree.

Artistic yet perfect.

Gavin smirked. "Have fun working?"

"As a matter of fact, yes." Despite the one-sided nature of it, I'd spent three glorious hours helping Chase.

It suited me very well, and I wouldn't let some jealous divine ruin my good mood.

"We saved you some chicken," he added.

I scratched murdering said jealous divine from my schedule. "Thank you. How long are you sticking around for this time?"

Caleb froze at my question.

"A while."

"You still have that loft near Caleb's school?" To give

credit where credit was due, Gavin kept a property in New York City where he could spend time with Caleb without me underfoot.

"Of course."

Of course. Divines conjured money at their whim. "If you swear to get Caleb to school on time every day and bring him back sometime Christmas morning, go do whatever it is boys do in December without me getting in the way. Morning is a period of time up until noon, not one minute after noon, not exactly noon. Before noon. Caleb, you're responsible for reminding your time-impaired father which day is Christmas."

Caleb's OCD would keep them around for at least six more hours as he wouldn't cut corners to leave earlier unless I took steps to break the cycle. "I'll finish decorating the tree, Caleb, so please leave notes on how you want it decorated this year, and I'll make sure it's done properly."

"You mean it, Mom?" my son squealed.

I wasn't sure which excited him more: going with his father or knowing I'd finish for him to his standards rather than mine.

"I mean it. Can you handle him for a few weeks, Gavin?"

"Will you provide an instruction manual if I require help?" he countered.

"You can call me. You can also ask Caleb. Despite his short stature, he can handle the basics with minimal help."

"You're never going to cut me any slack, are you?"

"No."

"Mom," Caleb complained.

Why were they both complaining at me? I stole the bucket of chicken and checked to see how much the gluttons had left for me. Amazingly, I'd have leftovers tomorrow, and I spied at least three drumsticks demanding my immediate attention. "I'm not even going to be upset if you leave the decorating to me and go get packed."

The instant my words left my mouth, my son bolted for his room.

"You're such a liar," Gavin muttered. "You're going to be sobbing your eyes out the instant we leave."

I grabbed a drumstick and pointed it at the divine. "But I'll do it with fried chicken in hand."

"How classy."

"Just remember the rules, asshole. No teaching him bad habits, he'd better be the happiest young man in New York, and if the cops call me again because you got him into trouble, I will end you."

"You're blowing that out of proportion."

"A police chief came to my house to tell me I had to bail your divine ass out of prison. He laughed at me."

"He was laughing with you until you transformed into a chameleon because of a cute cop. Also, that cop? Total dick. You should be thanking me for the curse for that time."

"I wouldn't have cared if Caleb hadn't witnessed the entirety of that fiasco."

Gavin smirked. "I know something you don't know."

"You know a lot I don't know. You're a god. I'm not."

"You could just agree to marry me, you know. You'd save yourself a lot of hassle. I'll even behave for however long you live."

Remaining loyal for my lifespan wouldn't be too much of a burden for a divine; from what I could tell, Gavin counted his age in millennia. I'd die in a blink of his eye.

I took a bite out of my chicken and arched a brow. Then, solely because I knew it drove him to the brink of insanity, I chewed and chewed and chewed until he started twitching. "While I appreciate your contribution to Caleb's life, you and me are a disaster waiting to happen. You sampled the wares, got bored, and wandered off to sample more wares. Had you only sampled my wares and stuck around like you meant it from the start, you wouldn't be regretting things right now. That's fine. I can handle it. You piss me off most of the time, but I'll never regret having Caleb, and to have Caleb, I needed you. But you're not husband material, Gavin."

"Harsh."

"But true. Treat Caleb right this Christmas, and try to spend some time with your other kids, too. When you bother to show up, you do the dad thing fairly well." I could give him that much.

He tried.

"He'll be safe with me." Something in Gavin's expression darkened, and his blue eyes took on a shadowed, haunted glaze.

"What's wrong?"

Gavin sighed, and the humanity of the sound startled me into narrowing my eyes and looking him over.

Divines rarely showed the remnants of their humanity.

"Gavin?"

"Caleb's the only one of my children left."

People died, children included, and being the child of a divine didn't grant long years or immortality. My heart ached for him. "What happened?"

"It's why I didn't show up last year. My last daughter died a few days before Christmas."

I added my name as a candidate for Asshole of the Year. Trying to imagine a life without Caleb hurt so much I struggled to breathe. "I'm so sorry."

"Icy roads, unexpected storm. Her and her mother died in a car accident." He paused, and he pressed his lips together into a thin line. "Neither suffered."

Some days, I wondered what it would be like to live forever—or at least for a few millennia. But then I remembered a simple, agonizing truth: the divine had rules, and those rules dictated when and how they could meddle in mortal affairs. One day, I might understand how he could curse people like me but couldn't save the lives of his children. "I'm still sorry."

"I can magic a pine tree to never burn, but I can't fight fate. I can't change circumstance. I can't circumvent choice. I can't bring back the dead, and I can't work miracles, not like others can."

"Still. That must be hard."

While the scale differed, I thought I could understand. I raised the child of a god, and Caleb came bundled with more problems than I liked admitting. He was as much my son as Gavin's.

Gavin had OCD tendencies, and I suspected it had something to do with his portfolio. One day, maybe he'd share the truth with me.

"It is. I am always with my children when they die. They didn't know I was there, but I watched over them all the same."

My traitor heart broke for the divine, and while it wouldn't change anything between us, I couldn't ignore what was written between the lines and in the words he wouldn't say.

"You should tell Caleb, Gavin. He's old enough to understand. You'll never be my husband, but I'll work on pretending I don't hate sharing space with you when you come to see him."

It was the best I could offer him without it becoming a lie.

"I'll accept a cranky friendship."

"If you disappoint our son, I'll find some way to make you pay for it. Just to be clear."

"Understand. And just to be clear: I'm not removing the curse. If any man wants to be your husband, he better be worthy."

"I hope you'll accept a very cranky friendship punctuated with murder attempts."

"You wouldn't actually try to kill me. You'll just think about it."

"Often."

"I wish you luck finding a man capable of loving a woman who turns into a lizard in his presence. You'll need it."

"Not all men are sex-driven freaks like you."

"You're being mean again."

"But honest."

"But honest," he conceded. "Hey, Miriah?"

"What?"

"Are you ever going to show me that tattoo you keep taunting me with?"

"Not a chance in hell, Gavin." I checked to make certain Caleb was still in his room. "Only he who breaks my curse gets to verify my tramp stamp, and he who placed the curse never gets to see it. You're just going to have to wonder."

"I could cheat if I really wanted."

"You could, but it would be an empty victory. No tramp stamp for you."

"I'm not sure if I'm the right person to tell you this, but I don't really think it's a tramp stamp if you're not a tramp, Miriah."

"You're the second person to tell me that today. Technically, it's a tramp stamp because of its location, but unless you're getting a piece of this, you're not seeing it, so you'll just have to wonder. When I get this tramp stamp properly verified, I'll do the tramp part of it justice, just you wait and see."

Gavin chuckled. "You'd make a terrible tramp, Miriah. Anyway, this might make you feel better about things. It's not a curse. It's an insurance policy. Only a good man gets to call Caleb his son. And never fear. I'll demand my visits as always."

Jerk divine. "You're putting the cart before the horse again."

"I just refuse to underestimate you. You told me no."

"I enjoy it."

"Just don't cry on your chicken when we leave."

Caleb barreled out of his room, paused long enough to kiss my cheek, and plowed into his father. "Hurry up. We need to get out of here before she changes her mind."

"I left your present in the kitchen, Miriah. We'll see you Christmas morning, which will be no later than a minute before noon."

"Call me, Caleb," I ordered.

"Every night before bed," he promised.

I loved my little liar of a son. He might call me. Maybe. "No trouble, and no cops."

Gavin grinned. "I'll try, but no promises."

I rolled my eyes and evicted the pair from my apartment. As I lived to defy the divine, I sat on my couch and cried while eating my favorite fried chicken.

THREE

I know you like Prince Charming, but it's hopeless.

I DRESSED my best for my date with disaster, and the instant Tiana approached the office building where Chase worked, I transformed into a chameleon.

"Your curse range is getting broader, I see. That'll be trouble. At least the baby daddy has your kid until Christmas. You can get the real work done after Prince Charming leaves the office. He's gotta be like Alex. He's only around for half the day and doing whatever it is hotshot CEOs do when they're not in the office. Fortunately, I'm well prepared. Alex gave me his parking pass for this joint until you're done fixing your Prince Charming's numbers. Don't ask me why Alex has a parking pass. Alex glared at me when I asked. Obviously, it's not to be discussed. Ever."

I thought it was odd Alex had a parking pass for the building, too. I added Tiana needing to have a parking pass for the building to Gavin's list of sins. Without him, I'd be the one with the parking pass.

"You're totally jealous. You've turned green. I know you like Prince Charming, but it's hopeless. You may as well just marry the damned god stalking you. He's gotten better in the loyalty department."

I hissed at my friend and opened my mouth so she could see my teeny tiny teeth.

"Or not. You wouldn't be cursed any more. Give me a break, Miriah. He'd obviously remove the curse if he was the target of your affections. Probably. Then again, he was stupid enough to cheat on you in the first place."

While true, I couldn't imagine myself loving Caleb's father. I doubted I'd handle a cranky relationship with him well, but I'd try.

To vent my general frustration with the situation, I crawled across the console and gnawed on Tiana's seatbelt.

"I should get mad at you, but I don't want to be bitten. Maybe you'll get lucky this time. Prince Charming hasn't run off yet. That might count as a miracle."

Tiana pulled into an underground garage and parked in a reserved spot, hung a plastic tag from her mirror, and scooped me up, placing me on her shoulder. "Maybe if he kisses your scaly nose, he'll break the curse."

While Gavin would do something like that, I had my doubts. A kiss seemed too easy.

"Anyway, you'll be fine. Alex will get cranky if Prince Charming hurts you, and while rivals, they're also friends. In addition to this, the charity drive is important to both of them. Relax. Do your job. You'll ace this and come back to work in no time."

Doing my work might distract me from the recent developments in my life. Caleb being with his father until

Christmas unnerved me. On the bright side, I wouldn't have to work hard to hide Caleb's presents for a change. Even better, I'd have all the time in the world to plan the perfect Christmas.

My life was a mess, but Christmas would be perfect.

Tiana locked her car and carried me into the building. The security guards in the lobby stared at us until Tiana waved an orange pass at them. Without caring if they scrutinized her, she strolled down a hallway lined with elevators. "This building has a fancy elevator. You need this pass to go to the top floor. There's a secret staircase, too. The pass will let you access it."

My friend swiped the card against a silvery panel which summoned the elevator. Inside, bright, spotless mirrors reflected our image, and I camouflaged and hid beneath Tiana's hair.

"You're a goof, Miriah. They're mirrors. They're not going to hurt you. And no matter what you think, you're pretty for a lizard. It could be worse."

Sure. I could've transformed into a slug.

The elevator zipped to the top floor and opened to a reception, the marble floors polished to a blinding shine. Tiana marched to the oversized mahogany desk and engaged the pretty blonde behind it in a staring contest.

Tiana must have been to Chase's office before, because the two women glared with far more heat than strangers meeting for the first time.

Tiana won; the receptionist sighed and asked, "How can I help you?"

"Tiana Harting to see Mr. Butler, please. He's expecting me."

The receptionist's scowl deepened at the mention of Chase expecting Tiana, which likely cut off her easy way of being a jerk. No matter how many times I witnessed Tiana facing off against executives, their haughty receptionists, and society in general, it never failed to make me uneasy.

When human, I could stand firm with my long-time friend.

I ignored my urge to hiss at the receptionist. If Tiana wanted my help, she'd ask for it. Until she asked for it, all interfering would do was annoy her.

The staring contest resumed, but after an uncomfortable wait, the receptionist managed to smother her scowl and forced a smile. She rose from her seat and gestured to a door behind her desk. "This way, please."

The receptionist led us through a maze of cubicles and hallways to a pair of wooden doors. After knocking twice, she entered. "Mr. Butler, Miss Harting is here to see you."

"Thank you, Denise. Please let her in. Until she leaves, I'm not to be disturbed."

"Yes, sir." The receptionist fled, which intrigued me.

Chase waited for the woman to leave before striding over and closing the door behind her. He rolled his eyes so hard I worried he'd faint or hurt himself. "I apologize, Miss Harting. Can I call you Tiana? Please call me Chase. I've got enough boot lickers around here."

Tiana laughed. "You must've told Miriah to call you Chase; she's the only one in our office who does. I'd been wondering about that."

"Well, the few times I've met with her while she's been human, yes. Of course." Chase returned to his desk, trailing his hand along the polished surface. "I opened an office for

Miss Cox on this floor. I suspect the person sabotaging my data is working within my marketing department, although there are some other potential candidates. Poor work performance is grounds for firing here, but it takes a lot for me to fire someone, even accounting for poor work performance. I give everyone a chance to improve. Corporate sabotage is an instant firing offense without warning or notice. As such, putting Miss Cox on this floor will give her an opportunity to observe the potential culprits with ease."

"She likes being called Miriah," Tiana announced.

Sometimes, I hated my friend. Other times, I adored her.

Chase's chuckle captured my attention. "I'm aware, but I'm trying to be polite, especially as it seems she's hiding in your hair."

"She has a mirror complex. Karma chameleons are easily startled. Also, don't even think about biting me, Miriah."

I tucked my tail close so I wouldn't lose it.

"Anyway, until the culprits are identified and I have proof of wrongdoing, pretend everyone is guilty. Several employees across multiple departments have access to the data. My primary systems administrator is creating a database from the unaltered server logs; it should be pristine, original data untouched by anyone. I've been told I should have it by the end of the day if nothing goes wrong. Unfortunately, we'll need to manually retrieve some of the data from outside sources. I should have that data in raw form tomorrow."

Tiana frowned and rested her hands on her hips. "How are you getting the raw data?"

"The companies send us statistics. I either have the login information or the original files from the mail server."

"That should work." Tiana plucked me off her shoulder and placed me on Chase's desk. "Feeding her lunch is your responsibility. She'll eat just about anything, but karma chameleons aren't restricted to natural chameleon diets. If you try to feed her insects, she will bite you. She'll try to claw you, too. She gets downright vicious if an insect is brought anywhere near her. Her favorite food is fried chicken, but she won't say no to salad and healthier foods. It's unlikely she'll return to human during daylight hours. This time of year is the worst for her."

Chase held most of the responsibility for my inability to return to human, although I assigned myself some blame for mouthing off to Gavin in the first place. To reclaim my humanity, I'd need to find Chase's fatal flaw, roll around in my misery for a while, and accept he was like every other attractive man who'd crossed my path.

"What can you tell me about this divine?"

Tiana snorted, shook her head, and perched on the edge of Chase's desk. "He's protective, jealous, and a bed hopper. She's loyal to her man of the hour, hates cheaters, and has one focus in her life: her son. Frankly, I'm amazed she let Caleb go with Gavin. I suppose she wanted him to have the best Christmas possible, and he doesn't get a lot of time with his father because he's not usually around. Anyway, Miriah refuses to marry him, and he doesn't think any other man is worthy of her. Whenever the human species gets lovey-dovey, she sprouts scales. Christmas and Valentine's are the bad ones."

"How charming of him."

"For a one-time fling, sure. Husband material, however, he is not." Tiana waved her hand. "In that department, he's junk, and my girl here has her head on straight. That's what got her cursed, actually. She told him he was shitty husband material to his face."

"Very gutsy of you, Miriah. I'll endeavor to make your time here as pleasant as possible. I've had the temperature in your office raised to seventy-eight degrees. There's also a heated blanket set to eighty-five available if you get chilly. I also took the liberty of installing a jam so your door can't fully close until you've finished your work here. That'll make sure you don't get stuck."

Tiana reached over and poked me. "Wasn't that nice of Chase? He made you a special chameleon-friendly office. If you don't need anything else from me, I'll be back at five to pick you up."

"I can handle things from here, Tiana. Thank you." Chase reached across his desk to shake hands with my friend. "I appreciate you bringing her here this morning."

"Glad to help. Call me if you need anything or have any questions."

"Will do." Chase waited until Tiana bounced out of his office to chuckle. "Your friend is quite enthusiastic."

That she was.

"Before I take you to your office, I want to give you a virtual introduction to the individuals behind the falsified data." Chase settled in his high-backed leather chair and pulled a tablet from a locked drawer. I skittered across the polished wood to peek at the screen.

The faces of seven women and nine men greeted me. With sixteen candidates to deal with, I needed to keep a close eye on everything I did. If I became human in his office, I'd have to pay attention to my every word. I pointed at the first in the lineup, an older woman with dark eyes and a weary smile.

"Miss Hefner is the company's Event Coordinator. She's been with us for three years. The issues seem to have started in January following the charity drive last Christmas."

I found that odd. Why would someone start sabotaging the company after the charity drive rather than during it? Then again, when I'd been hired by Alex, I'd spent the first month of my employment evaluating the company's charity drive performances in preparation for future events.

After evaluating the charity drives, I had worked on evaluating general campaigns to get a feel for how special drives should perform.

Why would the culprit wait until after the easiest opportunity to cause Chase's company trouble?

One by one, Chase described his suspected employees, offering his opinions on why each might adjust performance numbers. Two candidates worked in technical fields, which caught my attention, especially when he revealed their personal relationships with women in the marketing department.

Using a text editor, I asked about his company's upper management; beyond his Event Coordinator, none of the upper management had made his list.

"That's a tough question. It's not outside the realm of the impossible, but I don't understand what their motives might be. Most of them have been employed since my father was in charge of the company. My CFO might have motive, but like the others, he worked for my father and has been with the company for over forty years. He'll retire soon. Screwing up the financial numbers doesn't help him. He'd lose a lot sabotaging us."

After he finished giving me the breakdown of his company and the potential culprits, I thought about it. Personal grudges happened, but I wasn't quite ready to suggest that as a motive. Sometime after solving Chase's data mystery with my analytical skills, I needed to tell my boss I sucked at catching people red-handed. My son served as living proof of my failings as a culprit catcher.

Damn it. I still needed to decorate the tree. If I screwed up any of the measurements, I'd be the one to blame for ruining Christmas entirely.

Remembering my promise to give Caleb the perfect Christmas, I forced my attention back to my task, determined to find the culprit so I could return to my real job—and my human form.

MY OFFICE WAS LOCATED three doors down from Chase's, and a chameleon paradise waited for me. A smaller keyboard with separated numeric pad would make typing easier, and I'd do my work from a heated nest. The small display amused me, but I appreciated it, too. Larger screens made my head hurt.

Obviously, I needed to work at Chase's company when stuck as a chameleon for the rest of my life.

On second thought, I needed to hurry up and find Chase's dark, dirty secret so I could get on with life—as a human. One day, maybe, I'd stop falling for men utterly out of my league.

With my crap luck, Chase was married with children.

Chase brought me a tablet, a key card small enough I could use it if I could reach the pads, and a two-way pager. With a few button presses, I could reach him if needed.

I made it my mission to not need a single damned thing until I figured out what was going on at Chase's company and why. As little exposure to him as possible might help.

Damn Gavin and his stupid curse. I hoped Caleb pulled out all the stops and drove his father crazy until Christmas. Then we'd both enjoy having plummeted right off into the deep end in equal measure.

I began with an audit of the incorrect spreadsheets to familiarize myself with their system and numbers. A horror show of calculations promised migraines in my future, and the jerk responsible for the formulas deserved a trip to hell without the benefit of a hand basket.

If it turned out poorly written formulas held the blame, I'd karma chameleon some marketer's ass for overcomplicating my life. At the rate I was going, Gavin would need to bail me out of prison.

Prison seemed preferable to correcting blatant incompetence.

As I refused to be defeated by a damned spreadsheet, I went to work. Within ten minutes, I gave in to the inevitable: I needed to rebuild the damned spreadsheet from scratch. Within an hour, I caved to reality.

The next few weeks of my life would suck even worse than Gavin's curse.

It would take a lot of work to locate the silver lining in my cloud, but I'd do my best.

FOUR

Merry Christmas to me.

SOMEONE WANTED TO KILL ME, and a glass of ice water almost accomplished the deed. Frigid liquid tossed onto a chameleon needed to be made illegal. The glass cracked into me, smacked me into the monitor, and knocked my lizard lights out.

Torpor sucked as did the unpleasant process of emerging from it. Concussion-induced headaches came a close second. Until I warmed, I tended to function on auto-pilot while seeking the nearest warmest object.

The object proved to be Chase Butler, and the warmth was his naked chest, as he'd decided to stuff me into his shirt.

Merry Christmas to me. I forgave the glass-lobbing asshole on grounds of having a once-in-a-lifetime chance to snuggle with one of my crushes.

He smelled like vanilla.

"Do you think this will actually work?"

Chase peeked into his shirt, and he startled a hiss out of me.

"I take that back. Never mind. She's hissing at me. What do I do now?"

Tiana's giggle from somewhere nearby promised I'd never live down the day someone had chucked a glass at me. "Wait until she comes out on her own. She's bitchy during torpor. She's usually gentle, but her nips can hurt. You said you found her with a broken glass?"

"And ice. She was cold when I got to her."

"Torpor. She can't warm herself up. But ice? That means someone did it on purpose. When she wants water, I give it to her in a shallow bowl or saucer. She'll email or text me and hiss until someone figures out she needs help. She likes her water warm when she's a lounge lizard. Was she cut?"

"Fortunately not, but her monitor and electronics were trashed. I think the glass broke after it bounced her into the screen, but that's only a guess."

"Well, I have no doubt someone doesn't want Miriah to learn who is behind your discrepancy. You should move her into your office. Do you want me to come over to help take care of her?"

"No, I can handle this. I'll need to know where she lives so I can take her home." Something about Chase's tone promised he refused to compromise.

"I don't have a spare key, and until she transforms again, she can't access hers. Her son is with his father, so why don't you take her home with you? There's one issue, though. She's been planning to volunteer at one of the shelters."

"That's not a problem at all. Do you know which shelter?"

"I'll forward her email to you. It has her volunteer schedule in it, but there's an issue."

"What issue?"

"She's planning on adopting a dog for her son for Christmas."

Maybe Tiana enjoyed yanking my chain whenever possible and drove me to the brink of insanity, but she understood what mattered.

It was a good thing chameleons couldn't cry, or I'd bawl and humiliate myself in front of Chase.

"That's going to be hard while she's stuck as a chameleon, Tiana." Chase clucked his tongue. "I'll figure something out."

"Expect escape attempts. She'll try to find a way. By herself."

"While a chameleon?" Chase blurted.

"I never said it made sense, but she takes her boy's Christmas seriously, and she planned on getting him a dog."

As always, I couldn't tell if Tiana helped or hindered, but from that moment, I decided to enjoy my warm location in Chase's shirt. I'd—maybe, eventually—ask her what she thought she was doing. I could thank her and yell at her at the same time for making my Christmas plans more difficult.

"All right. So, she'll need help with her shelter work and finding a dog for her son. I can work with that. Anything else I should know?"

"She gets cranky when startled awake, frustrated when she can't talk, and eats a lot while a chameleon. Fried chicken calms her. It's her favorite, but it's special occasion food because the kind she likes is expensive."

"What kind?"

"There's a Ma and Pa joint near her house. Why don't I

meet you there after work? I'll try to get a key for her place, but I wouldn't leave her alone if someone's already started throwing things at her just for evaluating statistics."

"I wasn't planning on it."

"I'll email you with the address."

"Perfect. Thank you for your help, Tiana."

I wiggled, poking my head up to peek out of Chase's shirt. He reached across his desk and pressed a button on his phone. "You've been taking a glass-induced nap for three hours."

Ouch. I'd spent three hours unconscious in Chase's shirt, cuddled against his warm, smooth chest?

I didn't like someone smacking me with a glass full of ice and water, but I clung to my new favorite silver lining: Chase's perfect chest.

A chilly, wet lizard couldn't have been comfortable for him. Careful to avoid scratching him, I climbed to his shoulder. Before I could settle, Chase picked me up and placed me on the electric blanket folded on his desk. Heat seeped into me, and I plopped, stretched out, and basked in the warmth.

He stroked a finger along the length of my back. "Your job for the rest of the day is to rest. I'll work to figure out who threw a glass at you and why. I can guess as to the why: word of your presence spread, and someone told someone else why you're here. There are only three people who knew you'd be here starting today, and only one is aware of your species. I'd asked for confidence. Everyone will learn soon enough this is unacceptable."

As I didn't want to be the target of Chase's displeasure, I made a mental note to avoid betraying his confidence. Without a task to do, my head throbbing from a close encounter of the glass kind, and no desire to stir Chase's ire, I took a nap.

CHASE'S IDEA of lizard sitting involved taking me everywhere he went, even the men's bathroom, which was a lot cleaner and nicer than I expected. I hung out at the top of the stall and covered my eyes.

While tempted to peek, I behaved.

Long after normal people ate lunch, he ordered delivery. The lack of fried chicken saddened me, but he shared his Chinese without complaint, bringing me a plate and cutting mine into bite-sized pieces.

Lazing about annoyed me, and I took my temper out on my food rather than Chase's hand. Normally, I would've nipped Tiana and run the high risk of losing my tail to her wrath.

A steady stream of people invaded Chase's office, and I observed from the heated blanket, matching the gray of the blanket while fighting the urge to hiss. Most stared, likely wondering why their boss had a lizard on his desk.

One girl screamed and ran away, returning a few minutes later to continue the conversation from the doorway.

Determined to stay on Chase's good side, I feigned sleep whenever I wasn't dodging my headache through actual naps. The warm blanket helped. All wise lizards napped when opportunity—and a good heat source—knocked.

Sometime after six, Chase put his work away and poked me in the ribs. "Ready to go?"

No. I would never be ready to leave my warm, cozy nest.

To indicate I would, with minimal fuss and protest, I stood and stretched. He picked me up and placed me on his shoulder. "You'll have to ride in my jacket when we get to the restaurant."

How terribly tragic. Coping would test me.

Not.

The office seemed empty, but an older, gray-haired man sat at the receptionist's desk fiddling with his phone. "You're leaving earlier than I expected."

"Going to get dinner for Miss Cox and take her to a doctor's appointment," Chase replied, halting beside the mahogany desk.

"Harvey called to say you'd be stopping by his place."

Chase plucked me from his shoulder and handed me over to the man. "I want to do a round of the office, and I'd rather leave her here if I run into any trouble."

"Sure. If you do find any proof who caused you problems today, hold your temper."

"If I find proof, I'm calling the police."

I hissed at the thought of anyone calling the police about someone throwing a glass at me.

Chase arched a brow and stared me in the eyes. "I already called them, Miriah. Dispatch was the one who suggested I stuff you into my shirt to warm you up. You were still out when they were here, and as you seemed to be alive and comfortable where you were, they instructed me to keep an eye on you. I only called Tiana because it'd been three hours and I was getting worried."

Damn. I sighed and bowed my head.

"I'm sorry for embarrassing you, but I need the paper trail."

I understood. As I understood, I cooperated with Chase's wishes, wrapping myself around the older man's wrist, careful of my claws.

"Go do your round and satisfy yourself. I'll keep a close eye on her."

"Thanks."

After Chase vanished through the door, my new lizard sitter lifted his arm. "You're interesting. It's not like Chase to willingly keep company with a woman. It's definitely not like him to take work home with him. Well, the kind of work capable of talking back."

I hissed and added a few soft clicks and growls to the mix, although the effort made my throat ache.

Normal chameleons could barely handle hissing.

"In English."

Foiled.

"He's paranoid at times, and for him to leave you with me, he's not taking any chances—again, a little unusual. He tends to meddle with more subtlety."

Interesting. I wondered who the old man was, settling on a family member of some sort—or the CFO Chase had mentioned. Leaning back in the chair, my lizard sitter used his phone and ignored me.

I contemplated making an escape to discover how Chase would react. If the walls weren't too smooth, I could climb to the ceiling out of reach.

Chase returned while I contemplated the best way to dodge my lizard sitter. He picked me up and returned me to his shoulder. "No trouble?"

"Only an idiot would start something with me. It's been a long time since I've gotten to put someone in timeout."

"No."

"Would you please stop ruining my fun?"

"No, Dad. You're not putting any of my employees in timeout."

"I really don't see why not."

"Unless you're restraining someone posing a risk to someone else's safety, keep your magic to yourself."

I had no idea what they meant by timeout, but I'd had enough of magic for one lifetime, and I hissed my dismay that the pair could use offensive powers.

They ignored my complaints.

"You're being unreasonable about this. I visited to help."

"You visited because you like to annoy me, you're not convinced I can do your job, and you're bored. If you're tired of retirement, get a hobby that doesn't involve pestering me at work."

Chase's father pouted. "You're being unreasonable."

"Get out of my office, Dad."

"How rude."

"Don't make me deactivate your pass."

"You wouldn't do that to your old man."

"I really would. Are you convinced I'm hale and hearty yet?"

"I'm thinking I should tag along for a while just to be certain."

For the first time in my cursed life, I was grateful to be a chameleon. Laughing at Chase wouldn't earn me anything, but the father and son seemed so normal. And funny.

I missed normal. My parents did normal well enough for resolute Catholics clinging to the hope magic would disappear. Add in my status as a single mother, and I made Christmas Eve Mass entertaining for the resident gossips.

Caleb enjoyed attending Mass. The ritualistic structure appealed to him.

"Please don't," Chase begged.

I wished Chase well. I recognized the tone Chase's father used. I used it when I refused to change my mind.

"If anyone tries to hurt your lizard again, I can put them in timeout. I'll enjoy it."

"First, she's an employee of Price Financial Industry Solutions. Second, she's a woman. Her name is Miriah Cox. Third, I won't say no if you decide to visit during working hours until Miss Cox is finished with her work. She'll be sharing my office starting tomorrow."

"That should limit potential incidents."

"That's the idea. It also confirms someone modified the data."

"But who?"

"I'm hoping Miriah can help us figure that out."

"I could figure it out."

Chase sighed and shook his head. "No, Dad. You may not put any of my employees in timeout and interrogate them without just cause. Where's Mom?"

"Preparing an ambush in case I don't report to her with satisfactory news."

If Chase kept sighing, I worried he'd break something in his brain. "Can't you take anything seriously?"

"No. I'm too damned old for that shit. So, where are we going?"

"To eat fried chicken. You'll hate it."

"I refuse to listen to your lies and blasphemy."
"Don't whine later that I didn't warn you."

FIVE

You always get into so much trouble.

CHASE'S SOLUTION to protecting me from the winter chill involved his jacket and chest, and whoever had thrown a glass at me took a temporary top spot as my favorite enemy. I kept warm and cozy for the hike between Chase's car, a surprisingly sensible albeit luxury family car painted red, and the restaurant. Once inside, I gripped the collar of his coat and poked my head out.

"Mom!" Caleb pounced, plucking me out of Chase's coat. "You always get into so much trouble. Sorry, mister! She really doesn't like the cold. I'm Caleb. This is Miss Tiana, and this is my dad."

The inevitable ruination of my outing strolled over and eyed Chase. "I'm Gavin. Who, exactly, are you?"

So much for divines knowing everything. I stuck my tongue out at Caleb's father and added a hiss for good measure. An unrepentant Tiana waved from a table near the swinging kitchen doors.

No matter how I looked at the situation, my life was over. I'd either die of embarrassment, Chase would pick a fight with Gavin because that's what men did when given an opportunity and a motive, and my son would witness it all, learning bad habits I'd be hard-pressed to change.

"You're the one who cursed Miriah." According to Chase's tone, the temperature in the restaurant should've dropped by twenty degrees. "I'm holding you partially responsible for the current situation. She was fortunate. That may not be the case if there's another incident."

I reached for Tiana to rescue me from hell. My son tightened his hold to keep me from wiggling off.

My best and worst frenemy refused, grinning from ear to ear while shaking her head.

"I am," Gavin confirmed.

Jerk divine. Since I wasn't escaping from my son, I hissed at Gavin to make it known I still hated him.

Caleb cradled me against his chest and ignored my temper tantrum. "Dad just doesn't want Mom to like someone stupid. She has malfunctions."

Yep, Gavin had been teaching Caleb bad habits. To be fair, I supposed a tendency to have crushes over bad boys with few redeeming qualities counted.

"Yes, it does," Gavin confirmed, arching a brow and staring at me. "Maybe if you did things logically, you wouldn't be in your current situation. Alternatively, you could just agree to marry me."

Technically, chameleons didn't have thumbs; bilateral hands made for climbing could still manage a thumb down with some work. I regretted my lack of a middle finger, as I would've enjoyed flipping him off.

In the grand scheme, teaching my son one extra bad habit wouldn't hurt much.

My son sighed and rolled his eyes. "We've talked about this already, Dad. You're no good for Mom, either."

"That's not at all fair. I'm totally good enough for your mother. I'm a god."

"And?"

Ouch. Caleb's tone implied he was less than impressed with his father. He carried me to the corner table and set me down beside Tiana. "I'm sorry my dad's annoying, Miss Tiana."

"He's fine this time. He's just worried about your mom in his twisted way. Come sit, Chase. Who's that with you?"

"My father. If you ignore him, he might go away. After dinner, I have an appointment with our family doctor for Miriah. I want to make sure nothing's wrong. As far as I can tell, she's fine. She spent most of the day basking on my desk."

"Mom loves basking, but she's going to be upset if she falls behind on work. Really upset. Like more upset than if I reorganize the apartment without telling her I'm going to do it first. It's not my fault she doesn't understand where things should go."

Chase took the seat nearest to me, and I liked how he ignored Gavin's presence. "Your mother has nothing to worry about. She's already confirmed a few invaluable things for me. Thank you for the invitation, Tiana."

"Not a problem. How was Miriah the rest of the afternoon?"

"She seemed to like the nest I'd made for her."

I wondered if Chase meant in his shirt or on his desk. I'd liked both, but in his shirt had been my favorite of the two.

"Cranky, cold lizards like warm places. I got the key for you, but Gavin insisted on tagging along and being annoying. He claims he wants to check on her in person."

At the rate everyone kept rolling their eyes, they'd develop headaches.

Chase relaxed in his seat, and while most of his attention stayed on Tiana, I caught him sneaking peeks at me. "She seems fine now. Someone threw a glass of water and ice at her. While she got cold, I think she escaped generally unscathed. I'm handling the matter personally."

I expected Gavin to protest or complain, but he took a seat on the other side of the table and nodded. "I trust you won't permit something like that to happen again."

"She'll be working in my office and generally staying with me until the culprit is identified. The doorway of my office is always monitored, so she should be safe even if I'm not with her, which won't be often."

"That should suffice."

I gaped at Gavin. Alien? Imposter? Inflicted with some form of mental illness? Under the influence of an odd drug? The Gavin I knew never cooperated with anyone I liked.

Gavin arched a brow. "No to all of that, Miriah. Really. I'm not that bad."

Like hell he wasn't. Damned, nosy mind-reading divine.

"That part is true."

Caleb sighed. "Dad, be nice. I'm sorry. Dad picks out Mom's surface thoughts when she's a chameleon. He'll translate if needed."

"She's just giving me a piece of her mind as usual. It's nothing to worry about," Gavin reported.

"If you'd stop annoying her, she'd stop lecturing you." Caleb grabbed the menu and offered it to Chase. "You want the quarter chicken special unless you eat like a horse. Mom eats like two horses, so she gets the whole bird."

Chase arched a brow, and his mouth twitched. He lost the war, grinned, and accepted the menu from my son. "Thank you, Caleb. I'll order for her. Thank you for telling me what she likes."

"She probably won't eat it all," my son confessed. "She really likes the chicken here, so she wants leftovers to take home. She'll eat more than usual today, though. The transformations really tire her out."

I had the best son, and I even gave Gavin some credit for how Caleb had turned out.

"Just get a bucket to go," Gavin suggested.

For that suggestion, I'd cut off a day of being cranky at the divine for cursing me in the first place.

Chase fought his smile, finally won, and nodded. "Consider it done."

I almost pitied Chase's wallet—almost. If he got a bucket every day, he might run out of money one day. Maybe.

Gavin burst into laughter. "No, Miriah. If all it takes to make you happy is chicken, I can promise a lifetime supply if you marry me."

"No, Dad. Leave Mom alone. Can't we have one family dinner without you trying to provoke her?"

"It's not my fault she's obsessed with the chicken here."

"But it is your fault she's a chameleon right now."

"Actually, it's—"

I lunged for Gavin's face, hissed, and did my best to scratch out his tongue so he wouldn't betray my secret.

TO KEEP me from trying to kill his father, Caleb caged me in an overturned but unfortunately empty bucket and stacked something heavy on top. With tween ingenuity, he cut a slit in the cardboard so I could watch some of the goings on at the table. When I didn't hiss, my evil captor of a son fed me chicken while Gavin laughed.

"I'm sorry, Mr. Chase. Mom and Dad aren't very good at sharing space together, and Mom gets moody when she's cold."

"She's not cold," Gavin muttered.

"Divine magic, I presume?" Chase hummed a few notes of some slow song I didn't recognize. "As long as she doesn't get cold."

If I could ride in Chase's shirt again, I had no problems with getting cold.

Gavin's snicker confirmed the dastardly divine was listening in on my thoughts again.

Someone offered a steaming piece of chicken through the slot in my prison, and I snapped my teeth, growling when my torturer didn't relinquish it. I grabbed hold with my claws and pulled.

"She's surprisingly strong," Chase observed.

Well, then. If he didn't want to let my dinner go, I'd just have to eat out of his hand. I tore at the meat, swallowing whenever I tore off a piece of my prize. When finished, I thumped the bucket in demand.

"Mom, don't be rude."

"I'm thinking she's justified," Chase admitted. "I didn't let it go."

I smacked the bucket again and waited for more chicken to appear. The game of tug of war resumed. When Chase refused to give me my dinner, I landed a nip and managed to claim my meat before he escaped my reach.

"She's made a rule," Gavin reported. "It's her point if she lands a nip, yours if you escape."

"This game seems a little more dangerous than a minute ago. Those little teeth hurt." Chase offered another piece of meat, and I attacked from the side, chomping the tip of his finger in my rush to claim my meal. He yelped and dropped the chicken.

I took it to the other side of the bucket and hissed.

My chicken.

"Mom! Be nice. I'm so sorry, Mr. Chase. I don't know what's gotten into her today."

"Let this be a life lesson for you, Caleb," Chase replied. "Women are always dangerous, and perhaps I shouldn't tease your mother when she's hungry in the future."

Another piece appeared in the opening, and I darted forward to grab it, dragging it to my other prize.

"Give her a few minutes to eat that," Gavin suggested. "While she's in your care, there are a few things you should be aware of. Most importantly, she'll never shift if there isn't sufficient space for her human form."

Huh. I hadn't known that, but I approved. I'd always wondered what would happen if I'd shifted in a small space. For the first few weeks of the curse, I'd suffered from nightmares about melding with the nearest solid surface, resulting in a quick but messy death.

"Second, she needs to eat a human diet in human quantity —perhaps a little higher than human quantity. She's still human. The magic merely alters her anatomy. The cold isn't as much of a danger to her as it is in natural lizards, but she will hibernate until she warms up. Despite her opinions on snowbanks, falling into one won't actually kill her. She'll just be very unhappy and easy prey for someone. She's much more durable than a natural chameleon."

Tiana snickered. "Karma chameleons make great starter pets."

I loved my bitch of a friend, but I wanted to bite her. Hard.

"Third, her belongings transform with her. If you want to be able to access her phone or keys, make sure she's not carrying them before becoming a chameleon again."

"She'll return to human, then? This isn't a permanent condition?"

"It's not a permanent condition," Gavin confirmed.

It wasn't? Since when?

Someone poked the bucket. "Consider this an early Christmas present, Miriah. You'll shift back to human when you're doing your evening holiday project. I'll need your schedule for it. Otherwise, the same rules apply."

As I was limited in vocals, I forced a squeak to show my appreciation that my entire holidays wouldn't be ruined.

"You're welcome. Plan an outing with fro-girl here, too. I'll add one other exemption because I'm feeling generous. That, plus I'll never hear the end of it if you don't get your Christmas shopping in."

"I'm free on Sunday," Tiana said. "And you just wish you could rock a fro half as well as I do."

"I should curse you to have straight, boring hair for eternity."

"Don't you even dare," Tiana hissed. "You leave my beautiful hair alone!"

I willed Gavin to stop teasing my friend and stealing my nicknames for her.

"All right, all right. Eleven in the morning until midnight," Gavin replied. "Don't lose her in a snowbank."

"I wouldn't!"

She would, but I loved her despite her tendency to cause me trouble for the fun of it.

Chase cleared his throat. "Anything else I should know?"

"She's a walking catastrophe. She's allergic to almonds, but they're one of her favorite foods."

I hissed. Stupid, delicious almonds. They made me itch, but I loved them. Traitorous, wonderful almonds.

"No almonds. Got it. Anything else? What about other nuts?"

"She's allergic to cashews, but she doesn't love them nearly as much as almonds. She doesn't have problems with any other nuts. I'll have Caleb call in the evenings. She'll be easier to handle that way."

I could think of one nut I had a problem with: Gavin.

The divine sighed.

"I'll give you my number in case her phone is inaccessible," Chase offered.

"Perfect. Oh, one last thing. Take some work home for her. It's a coping mechanism. That, plus I expect you'll get annoyed with the intricacies of chameleon care. The sooner she's finished, the better off you'll both be."

I hated that Gavin was right, and to hide the sting and pretend the truth didn't hurt, I thumped the bucket to demand more chicken.

Gavin kept my thoughts secret, for which I was grateful.

I INHALED a ridiculous amount of chicken, and when I couldn't handle another bite, I curled up for a nap.

"Miriah's done," Gavin announced in a soft voice. "It's probably a good time for us to get out of here. Caleb has school in the morning."

Gavin was a lot of things, but he took his son's future seriously. I understood. I expected Gavin would be underfoot more than usual following the deaths of his other children.

Some things I could never begrudge, and while we had problems, if Gavin wanted to see Caleb and Caleb wanted to see his father, I wouldn't get in the way.

Chase peeked beneath the rim of my bucket. "I think you're right. This works well enough. She doesn't need to be awake for the doctor to check on her."

Chase's father chuckled. He'd stayed so quiet throughout dinner that I'd forgotten about him. "He feels responsible, and he won't be satisfied until someone he trusts convinces him she'll be fine. Well, I never thought I'd have dinner with a divine. It definitely wasn't what I was expecting."

Caleb giggled. "Dad's playing pretend. He doesn't like freaking us weak-willed humans out."

"Yet he cursed your mother so she becomes a chameleon," Chase muttered.

"Dad has issues, Mr. Chase. Sorry."

So did I, and so was I.

Tiana snickered. "Don't worry about it, Chase. He's an idiot. Sometimes, I even think he means well. Sort of."

Traitor frenemy. I stuck my tongue out at her.

Chase chuckled and flagged down the Pa portion of the Ma and Pa joint, and he ordered a bucket to go and the bill.

Damn it. How was I supposed to dislike him if he got an entire bucket of my favorite chicken for the road? At the rate I was going, I'd be stuck as a chameleon forever—or for as long as Chase stuck around.

Gavin laughed, said his farewells, thanked Chase for picking up the bill, and herded our son out the door. Tiana followed, winking at me before making her escape.

While we waited for the chicken, Chase eyed his father. "Thoughts?"

"Someone's hiding something big enough they're willing to stoop to murder to keep it secret. That they acted so early tells me they believe your chameleon can expose them—probably with general ease. My bet is on someone attempting to skim corporate accounts. You're lucky it was noticed before January. If someone in accounting is attempting to skim, they'll act near tax time."

"And get caught," Chase grumbled.

"You know that. I know that. Whoever is behind this likely has no idea how hands on you are with the tax accounting each year. It's likely more than one person, too. I'd put my bets on someone in marketing, and I wouldn't be surprised if they're working with someone else in a different department to make their work easier."

"Or they're working with an outsider and overcharging the accounts. They'd be faking statistics to keep the money flowing."

"That's also a possibility. That divine had good advice for you. Take your work home with you this once. No one will expect that, you'll find the culprit faster, and you'll be happier for it. I'm not suggesting you do this all the time, but I feel the situation likely warrants it."

I appreciated Chase not wanting to take work home with him. When I worked from home, I recognized every minute it took away from Caleb.

"I don't like it, but all right."

"Good boy. Now, tell me about Miss Cox. You're not usually so interested in employee acquisitions unless you're looking for a new assistant."

"Alex recommended her. He likes her work a lot, and her spreadsheets and general reports are logical. And sane. You don't need a math degree to get the idea."

Chase's father laughed. "She managed to dumb it down enough you understood it without needing a meeting?"

"There's a reason I don't invite you over for dinner, Dad. Could you not be a jerk today?"

"Me being a jerk keeps you on your toes and prepares you for handling the assholes in charge of other companies. I'm helping you succeed at life. Go on. What else?"

"Miriah did a full evaluation of Alex's business when she was hired because she wanted to understand the company's dynamic. He thought it was a good idea, and he was impressed she wanted to get a good view of the company's history. Of his staff, Miriah's one of his quickest thinkers, and because she did do the background work, she was able to build some pretty accurate projections. She also has a good eye for any oddities in the numbers."

"She's a basic number cruncher?"

"She's hardly basic," Chase snapped.

If he kept stroking my ego, I'd become as insufferable as Gavin within a week.

"Chase. She's a low-level employee of Alex's. That makes her a basic number cruncher. She's not in management, and she's not a team lead."

"A divine who doesn't want to take no for an answer wouldn't be interested in someone basic."

"In the employment field, Chase."

"She's a number cruncher."

"How did you convince that scrooge to part with one of his number crunchers, anyway?"

"I asked."

Chase's father snorted and leaned back in his chair. "Boy, he would've laughed me right out of his office if I'd asked."

"Maybe if you stopped putting people in timeout when they annoy you, they wouldn't laugh at you when you ask them for help. Let me remind you of something: you put Alex in timeout three times before you finally retired. In the same week."

"If they didn't annoy me, I wouldn't put them in timeout."

"I get tired of listening to Mom complain you've added more time to your community service. Please stop putting people in timeout."

"Why are you siding with her?"

"I retrieved you from jail four times last month. The

police have my number on speed dial. This isn't something to be proud of."

I watched Chase's father, and it occurred to me I needed to make certain he didn't teach Tiana any bad habits—or Caleb. Or Gavin. Or anyone else I knew. Men like him meant trouble for me, and I didn't need the help of some dumb curse to recognize that.

If Chase's father had polluted Chase with his trickster ways, I'd be in even more trouble. I liked tricksters who didn't actually hurt anyone. I'd need to do some research to discover what the pair meant by timeout and why the older man kept getting arrested for doing it.

The two glared at each other, and Chase's father finally scowled, turned his head, and muttered, "Nonsense."

"Dad, you're supposed to be a mature adult. Stop getting arrested."

"Why must you insist on ruining my fun? I'm retired. Life during retirement should be enjoyed."

"Can you be serious for just this once, please? Someone threw that glass hard enough it left a chameleon-shaped imprint in her monitor. This isn't a game."

"I'm aware. It's likely someone is trying to skim company funds. People will do a lot to get money, and throwing a glass at a lizard to protect their secret? Doesn't even register to most people as a crime. They either don't know or don't care she's human. In your shoes, I'd audit the entire accounting and marketing departments, and I'd take a closer look at the system administrators, too. The secretarial and coordination staff might have access, but I'm not sure they'd have the skills needed to pull it off. Your first job is to identify who could pull it off, and I'd put together lists of people you think might work together to make it happen."

"Likelihood it's a collaborative effort?"

"How much are you estimated to be bleeding?"

"Enough I'm worried about it. A lot."

I estimated the figure to be in the millions, possibly into the tens of millions if I assumed all accounts were skimming ten percent in extra expenses. I hadn't checked the total amounts, but the accounts I'd investigated were worth millions—each.

"A lot divided by five people is still a lot."

Chase sighed and rubbed his temple. "There are enough people involved they might need to work for ten years to make this worth their while. Each."

"How the hell did you misplace tens of millions of dollars?"

"I think the problem existed while you were still CEO, old man." Chase pointed at me. "She pinpointed an issue with the extra expenses fund, and whoever is doing it knows enough about how we check for red flags to be working that fund—likely working with the companies to get a prettier piece of the pie."

"The extra expenses account? That's where the hole is?"

"Miriah discovered that sometime in January this year, someone began adding the extra expenses fund into the campaign totals. That's why the projections and the actual earnings dive-bombed."

"Because when you add an extra ten percent to the campaign costs, the campaign no longer looks like it's performing as well, does it?" Chase's father grimaced. "All right. If the issue is with the extra expenses fund, I'm partially to blame. That whole category was my idea so I'd have to stop signing as many damned authorizations."

"You could have just hired someone to handle the extra expenses authorizations, Dad."

"You're right. And it seems obvious I should have. Any ideas on who or why?"

"No, but I'll be getting Miriah all the data she needs to figure it out tomorrow. With luck, we'll be able to bury this before the end of the holidays—or at least cut off that funding leak."

"How the hell did you bleed out millions, Chase?"

"I wanted to ask the same of you, as it seems I may have inherited the issue."

I watched them with interest, wondering who would emerge the victor of the escalating dispute.

"All right. How the hell did we lose millions out of the extra expenses account?"

"Well, before I asked Alex for help, I had no idea it was from the extra expenses account. That's why I asked Alex. I couldn't figure it out. The accountants swore all the signed invoices matched the accounts, but the numbers on the account performance reports seemed off."

"How off?"

"When I estimated, before Miriah discovered the altered formula from January, I was looking at around three million."

"Any of it from the charity funds?"

"That's what caught my attention. I believe that the charity campaigns were unaltered; their performance for this year so far is off compared to regular campaign perfor-mance—by around ten percent."

"The allowed maximum for our extra expenses account. So, it seems you have a case of an almost ethical crook."

"Or they're not directly involved with the charity drive."

"That's always a possibility. Tell you what. I'll send in a friend of mine. She'll play number cruncher while your real number cruncher works on isolating the true source of the problem. My friend is quite capable of protecting herself. She's also very observant. If someone at your office is going to continue targeting those getting close to the discrepancy, she'll be able to handle the issue."

"I'll think about it."

The arrival of a bucket of chicken ended the discussion, and without another word, Chase tucked me into his jacket, paid for dinner, left a tip, and braved the cold to return to his car.

Either he forgot about me or liked having a lizard in his coat, but Chase neglected to put me on the seat like he had on the way to the restaurant. Or he suspected I'd dive into the steaming bucket of chicken and resume my feeding frenzy.

Chase was a wise man.

SIX

I'd save hurting someone for when
chicken was withheld from me.

THE DOCTOR LIVED in a nice townhouse in an even nicer part
of town, which did a good job of confirming Chase lived in
an entirely different world, one where money mattered little
—unless it was stolen from his company. I found the whole
situation absurd.

Then again, I found the whole idea of someone trying to
kill me over Chase's money absurd. Money would make my
life easier, but I didn't understand why someone would hurt
someone else to get it.

I'd save hurting someone for when chicken was withheld
from me.

A light snow fell, and I hissed at it, retreating deeper into
the safety of Chase's jacket.

"You'll survive." Chase grabbed the bucket of chicken and
carried it to the front door. He knocked twice before giving
the knob a twist. The door opened.

What sort of crazy person left his front door unlocked in New York City?

"I'm in the study, Chase," a man boomed.

"Harvey's convinced I'm deaf along with everyone else. He refuses to acknowledge he can't hear anything in his left ear. One day, he'll have someone look at it. He's talented with his magic, but it comes at a price: he can't use it on himself. It drives him right up the wall, too."

I wiggled so I could peek out of Chase's coat. The inside of the townhouse was even nicer than the outside, and the owner liked antique everything.

I'd do my best to stay in Chase's shirt for the duration of the visit so I wouldn't break something I couldn't afford, and I was fairly certain I couldn't afford anything in the doctor's home.

A white haired black man with the wispy start of a beard hopped to his feet when Chase strode into the study. I'd seen libraries with fewer books, and hundreds of volumes resided in neat piles on the floor. "Where's this cursed chameleon of yours, boy?"

"In my jacket."

"Well, that should be warm enough. Trot her on out and let's have a look-see."

Chase obeyed, wrapping his hand around me and dislodging me from the warm confines of his jacket. "Her name is Miriah."

The doctor strolled over and leaned close. "Well, there's definitely a lot of magic at play here." He plucked me out of Chase's hand, and I hissed my alarm. "Most interesting."

"The curse?"

"I'll get to that in a moment. I'm curious. She's rather

vocal for a chameleon. Sure, some hiss like she does, but she's rather loud. She's similar to a few natural species, but she changes colors faster than mundane chameleons, too. Does she make any other noises?"

"I heard her squeak a few times, and she growled some in her sleep."

"The growling was likely some form of respiratory distress. How long did it take to clear up?"

"It stopped after she woke up and started moving around on her own," Chase reported.

"Call me if she starts growling again. Growls aren't part of a chameleon's vocals, so we'll need to figure out if she has different vocal cords than a standard chameleon. They're usually silent unless hissing because of being agitated, and they're usually much softer."

"Since when did you become a reptile expert?"

"Since you called me and notified me you'd be bringing me a chameleon. I called a friend, and I had a long chat with someone who knows chameleons. Record the sound if she makes it again, and I'll pass it along to see if it's something to worry about. How has her climbing ability and balance been? Her ability to move?"

"She landed a few bites when I didn't give her her chicken fast enough." Chase lifted up the bucket of chicken. "This is her dinner and her breakfast, as I've been informed she eats human food and not chameleon food."

"You're feeding her chicken?"

"When I'm told her favorite food is this specific chicken, I'm providing."

"Fair enough."

"What can you tell me about the curse?"

The doctor turned me over in his hands, and I hissed at him, snapping my teeth at his fingers. "Yes, she's quite agile for a chameleon, and she's rather aggressive. Unsurprising, really. I'd be agitated, too, if someone I didn't know handled me without permission. The curse is a curious one—if you want to call it that. I'm not convinced. I can see the shadows of injuries, particularly along her back and side, but this 'curse' magic is repairing it. She'll be as good as new by morning. I don't even need to do anything. It looks like the magic is tapping her natural energy reserves, though, so make sure you feed her extra."

Chase gave the bucket a good shake. "I think I'm covered, and if not, I have plenty in the fridge I can cook up if she eats the entire bucket."

Dr. Harvey sighed. "Did you not learn anything from observing your mother?"

"I'll acknowledge I should have paid more attention."

"Women are simple, Chase. Feed them at appropriate intervals, tell them you love them at least once a day, do not steal their food, do not ever, ever steal their food, don't make messes they need to clean, and there's something about pillows and thermostats, but I'm choosing to forget what."

"Do not make me come in there!" a woman howled from somewhere deeper in the house. Upstairs, from what I could tell. "If I wanted to live in an icebox, I would've bought a walk-in freezer."

"Ah, that's right. Don't adjust the thermostat to save money on the heating bill. Don't ask how much it costs to run the AC in this place."

"Good to know. Anything else I should know?"

I had a thought: Chase needed to pick who he took advice

from with a little more care, although Dr. Harvey's points on not stealing my food were amusingly accurate.

"I hear paying close attention to when they complain helps but if you really want to impress her, you stop what was causing her to complain. Marigold wants me to see someone about my ear."

"The poor boy's going to go deaf, too, if you keep shouting at him!" the woman screeched as the sound of her voice drew closer.

Steps creaked overhead, and I blended in with the doctor's hand just in case his wife came into the study ready to wage war.

Chase chuckled, and his expression relaxed. "Do you need a lift to the specialist?"

"Maybe."

"Yes, please!" Marigold screamed.

I wondered if the woman held some responsibility for the doctor's hearing problems.

"Tell me when. If I'm not free, I'll have Dad play driver for you."

More thumps warned me the woman was on the move, and several moments later, a little, gray-haired lady with a glorious, golden tan leaned into the room. "Thank you, Chase. Dear lord, Harvey. Do you have a tumor on your hand?"

"She's a chameleon, and she's changed colors as it seems your ruckus alarmed her."

"Well, that's something. Last time our boy here brought a little white girl along, she done made it halfway to Jersey before he caught up with her after she got told off for her language and actin' like she ain't ever seen a mixed couple before."

Chase sighed. "That little white girl was my niece, Marigold. Miriah isn't a little girl. She's a woman. Anyway, my niece earned a tongue lashing for being nasty, and she won't do it again in front of me if she's got half a brain. Unfortunately, there's also a reason my sister won't visit me right now."

I assumed nasty meant rich, white, and prejudiced, a common enough affliction in New York.

"Well, sure. You told that little girl if you ever heard such a slur come out of her pretty little mouth again, you'd hang her by her britches from the Empire State Building. Be fair, Chase. When you make threats, you typically mean them. She probably worried you'd actually do it, so she ran off down the street like she meant it while her parents watched all aghast. Anyway, thank you. If you're taking him to the appointment, he won't back out of going. Again."

"You're welcome, Marigold."

The doctor scowled. "That's right, side with her."

"Keep your voice down, Harvey. He's not deaf, not like you. I can't hear my show over your howling." Marigold darted off with far more energy than I expected from a bent woman who couldn't stand perfectly straight.

Chase leaned out of the study and called out, "Same goes to you, Marigold. Tell me when you need to go in for your back. And don't even try to tell me it hasn't gotten worse."

"Old can't be cured, boy."

"But old, bent backs can be straightened if you go to a specialist. An appointment, Marigold. Not excuses. Call me after you make an appointment."

"Fiend!"

I questioned who was the adult in the odd relationship between Chase, his doctor, and his doctor's wife.

"How severe do you think her injuries were?"

"Severe enough, but she's in no danger and is healing well. Feed her, let her rest, and keep her warm. With magic that strong on her? It'd take a lot to actually hurt her. I'm assuming the divine wanted an insurance policy; his curse isn't much of a curse if his victim dies while transformed. The real risk is her getting too cold, and it's only a risk because she'd be helpless. I don't think it would do any lasting harm to her, but she'd be unable to defend herself. Of course, this is just a guess. The magic on her is strong enough to make seeing anything else difficult at best."

"I think your guess is right. She was helpless after she got clobbered with a glass full of water and ice. It took her hours to warm up, too."

"Get out of here, go home, and make sure you take your vitamins. You also need to get sleep. If your next bloodwork comes back like you lick your food instead of eating it, I'll have your daddy pop you one."

"Ouch. I'm eating properly now, I swear."

"Account for any gym time. Protein supplements are encouraged for a reason. I even gave you a convenient chart to tell you exactly how much you need."

"That protein supplement tastes like chocolate left out to rot in the sun for a month."

"Chug it down and chase it with some real chocolate milk if it bothers you that much."

Chase scowled. "You're cruel and heartless."

"Just take the damned supplements if you work out at the gym."

"Fine, I will." Chase reclaimed me from the doctor, and I curled around his wrist. "Thanks for having a look at her."

"Of course. Bring her over if you have any issues or hear her growl again. I'll also ask around to see if there's anyone who might be able to break that curse."

"Don't bother. A divine placed it, and he's actively meddling. It would take another divine to do it, and he's masking his portfolio."

"Already looked into it?"

"I tried. I can't find anything on him, but whoever he is, he's definitely a divine."

"How'd he register to you?'

"Neutral with annoying tendencies," Chase grumbled.

"You're much grumpier than I expected over this."

"This curse made her vulnerable at my company."

"You can't beat a divine, Chase. I know you have opinions on workplace safety, and I know you really don't like when someone who is your responsibility is threatened, but you need to hold your temper. Do what you can. Otherwise, let it go. She needs sleep and food, and as I see you're on top of the food issue, you don't need me for anything else right now. Go home. Leave the divine alone."

Chase grunted.

"You think you're all that and a cup of Marigold's coffee, boy, but you can't beat a divine. Give it up."

"Like hell I can't," Chase snapped. "Fine. I'll call you if there are any issues."

The doctor stepped forward and prodded Chase's chest with a finger. "Leave. The. Divine. Alone. He's obviously taking steps to protect her. All you're going to do is get your ass kicked. By a divine."

"Because of that divine, someone almost killed her at my company."

"Deal with that issue. The divine is not the reason that issue happened. Be grateful that magic was in place. Had she been human, I make no promises it would've ended as well for her."

Chase clacked his teeth together. "Dad's sending someone in to draw fire."

"Good. That'll keep him busy for a while. Head on home and keep an eye on the weather. We're in for a bad blow in the next few days."

"Great. Just what I needed. More snow on top of trouble at work."

"Take your bah humbugs elsewhere, you."

Chase muttered curses all the way back to his car.

LIKE HIS DOCTOR, Chase lived in a townhouse perfect for the rich and famous not far from his office building. He'd never seemed like a fan of the holidays to me, but lights decorated his handrails and windows, the LED type I preferred. He even had a Christmas tree in his living room, one made of plastic and in dire need of some tender loving care from me. While he had ornaments, tinsel, and lights, he'd tossed them on at random.

The poor tree needed to be groomed properly.

I blamed my son for my automatic need to make a Christmas tree presentable.

Chase locked his front door behind us, turned the thermostat up, and pulled me out of his jacket. "Go ahead and explore. I'll make you a plate of chicken and get the heated blanket set up for you."

He bent over and set me on the hardwood floor. I scampered to the tree, climbed up, and blended in, which didn't work well thanks to the color-changing lights.

Chase's laughter warmed me. "And to think I had doubts about putting up a tree this year. Enjoy."

When he strolled down the hall, I admired the view. Him in a suit kept my attention, and unlike every other man I'd developed a crush on, I hadn't found a single fatal flaw within several hours of serious exposure yet.

There had to be something wrong with him. Time would tell what.

Technically, I'd discovered one flaw: he could curse with the best of them when annoyed. A good vocabulary didn't count as a fatal flaw. I viewed it as additional coloration.

To some women, his protective streak would count as a fatal flaw, but I liked it. A man protective of people would be protective of his family.

I wanted someone who would protect me and Caleb, especially as I had a poor track record of protecting myself. Sometime after I returned to human for extended periods of time, I'd have to do something about that. A few self-defense courses would work, and maybe I'd ask my best frenemy for advice on the man department. Tiana managed to date without running into trouble.

Maybe she could teach me which men to avoid.

Once certain he was gone, I went to work tidying his tree, settling into a routine of climbing down, picking a few ornaments to move, and climbing up to gingerly relocate them to their new homes. The work soothed my nerves and offered hope I could still give Caleb the perfect Christmas. How I'd top several weeks with his father remained a mystery, but I'd figure something out. Picking a good dog for him might work. Maybe. I cringed at the thought of disappointing him.

He'd spent weeks depressed over his father's failure to show up, although knowing the truth made it a little easier on me. If Gavin didn't tell Caleb the truth, I would—sometime in May. Or June. Maybe July.

It'd take that long for me to work up the nerve to do it.

"You really love Christmas, don't you?"

Somehow, I kept hold of the glass ball, twitching at his voice. I dragged it to its new spot and hung it, giving a tug to make sure it'd stay in place. When finished, I gave Chase my complete attention, and nodded to answer his question.

"Well, redecorate to your heart's content. I brought you a piece of chicken and broke it up for you. Since you like the tree, I'll bring the blanket in here in case you get cold. I tend to be an early riser, but don't worry about it. If you're still asleep when it's time to head into the office, I'll wrap you in the blanket so you can rest. A replacement computer should be ready for you by the time we're there, but it might take until noon at the latest. One of the techs messaged me to let me know they were able to recover all your work."

I'd appreciate that tomorrow, and I clapped to indicate my approval.

"All right. I'll have an unlocked tablet on my nightstand. If you need anything, use it. It has an alarm app and a notepad running. Enjoy working with the tree. Remember, if you need anything at all, wake me." He offered a smile before strolling out of the living room, leaving a plate piled with shredded chicken near his coffee table.

I needed my heart back, but he'd only think I was crazy if I told him the truth. No, I'd wait for him to show his true colors.

Gavin understood me better than I liked.

I always picked the wrong men. Always.

A little normality went a long
way in my complicated life.

In the dead of night, I transformed back to human. Uncertain how long the respite would last, I ditched my purse on the coffee table and sent Gavin a text threatening death if I shifted during my shower. His reply promised a shower and a chance to get dressed but nothing else.

I could work with a shower and a chance to get dressed. It took me a few minutes to squish my pride, but I thanked him for not being a complete jerk.

Tip-toeing around Chase's home seemed wrong, as did borrowing his shower without his permission, but I ignored my misgivings. Even an hour as a human would restore my sense of normality.

A little normality went a long way in my complicated life.

Unfortunately, Chase's ridiculous bathroom with its massive shower ended my dream of indulging in peaceful, quiet normality. The damned thing had buttons, and I lost ten minutes figuring out how to turn it on. I stole his shampoo, the source of his vanilla scent, and turned the heat up as high as I could tolerate.

I'd miss his shower when I returned home.

I made it through my shower, got dressed, and dared to invade Chase's kitchen to devour half a bucket of chicken. I even returned it to his stainless steel refrigerator and cleaned up all evidence of my chicken thievery before Gavin's curse snapped me back to a chameleon and dumped me onto the tile floor.

I wanted to call him rude, but rude would've been forcing me to transform with my head stuck in his fridge.

Determined to make the most of my situation, I retreated to the living room to nap. The heated blanket made an ideal nest, and I settled in to wait.

The night passed, too quiet and tranquil for my liking. I missed my son's restlessness, his quiet snore, and his tendency to creep out of bed to fix something askew he'd noticed somewhere in our cramped apartment.

I could get used to the quiet. It would take a few days, that was all. I wouldn't hunker in my warm nest and whine that my son was enjoying the weeks leading up to Christmas with his father and without me.

Around dawn, I discovered the truth about Chase Butler. Not only did he rise early, he redefined cranky, transforming into a snarly scrooge. I observed him from the safety of my nest while he stomped around in his boxers.

I waged a quiet war with myself, losing the battle for a chance at a better view. Taking my time, I emerged, crept along the couch, and stretched out so I could peer into the kitchen.

Did Chase believe flexing his muscles and stomping

around would make his morning better? He could flex all he wanted.

Early, grumpy riser went into the con category, but Chase wearing boxers while grumpy and stomping around might ruin me for life, convince me he was worth being cursed for, and ensured I'd consider performing acts destined to put me on Santa's naughty list.

Permanently.

Chase wasn't safe for work or anywhere other than the bedroom when wearing boxers, and I foresaw weeks of silent suffering, enduring a heavenly view without complaint.

Upon closer observation, I learned tea tamed the grouchy beast. Satisfied he wouldn't play a game of kick the chameleon, I approached so I could admire him up close and personal. He sipped his tea at the counter, yawning while fiddling with his phone.

As chameleons were rather limited in the vocals department, I hissed to get his attention.

He hissed back.

Okay. I could work with a morning battle of the sexes. I eyed his bare toes, debating which one to nip.

"I'll feed you breakfast after I have my tea."

Would making tea at stupid AM tame Chase every morning? I stood and lifted my paws to indicate I wanted to be picked up. He sighed, set his mug down, and complied, setting me on the counter. I investigated, taking inventory of everything I would need to make him tea. An electric kettle waited near the sink.

"Please tell me you're not a coffee drinker. I don't have any coffee."

While I considered the lack of coffee unfortunate, I'd compromise. I pointed at the kettle. Tea would do.

I hoped.

Chase sighed, slid his mug out of the way, and reached for an upper cabinet to fetch a second mug.

As I liked the idea of questing for a top spot on Santa's naughty list, I investigated his tea with my tongue.

Tea tasted better than I expected, so I dunked my head in and drank in large gulps, determined to get as much into my stomach as I could before he stopped me.

"This is entirely my fault. I didn't leave anything out for you to drink last night, did I?"

While he hadn't, I hadn't noticed. I gripped the rim of his mug to indicate the transferal of ownership and embarked on my mission to empty the mug.

Chase made himself a new cup of tea, and I observed where he kept everything between swallows. With the exception of the mugs, I could reach everything else with a little work.

Once he finished his drink, he opened the fridge and pulled out the bucket of chicken. "What the hell?"

I drank Chase's tea and pretended I hadn't gone on a chicken binge in the middle of the night.

"You're a foot long. How did you get into the fridge?"

I lifted my head out of his mug, tea dripping from my chin.

"Better question. How did you eat half a bucket of chicken?"

Tea tasted great when accompanied with early morning entertainment. I'd have to ask—possibly beg—Gavin to let me have future adventures in Chase's home in the middle of the night.

No wonder Tiana enjoyed causing so much trouble. Pleased with my first foray into harmless naughtiness, I drank the rest of Chase's tea and plotted my next act of disobedience.

IT TOOK Chase three cups of tea and a shower to become the social man I couldn't help but admire. I particularly enjoyed his habit of walking around in his underwear. I couldn't fathom why, but he saved dressing for absolutely last.

I wouldn't complain. If the man wanted to prance around in his boxers for my enjoyment, he could. He knew I was, when Gavin wasn't being a complete jerk, a woman. He even knew I was a woman with a son.

To keep me nice and toasty, he packed a small duffle lined with the heated blanket and a throw, which I nested within. He zippered it closed when outside and opened it inside his car.

"We'll come up with a better plan at work," he promised.

I planned to solve his numeric mystery, and I'd ignore the temptation to waste time so I could hang around longer. The rest of the mess, including the aftermath of my discoveries, would be his problem.

As always when put in a bad position, I cursed my stupid, pesky morals. Life would be much easier if I allowed myself to cheat a little now and then. Then again, anything other than doing my best would hurt him in one way or another.

Once I finished my work, I would go back to being human with occasional chameleon tendencies.

Chase didn't visit my real workplace that often.

If a severe case of grumpy and rising with the sun topped his con list, I'd have to avoid his offices. If he started showing up at work more often, I might need to find a new job, too. At the rate I kept falling for him, I'd never get over my crush.

Gavin might relent if I begged him enough—or found a potent enough threat. Maybe.

Later, I'd try, sometime after Chase clued in my purse and phone were on his coffee table rather than melded with my chameleon body. I assumed his case of the morning grumpies came bundled with impaired observation skills. While I added that to the con list, I slipped in a few reminders he spent most of his morning shirtless to the pro list.

Chase kept quiet the short trip to his work, and when we arrived to his office. I discovered a second computer, identical to the one destroyed, waited on Chase's desk near his. I scrambled out of the bag and went to work, delighted most of my spreadsheet and data gathering was intact.

It would take less than five minutes to restore everything to rights.

"I told you," Chase murmured, thumping into his seat. "I'll apologize in advance for the never-ending wave—"

Chase's father strode into the office armed with a steaming bucket of my favorite chicken. The older man joined the pro list, and I breathed in deep to enjoy the delicious aroma wafting in my direction.

"—of individuals determined to bother us. Where did you get that at seven in the morning, Dad?"

"I asked really nicely and paid for it. I called them last night after I left. This is a gift for your little lady for putting up with you. She needs all the gifts I can wrangle, as it seems you both survived an entire evening together. Consider it a celebratory present. If she agrees, you can even have some."

Chase leaned back in his chair and scowled at his father. "She stole my tea this morning and somehow got into the fridge last night."

"Poor Chase. Someone screwing up your precious morning routine is good for you. I came by to tell you that your second number cruncher is in her new office, and she's itching for trouble. Unfortunately, it seems the office has a healthy sense of self-preservation, as it appears no one is willing to anger the young gorgon."

Since I wouldn't be able to concentrate with them yapping, I stopped working and reached for the bucket. Chase's father removed the lid and used it as a plate, peeling off some skin and offering it to me. It crunched just the way I liked it, and while I waged war with my first bite, father and son shredded the meat for my enjoyment.

They offered me three big pieces.

Both men elevated themselves on the pro list, and I'd even ignore all the morning grumpiness if it got me fed chicken every morning.

"So, who did you bring in? You said she's a gorgon?"

"She's a young gorgon new to the area; she's been on her own for a while. She's too old to stay with her father's hive, but she's too vocal to easily find a new one. She's rather feministic for a gorgon, which means she doesn't fit in the gorgon family structure very well. She seems oddly monogamous, too—which will make having any children difficult for her at best. She needs the money, and she's reliable."

"It's probable I'll be hiring some new full-time employees soon. Train her in a solid role. If she does well, I'll make room for her."

"You need a proper assistant, Chase. You can't keep stealing interns or the receptionist in her downtime."

"I don't see why not. Anyway, I have a plan for my lack of an assistant. I'll let you know if it doesn't work out. Can you teach this gorgon the nuances of data gathering and reporting?"

"I'll add contract reading, invoicing, and fulfilling purchase orders to the mix. Her name is Michella Darven. She's twenty-three. As a warning, she hasn't graduated high school. Her hive had difficulties before she was essentially evicted."

"Pitch an opportunity to finish her diploma and continuing education. I'll adjust her hours if she'd like to attend school. How is she with animals?"

I paused in devouring my second breakfast to stare at Chase, unable to comprehend what animals had to do with data reports.

"I'll ask. Why do you want to know?"

"Our charity drive this year involves animal shelters. I offered a bonus to all employees who do fifty hours of volunteer work for the local animal shelters next year—and another bonus if they do ten hours this year. I sent a memo to all employees last month with a list of the eligible shelters."

"I'll let her know. Anything else?"

"For the record, I'm not paying you a bonus. I'm not

paying you anything at all. You're retired. Retired, old men do not come to work and get paid for it."

"You're moody this morning. I'm being helpful. I even brought your lady chicken."

"You're still not getting paid, you're not being hired in any capacity, and I fully expect you to go home to Mom sometime sooner than later. Bringing Miriah chicken ensured I didn't call security right away. As you brought her something she enjoys, I won't even complain if you linger. I'll even let you play on a computer in the empty office down the hall."

"If you'd hire an assistant, that office wouldn't be empty."

"Please go away so I can get some work done."

To my amazement, Chase's father obeyed.

NUMBERS ALWAYS TOLD A STORY, transforming themselves into an unbiased entity I named the truth. Using the database Chase provided, I found an old tale, one that would keep me awake at night. As suspected, someone was skimming money.

The amount paid to some companies worked out to be approximately ten percent higher than what was listed in the reports before January. It took some work, but I figured out the source of the discrepancy readily enough.

Chase's company used several reporting methods for performance, and every company seemed to have an extra expenses allowance. When I removed the extra expenses from the newer reports, the figures fell into line with the older reports.

I didn't understand why they'd excluded the extra expenses figures before January and added them during January, thus skewing the figures. I pinpointed the formula that drew in the extra expenses into the mix, but no matter how long I stared at it, the why of the tale eluded me.

One fact stuck out to me: long before January, the extra expenses figures for twenty key companies hovered consistently near ten percent—never over, and never far under. I could think of one person who could give me the intel I needed to solve the puzzle: Chase.

I left my workstation and sat beside his keyboard. His gaze remained locked on his monitor. Amused by the depth of his concentration, I observed him work for a few minutes. When it became clear he wouldn't notice me anytime soon, I reached over and tapped his hand.

Chase took flight, knocked his chair over, and yelped. The instant his feet hit the floor, he bolted to the door, skidding to a halt and reaching for the knob without quite touching it.

I longed for a camera to capture his expression, a mix of horror and embarrassment.

"I forgot you were there," he admitted. "Karma chameleons are quiet."

I pointed at his keyboard, hoping he'd understand I needed to tell him something.

"I'll be there as soon as my heart rate returns from orbit. I like working when it's quiet, but I forget I'm not alone sometimes. Would you be offended if I gave you a little bell to wear?"

I put his suggestion I should be collared with a bell at the top of his con list and hissed at him.

"I can work with a hiss instead. A very, very soft hiss. Very soft."

A better woman would've complied with his request. Me? I planned to find new and interesting ways to startle him when he forgot I was there. I wouldn't touch him, but I would reserve soft hissing for special occasions. If I startled him enough times in new and interesting ways, I'd see the real him, the one he surely hid from the rest of the world.

I patted the side of his monitor since his keyboard hadn't summoned him.

Chase straightened, adjusted his tie, dusted himself off, and returned to his desk. Shaking his head, he righted his chair and sat. "How can I help you?"

I shuffled to his keyboard and pointed at his monitor. He opened his word processor, saving me from a bitter battle with his mouse.

I typed up a brief explanation about the extra expenses category and made my request for additional information.

"I can find out for you, but I can tell you this much. We have that fund, and according to company policies, it shouldn't be heavily used. The only difference you noticed was a changed formula that included the extra expenses accounts?"

I nodded.

"This has been a problem for longer than I thought, then?"

I nodded again.

"Well, shit."

I understood. While I wanted to test his limits, I'd wait for a more appropriate opportunity. Skittering back to my computer, I returned to work.

EIGHT

I really doubt it's cyanide, Dad.

A MEETING CALLED Chase out of his office, and after one incident of assault, I decided to take no chances. The curtains made an excellent hiding place, and the heat vent below the window kept me almost as warm as the blanket on the desk. I picked the pleats at the top for my roost, gripping the material and metal rings holding the fabric to secure myself.

Snow swirled outside, heavy enough I suspected Chase might want to walk home rather than test his luck on the roads. I'd enjoy the trip if he insisted I ride in his jacket. I gave it equal odds of happening.

While the blankets inside the duffle would keep me warm, tucked close to Chase came with the added bonus of a sense of security, something I'd never admit to anyone.

The snow fell harder until it shrouded the city in a pale haze. I loved the sense of the world growing still and quiet around me, the wind and snow hissing against the window.

Winter always seemed to arrive on silent feet, taking me by surprise each time a storm rolled in and transformed the city into a sparkling paradise.

The door creaked open, and I peeked over the curtain.

Denise narrowed her eyes, took a long look around, and relaxed when she realized she was alone—or so she thought. She strode to the desk and headed for my workstation. At every job I worked at, the first thing I did was change the password on the computer so no one could meddle with my files. My habit served me well; after three failed attempts to gain access to my machine, she cursed and stole glances at the door, growing tenser with every passing moment.

Poking at my work didn't make her the primary culprit, but I'd be a fool to ignore the obvious. I doubted a receptionist had the skills needed to manage altering the complex report, which implied she was only part of the puzzle plaguing Chase.

When she couldn't unlock my system, she cursed some more, dipped her hand into her pocket, and sprinkled a pale powder on my keyboard and blanket, then she blew it around to mask her activities.

What a bitch.

Unwilling to alert her to my presence, I swallowed my desire to hiss and blended in with the curtain.

Denise left after wasting a few more minutes battling with my computer. She closed the door a little too hard behind her, and it bounced in the frame and popped open enough for me to slip out if I wanted.

What had she used on my computer and in my nest? That she'd go to such lengths bothered me. Was the substance toxic to humans, too? Was it toxic to me?

I assumed so.

I couldn't allow her to hurt Chase, not after he'd done so much for me. Climbing down the curtain, I headed for his desk and used his chair to investigate.

The alluring scent of almonds teased my nose.

Who had told her I was allergic to almonds? I hissed at the blanket and contaminated keyboard. Almond flour wouldn't hurt Chase, but I'd be miserably itching within minutes. Had only part of the conversation at the restaurant been heard? Inconveniencing me with almond flour made no sense. Anyone with a scrap of sense could figure out someone meddled. The flour left a residue everywhere. Had I been completely oblivious, I wouldn't have noticed before touching, but her blowing it around hadn't done much to hide its presence.

Stupid woman. Chase needed a new receptionist.

I also needed to resist almonds. Fortunately, I preferred my nuts intact and not in flour format, and the fear of full-body itching ensured my good behavior.

I settled with hissing my discontent while I waited for Chase to return, and I picked in front of his keyboard as my spot.

After an hour, which I timed from Chase's screensaver, he returned, and he frowned while closing the door behind him. "Did someone come in here?"

I crawled around his monitor, pointed at the blanket, which would be easiest to spot the powder on, and nodded.

With a frown fixed in place, he headed over. A single sniff transformed him from a calm, rational man into a raging, growling beast stuck in a handsome man's body. "Almonds?"

I slinked back to my spot between Chase's chair and keyboard, hunkered down, and kept a close eye on him.

"Did you see who did it?"

I nodded, and I pointed at his computer. Reaching around me, he unlocked his system and opened his word processor. I described Denise's behavior, quelling my initial urge to feel guilt over tattling. Chase grunted, picked up his phone, and dialed a number. "Dad, did you plant any intel about Miriah's allergies to anyone? No? Okay. We've got a possible bug or a clever tail. My office was dusted with almond flour while I was in a meeting. Miriah was in here alone, but she was hanging out on the curtain. Denise didn't notice her."

Chase's father talked for a long time, and Chase sighed. "I really doubt it's cyanide, Dad. But that said, I'll call in for a lab and pretend it is. If it is cyanide, I really doubt the culprit —yes, I know who it is—would touch it with bare hands. While I agree it's a desperate stunt, I'm not convinced it's to the point of accidently killing themselves over. That said, as far as I'm concerned, it was a murder attempt. As soon as I'm off the phone with you, I'm calling the police. Remember everything I said about timeout? Go ahead and ignore that bullshit. Start with the receptionist. Also, you know the rule: no questioning her. Put her in timeout until the police arrive, and when they give you directions, please listen to them for once in your life."

Damn it. I didn't want to deal with the police. I hissed my discontent.

"Sorry, Miriah. This is too serious to ignore."

To a point, I agreed. Being murdered would make giving Caleb a good Christmas impossible. I considered Chase.

Everything I'd witnessed pointed at the same conclusion. For the first time in my life, I'd fallen for a decent human being. No, not just a decent human being, but a genuinely nice one as long as I ignored his pre-tea grumpiness.

Good fortune came with buckets of bad luck. I flopped onto my side and waited for the inevitable misery of the police snooping about in my business.

"It'll be all right. I thought you'd be safe in here. I was wrong. I won't be making that mistake again. I'll get you a good laptop so you can work wherever I have to go, but you're not leaving my sight until this is resolved."

I foresaw a great deal of trouble in my future. How far would he take his edict? I'd experienced the men's bathroom enough for one lifetime, although I had to admit the urinals made excellent waste disposal facilities for karma chameleons.

Christmas would be an interesting adventure if I didn't get to the bottom of Chase's mystery. Would Gavin take pity on me for once? I needed to catch a break for a change.

I just hoped it wouldn't be a literal one. I had enough difficulties in my life already.

A PAIR OF COPS, two younger men likely new to the force, and someone with a lab testing kit invaded Chase's office. As only a fool would pour powdered cyanide out on a desk without heavy protective gear, the police suspected almond flour, a dangerous only-to-me substance that would waste them time and resources in an investigation they likely wanted nothing to do with.

They descended on my workstation with startling determination and efficiency. I scrambled off the desk, used Chase's leg as an escape route, and bolted for the safety of the curtain. I made it halfway across the carpet before Chase caught me and relocated me to his shoulder.

"Thank you for coming, officers. Please forgive Miriah. She's edgy. She's allergic to almonds, and someone targeted her yesterday. She's been cursed by a divine, so she's currently stuck in this shape. She typed up a recounting of the situation on my computer. I can send you a copy of the statement after you read it."

While young, the cops went to work with no outward sign of inexperience, photographing Chase's desk, examining my workstation, and otherwise poking their nose in my business.

The older gentleman with the lab kit also went to work, taking samples of the powder, sealing it, and stowing it away. "We'll run a full lab on this to test for additives. It's entirely possible there's something else toxic in the powder. At first glance, I'd guess almond flour. There doesn't seem to be any bitterness to the scent."

"Not cyanide, then," Chase muttered.

"Very probably not." The lab technician checked my message on Chase's computer. "Especially not handled so casually. That's a good way to take an express trip to the grave."

The cops both sighed and shook their heads. The younger of the pair, a handsome enough blond with bright blue eyes and a crooked grin, pointed at the desk. "Can you confirm everything that was dusted, please?"

Chase pointed at my keyboard and nest. "She left every

thing else alone. You can take both as evidence. We haven't touched anything since it was dusted. If you need to take the complete computer, we need to get a backup made of it first. That said, the woman responsible did attempt to access the machine without success."

"You can confirm she didn't succeed?"

"Yes, we can."

I wondered what Denise wanted from my computer. My work wasn't anything new; I merely confirmed the story the numbers told, none of which pointed at her as the culprit. The suspects belonged to other departments, although her addition to the puzzle would complicate matters.

Who did she work with?

Why?

The cops talked to Chase for a few more minutes, asking so many questions I wanted to go hide. Chase kept his answers short but cooperative, and most focused on him rather than me.

Chase's phone rang, and I hissed at the wretched device for startling a few years off my life.

"It's just my phone," he murmured, stroking his hand down my back before checking the display. He answered and said, "What do you have for me?"

While faint, I heard Chase's father announce he'd put Denise in timeout and that a bag of almond flour had spilled in the hallway. His father didn't sound very apologetic, not that I blamed him.

The almond flour in the reception would make my afternoon and evening even more difficult unless someone cleaned up the mess or I found some way to bypass it.

Chase chuckled. "Officers, the culprit was just detained

by my father in the reception, and she's in possession of almond flour. It seems there's a bit of mess out there. If you need us for anything, we'll be in here."

It amazed me the cops went along with Chase's implied suggestion they head to the reception, and they packed the keyboard and my nest and took them out in sealed bags.

I tapped Chase's shoulder, and once I had his attention, I pointed at the cops' departing backs.

"Oh. You slept through most of it yesterday, but they're the same folks who did the initial investigative work in the other office. We got to skip a lot of the extra bullshit and get straight to business. If we're needed, we'll be summoned. If they need your direct statement, they'll call in an angel—or subpoena that damned divine to reverse his curse during the questioning sessions."

I'd pay a great deal to watch that disaster.

"The tech team is going to love me in about ten minutes. I'm going to order a laptop for you along with a replacement keyboard. Damn it. I'm going to have to detox my entire office, too." Chase stood, checked his chair, and once satisfied it wasn't contaminated with almond flour, he placed me on it. Stomping to the door, he yanked it open. "Dad! My office. Now."

I admired Chase's ability to howl louder than my son during one of his temper tantrums.

"I'm a little busy right now," his father howled back.

Obviously, howling was a family trait. Were they lycanthropes? I could handle Chase being a lycanthrope.

Lycanthropes had zero loyalty issues, long life spans, and with my tendency to have disasters rather than dates, I might even survive a relationship with one. With my luck, Chase was an incubus, which would prove Gavin right—again—and leave me with more than a few regrets.

"Unacceptable," Chase replied, lowering his volume to something a little less offensive to my ears.

"Deal with it, brat!"

Life never made sense, and I doubted it ever would. As I'd somehow gotten lost in some odd version of reality, I decided to make the most of it, returning to my hiding spot at the top of the curtain to watch it snow.

A CIRCUS of men and women streamed through Chase's office, and one of the women was a gorgon with black snakes, all of which wore tiny hats with veils. Each hat had a bow of a different color. I counted snakes and estimated she packed thirty or so.

She must have spent a fortune of time and effort making thirty-something hats with little veils and adorable bows. Did it offend gorgons to ask about their snakes?

Did they have names?

Did they pick which color bow to wear?

Did they eat?

I could spend a lifetime asking questions without my curiosity being sated.

The gorgon lifted her chin, waited until everyone else left the office, and closed the door.

"I know why no one has discovered an issue with your financials until now," she announced.

Well, damn. The gorgon did a better job at my job than I

did. I'd only pinpointed the problem without coming close to learning the why of it.

"Have a seat. What have you learned?"

The gorgon sank into one of the chairs across from Chase and clasped her hands on her lap. "Your chameleon has excellent sight—of a magical nature. It's unlikely she knows she has it, either. It's not one easy to discover. Someone obscured the reports to draw attention away from their siphoning of funds and general performance issues. You're developing a resistance to it, which is why you noticed something was amiss. I have not. I only see the issues when I use her new reports. You're fortunate to have developed some resistance to it."

"How so?"

"From what I can tell comparing the reports, part of the magic creates an impression on its victims. Creating a new report won't be considered by most because of that magic, which is unusual in nature. Really, the interplay of magic and technology is fascinating. So, you have an interesting situation here. You would be wise to avoid trusting your eyes. They may deceive you. I would also guard your chameleon well. She's going to be a target for all those involved if they know she's capable of seeing through their magic. I expect without her you would be very frustrated. You would continue knowing something was wrong, but no one else would be able to find something amiss. Perhaps an angel. The magic is a lie, and they dislike lies. I've met a few angels. They would find this situation... interesting."

I decided interesting was the gorgon's favorite word of the day.

Chase grumbled a few curses and reached for his phone.

"I know one way to solve this." He pressed a button to activate the speaker and dialed a number.

"How can I help you, sir?" a man answered.

"Timothy, send a memo to the entire company for me, please. All extra expenses need to be approved by department management, on printed purchase orders, before being delivered to me for final approval. In addition to this, the basic extra expenses authorizations are revoked beginning immediately. All purchases, from office supplies to advertising campaigns, will need official physical purchase orders along with the digital copies. Management will need to justify all petty cash expenditures as well. Call me back when you've sent it. Finally, make certain all management confirm, in writing, their acceptance and understanding of the new policy."

"Yes, sir. It'll take about an hour. I'll have our attorney go over it first."

"Thank you." Chase disconnected the call.

The gorgon sighed. "That will anger those responsible."

"Good. You have my blessing to petrify anyone who even looks at Miriah wrong. I'll cover all of your fines and claim your community service hours as necessary. No one is to hurt her."

If everyone treated other people like they had real value, the world would be a much better place. I hadn't done anything to earn any of Chase's consideration or care.

If anything, I created more trouble for him at every turn.

"I'll do my best, Mr. Butler."

"Chase, please. Has anyone bothered you today?"

"Bothered? No. Investigated? Yes. I have pictures of

everyone who paid me a visit as well as recordings from hidden cameras I placed in the hallway. They're interesting."

I found her interesting. Were all gorgons corporate espionage queens? At least she knew what she was doing. I wondered about my suspected sight, though. Magic worked however magic wanted to work, but I didn't think I had anything magical about me beyond making a scanner beep whenever someone brought it next to me. I typically blamed Caleb and Gavin for the beeps.

I hadn't started beeping until I'd become pregnant with my son.

"What do you mean by interesting?"

"More people hovered outside of my door than bothered to come in."

"Well, you are new."

"But none of them tried to throw a glass at me. I'm disappointed."

"I'm sure someone will give you a valid reason to petrify them soon enough. Oh, would you please do me a favor?'

"What do you need, Chase?"

"Send me a copy of the reports you send to my father, please."

The gorgon grinned. "Of course. He hadn't told me I couldn't."

"Thank you."

Still grinning, she rose from her seat and left the office, and I admired her, her snakes, and their precious little hats. I would need to be careful around the gorgon. She was sneaky.

NINE

That escalated quickly.

TIANA SWEPT into Chase's office, struck a pose, and sang, "Where is my princess? We must go forth to the shelter to volunteer. Our time has come!"

"And so has a blizzard. To complicate matters for you, your princess isn't leaving my sight."

Wow. Hello, possessiveness. Since when did Chase involve himself with territory disputes over me? And since when did I actually enjoy it for a change? Obviously, my exposure to him had rattled my few remaining brain cells.

"That escalated quickly. Well, the whole my princess leaving your sight thing. The blizzard isn't really a blizzard yet. It's just a moderately angry snowstorm out for the city's blood. I called the shelter, and they're in a bit of an emergency situation, so we really can't skip on account of the weather. What did I miss?"

Chase sighed. "Almond flour while I was out of the office."

Tiana's brows rose, and she locked onto my computer, which still lacked a keyboard and a chameleon-appropriate nest. "I'd noticed a mess in the reception. Also, were you aware your receptionist is frozen near the front doors? There are particles of white dust floating in the air, too. It's really weird."

"Yes, I'm aware. My father put Denise in timeout." Chase checked his phone. "Was he still in reception?"

Tiana nodded and plopped onto one of the guest seats. "He was talking to the police, and they were discussing how to move her. They're arguing over her talents. Until her talent evaluation is done, your father doesn't want to remove her from timeout—whatever that is."

"It's essentially a time vortex. She's stuck in the moment my father used his talent on her. Think of it as conscious petrification. She's aware of everything going on around her, but she's frozen. Technically, she's not even breathing."

"That's horrifying."

I nodded my agreement and stayed where I was, safely out of reach of the crazy old man capable of freezing time.

"There's a reason I tell him to keep his magic to himself unless needed."

"Where's my princess?"

Chase pointed in my direction. "She's busy watching it snow. How far away is the shelter from here?"

"Ten blocks."

"Are you walking?"

Tiana frowned, and according to her expression, she was trying to figure out the politest way to tell Chase he'd lost his damned mind. "I drove to get here. The roads aren't that bad."

"The roads are that bad, and they'll only get worse. I'll walk with you to the shelter."

The moment Tiana recognized she was dealing with the son of a mad man likely as mad as the old mad man, her expression went blank. She cracked, and a giggle slipped out. "You want to walk ten blocks in a blizzard? Are you mad? We'll freeze to death."

I adored my best frenemy.

"Hardly. Did you bring a good winter coat with you? That little frock does not count as a good winter coat. That barely qualifies as a spring coat."

I observed the cage match between the rich, wealthy white man and the black chick who wasn't about to take any shit from the rich, wealthy white man with glee. Who would win? I would. Neither of the participants stood a chance of victory.

Tiana hopped to her feet and stomped her foot. "This girl fears no storm, and this frock is a Prada, thank you very much."

"It's a disaster waiting to happen and a vessel for hypothermia," Chase countered. "An expensive disaster second only to the hospital bill should you try to go outside while wearing it."

Burn.

"Don't be ridiculous. I'll drive us to the shelter."

"No. By the time we're done for the night, the roads will be unsafe. And anyway, in that getup, you'll freeze to death walking across the parking lot. Go home. I'll take over your shift at the shelter, and I'll take care of Miriah—and I'll make it clear to that Gavin fellow he won't be screwing with Miriah's shelter time."

"You're a brave man."

"Thank you for not calling me stupid or foolish, both of which are appropriate descriptors of my current life choices. I gave my word, and I have no intention of breaking it. Anyway, with the weather like it is, it's safer for you to head home now before the roads get worse. I have good winter clothes, and I can keep Miriah warm for the entire walk."

"All right. Call the shelter and warn them you might be a few minutes late. Leah will panic if we don't show up on time."

"I can do that."

"Okay. Good. Have fun, Miriah! Try not to adopt every dog in the shelter tonight. You need to pick one and only one. And no cats. If you get a single cat, you'll end up with ten cats, and you're crazy enough without the addition of cats to the mix."

What a bitch. I hissed at her to show her my exact opinion of her correct estimation of what I would do if allowed to adopt a single cat.

Caleb loved dogs.

I liked dogs.

Caleb tolerated cats.

I adored cats and wanted to take every kitten on the planet home with me, which ensured I'd never have a kitten of my own because there was no reasonable adult in my life to stop me after one.

"One dog, Miriah. One. You can pick the dog you want tonight if you really want, just make sure you tell Leah so she can draw up the paperwork. But only one."

"I'll make sure Miriah is reasonable about any selection of

dogs, and should she adopt a dog, it will be only one dog and not an entire pack of them."

"The dog is Caleb's Christmas present, and she's working at the shelter in part to find the perfect dog. The dog must be the perfect dog, Chase. Are we clear?"

"I see. Well, as Caleb is getting the perfect dog for Christmas, I better get her to the shelter so she has plenty of time to meet the candidates. Drive carefully, Tiana."

"I'll be careful," she promised. "Don't lose my princess in a drift."

"She'll be safe, sound, and warm with me," Chase replied.

He needed to stop being everything I had ever wanted in a man. If he kept it up, I wouldn't care if he had a fatal flaw.

CHASE WRAPPED me in a scarf he warmed on the heater before tucking me in his coat and zipping me in. While a snug fit, I enjoyed the odd sense of security.

"You could carry her in a duffle," Chase father's suggested.

"We have a ten block walk ahead of us. She might get cold in a bag. She won't get cold in my jacket."

"No, but she might get sweaty. With your sweat. That's a lot to ask of a woman you're not married to."

"Dad, stop. She's not right against my chest. She's protected by my shirt. She's not going to be covered with my sweat. Grow up."

Pity. I wouldn't have had any complaints being cuddled up to his sweaty chest. While I'd rather not be drenched in his sweat, I considered it a small price to pay for being close to him.

"If you're concerned about her getting cold, I have the SUV with me. I can drive you. That will be safer for her. You can leave your car parked here tonight, and when you return to work, I'll pick you up if the weather hasn't improved. I'll go tell the cops I'll meet them at the station to release your receptionist from timeout."

"Former receptionist. I have her firing letter already drafted." Chase returned to his desk, unlocked his drawer, and pulled out a sealed envelope. "You can deliver it. Make certain the police and her lawyer witness you delivering her notice of termination. Text me when she's opened it, and make certain she opens it in your presence."

"Having fired my fair share of employees over the years, I know how it works. What's my job position for this?"

"On my order, and I'm the damned CEO. You can be my assistant for the day. I'll even have HR draw up a temporary employment slip for you effective immediately." Chase muttered a curse, grabbed his phone, and said, "Tim, hire my father as my assistant effective this morning and pay the asshole minimum wage."

"Sir, we don't pay any of our employees minimum wage."

"Well, give him the lowest rate we pay and skimp on his benefits."

Chase's father laughed. "I don't need insurance. I'm already insured. Just put me on a contract for the next six months for half hours at minimum wage. I'll bail the brat out as needed."

"Sir?"

"Do it. Won't be the first time we've had a contractor. Get

him set up and send a contract for digital signature; I need him as an employee so he can deliver a firing notice."

"I'll have it sent to his email address on file within the next twenty minutes, sir."

"Thank you." Chase hung up. "Anything else I'm not going to like, old man?"

"Well, I have to go to the station to release your receptionist from timeout so she can talk. Things would be nicer if we didn't have to listen to her talk."

"You need to take ethics courses, Dad. She does get a chance to defend herself. Make it clear to the police we're prepared to request an angel to verify her actions."

"I'll make sure they know that," his father confirmed. "Get everything you need while I go tell the police I'm driving you to the animal shelter before meeting them at the station."

Chase sighed. "All right. Keep me in the loop on what's going on. If the temperature gets too low and you're done with the cops, I'll have you earn your money and pick us up from the shelter. If the weather isn't too bad, I'll walk home."

"Either way, be careful. If they're willing to come into your office attempting to get rid of Miriah through her allergies, they might go to the shelter."

"I may not be able to put people in timeout like you, but I'm not defenseless, Dad."

"I know you're not, but please be careful."

"Always."

Within ten minutes, we were nestled in an SUV on the way to the animal shelter, and Chase evicted me from his coat. The snow fell harder, but the drive didn't take as long as I expected; I assumed most had left work early to flee the storm, leaving only stubborn stragglers out and about.

Chase's father chuckled. "She likes the snow, doesn't she?"

"She spent most of the day watching it from the top of the curtains. After the almond incident, I thought it best to leave her to her watching. I'm going to set up a spot over the heater for her and bring her some hot chocolate tomorrow for when she's on break so she can enjoy it."

Chase would make concentrating on my work difficult with such a tempting bribe hanging in the air.

"You're not going into the office tomorrow. I already told HR to give everyone a paid day off. When they whined about you being the CEO and me just being a contracted assistant, I asked how they planned on getting to work through the estimated two to three feet of snow that'll be coming down tonight. That changed their tune without me having to say another word. I may have told them I'd handle any fallout with you. Go home after you've done your shelter work and stay home. I'd say go home now, but I know you won't listen."

"Point taken. I'll thank HR when I get a few minutes."

"What about me? Shouldn't you thank me?"

I descended from my perch near the window and crawled across Chase's lap. I hopped down to the console, stood on my hind feet and strained to reach Chase's father, cursing my short form.

Chase picked me up and held me towards his father. I patted the older man's shoulder.

"I can't tell if she's thanking you for me or if she's trying to tell me I'm being a baby and should stop whining."

"I can't tell if she's thanking you or being condescending, either," Chase admitted.

"Either way, she won that round. Oh, that reminds me. I asked your mother already. If you get tired of watching her, she's welcome to stay with us."

"No."

I appreciated Chase's immediate rejection of the offer.

"You're not being nice, Chase."

"I'm not going to get tired of watching her."

"Next you're going to tell me you want to marry her. You get tired of people being in your space within ten minutes. You always have. Have you asked her to marry you yet? Do you need help finding a ring? You need to have a ring to ask her. I know this sort of thing is difficult for you, but we're willing to help you."

"Dad, you're going to embarrass her. Anyway, if I even thought about that, you'd crash. The shelter's not far. Please don't crash indulging in your flights of fantasy. And anyway, if I were to propose, I'd arm myself with a bucket of that chicken. She probably wouldn't even notice the ring. She doesn't seem like the kind to be worried about a ring. I also suspect she's the kind of independent woman who'd want to pick her own ring since she's the one who will be stuck wearing it."

"Chase, Chase, Chase. You have this all wrong. Women want you to go through the hassle of trying to figure out what they'd like. I think you're onto something with the bucket of chicken, but make sure you give her a gift certificate for as much chicken as she wants for the duration of your relationship. As she's got herself a little boy, he's part of the package, too, so don't you forget to figure out how to earn your way into his good graces, too. A happy son makes for a happy mom, so you take care of that little boy, too. You can start by helping his mom find the perfect dog. Then you need to convince her to let you take some of the credit. Really, boy. You need to figure out what women really want, or you're going to be hopelessly single forever."

I stared at Chase's father in astonishment. For a man who presented himself as more than a little crazy, he had me figured out to frightening degree.

Chase's idea of arming himself with a bucket of chicken made perfect sense, and while embarrassing, I admitted he'd be well on his way to charming himself into the rest of my life with such a scheme. Therapy might help.

"I've had enough excitement for one day, Dad. Please just get us to the shelter intact."

"Just consider my advice. Also consider that your karma chameleon isn't protesting my suggestions."

Busted. I camouflaged and scrambled up Chase's arm and retreated into the safety of his coat to avoid any other discussions about what I wanted—and needed—in a man.

"Dad!"

"Relax, Chase. Maybe some time at the shelter will do you some good and give you some time to think. Miriah? If he bothers you, lock him in with an ankle biter and leave him there. It'll serve him right."

Poor Chase, stuck being related to such a strange man.

TEN

Horgis. Half husky, half corgi.

CHASE SLID out of his father's SUV, which was when Gavin's curse struck. It ignored my presence in his coat, and following a jerk, I shifted and landed in a snowbank with an unhappy shriek.

I viewed my removal from Chase's coat unacceptable, and I howled my fury over losing one of the few things that had gone right with my day. Snow infiltrated my clothes, and the shock of the cold whipped several extra curses out of me before I regained control over myself.

Chase grabbed my arm and hauled me to my feet. "Get inside before you freeze to death," he ordered.

Chase's father leaned towards the open passenger door and waved. "Have a nice night, Miriah," Chase's father said. "Go on and get inside."

"You, too—and thanks for the chicken. Drive safely." Pleasantries accomplished, I bolted for the shelter doors and barreled inside. The receptionist, an older woman and one of the shelter's few full-time employees, laughed while I stomped the snow off my slacks and shoes. "You forgot your coat, your gloves, and your scarf."

"Long story, Leah. How are you?"

"I'm good. What happened to your friend? I got a call that you were bringing someone else in with you?"

"The weather's bad enough she needed to head home, so I replaced her for today. He's outside chatting with someone."

"He?"

"Another long story. I heard none of the other volunteers are showing tonight?"

"No, not that I blame them. This weather is awful. We're going to have a busy night. We're packed with new animals. A puppy mill got busted, and we have fifty new dogs in, and they're all in bad shape."

Damn it. "What cretins."

"You don't have to dodge cursing around me, Miriah. I indulged for a solid twenty minutes this afternoon. The mill was attempting to breed designer dogs. They weren't doing a good job of it."

"What breed?"

"Horgis."

"What?"

"Horgis. Half husky, half corgi. They're younger dogs, ridiculously energetic, and have been going nuts because they're all crammed in the playroom. They've lived in cramped cages for their entire lives. They've finally settled down, but they've been romping. They all need baths."

I foresaw a wet, miserable evening. "Temperament?"

"Sweet, energetic, and most of them are so ugly only their mother could love them. We think the mill wanted to cash in on designer pups, got a few corgis and huskies, and bred them at random. They're cute in a fluffy and will love you to death sort of way."

Would Caleb like a fluffy but ugly dog? "Are they ugly or cute?"

"They're both. You'll understand when you see them."

"That sounds strangely ominous," I admitted.

"They'll be cuter once they're cleaned up and groomed. We've hosed the poor things off, but they need a lot of work."

"Those poor dogs."

Chase entered the shelter, and like me, he stomped the snow off before stepping fully inside. "He wouldn't stop talking."

Poor Chase.

"Try having a tween boy. Your father is an angel in comparison."

"Don't say such things about Caleb. Compared to my father, he's angelic—and he's definitely quieter than Dad."

"Go ahead. Try your luck, Chase. Invite Caleb over with your tree as it is right now. When he's done screaming, you'll be subjected to a lecture on the advantages of perfectionism."

Chase arched a brow. "Should I be concerned?"

"Only if he sees the tree in its current state."

I loved the sound of his laughter. "That explains your determination to redecorate. I can handle a temper tantrum. You don't need to redecorate unless you want to."

Leah stared at us with her mouth gaping open.

Introductions. Right. Damn it, Chase kept making me forget the basics. "Leah, this is Chase. He's standing in for Tiana so she could head home before the weather gets any worse."

"But what about you?"

I grinned. "I'm good. I'm going somewhere within walking distance."

"In those shoes?"

I stared at my feet. "Can we just forget today happened?"

Leah snorted. "I've a spare pair of boots that might fit, worst case, we've got rubbers you can borrow if needed."

Chase choked trying to smother his laughter.

Did perverted belong in the pro or con column? I needed to think about it later. "Come on, Chase. We have traumatized dogs to bathe. Are there enough kennels for them?"

"We've space for all but two, and one of them might be able to fit in a cat cage if we can find a pair of cats who can stay together, and that's after partnering up some of the smaller dogs that seem to get along well. We're going to have to find at least one foster."

"All right, Chase. Let's go clean some dogs."

THE SHELTER'S playroom didn't realistically fit fifty dogs, but the poor animals were so exhausted they slept on each other. Filth covered them, and I gagged at the thought they'd already been hosed off once already.

"It's not every day I contemplate murder, but I'm getting close," Chase confessed.

"Me, too." I wanted to drown the puppy mill operators. No, drowning killed them too quickly. I wanted to light them on fire and slowly roast them first. "Would you mind calling Gavin and asking for a stay of chameleon? I'm not leaving until they're all clean, and if I have to talk to him, I might add him to the people I want to kill today. I'll start with the first dog while you take care of him."

"Sure. I'll ask his divinity to bring you some winter clothes, too. I bet the bastard can teleport."

"Take a picture of the dogs, but warn Gavin that Caleb isn't to see the images. It'll upset him."

"Okay." Chase snapped a few photographs and headed towards the reception.

I cracked open the playroom door and snagged the nearest dog; she didn't even stir. I guessed she weighed about twenty pounds, and judging from the size of her paws, she had a lot of growing to do.

Instead of husky, I suspected the h in horgi stood for hulky; full grown, I wouldn't be surprised if she hit fifty pounds. The groom station included tall tub capable of containing small and mid-sized breeds, and I hauled the young dog in and rubbed her head until she woke up.

"Good girl," I soothed, petting her despite my skin crawling at the muck caked into her coat.

I grabbed the extendable faucet and turned on the water, careful to make sure it was room temperature. According to the horgi, I ushered in the apocalypse. She howled and ran from the stream. Pawing at the sides did her no good. I would win the war, although I'd try to win it with as minimal struggle and suffering for the dog as possible. Arming myself with the dog-friendly shampoo, I prepared to battle the unhappy animal.

"You'll be so much happier in twenty minutes," I promised.

The horgi didn't agree with me.

While she didn't enjoy her bath, she kept her protests to

agonized howls, notifying every animal in the shelter she'd endured torture at my hands.

"If you think this is bad, wait until you're being brushed."

Fortunately, her coat brushed out better than I expected, costing me only an extra ten minutes to transform her from a drenched rat to an ugly yet cute mess of fluff. With the stubby legs of a corgi, the ears of a husky, and a muzzle the awkward mix of both, she wouldn't place in a dog show, but I liked her black and tan fur, long enough to ensure her future owner would spend a lot of time caring for the pup.

Leah had it right. A dog could be devastatingly cute yet uglier than sin.

"Is that really a dog?" Chase asked, entering the grooming room carrying bags loaded with supplies. "I'm on collaring, walking, and helping with microchipping duty. Apparently, an aversion to injections isn't a permissible excuse, and I will be trained in how to safely assist them with chipping each dog and registering them in the system. Leah wants to finish traumatizing them in one fell swoop. The vet will be coming in the morning to handle all their vaccinations. I have more shampoo for you, and Leah thought you might need the clippers for some of the dogs. There's also medication if they have raw skin. Leah asked me to tell you to ask her if you need help figuring out which cream to apply. If you have to use the creams, you need to use the cones."

I worried what I would do if my night became any more complicated. "And Gavin?"

"He says it would be cruel to force you to transform while covered in that mess, so you have a stay of curse until after you can take a proper shower. He seems to think I'll be carrying you home sometime tomorrow, likely in the late afternoon."

Gross. "I'll walk. One of us covered in this is bad enough."

He nodded and shuddered. "This isn't what I imagined when I agreed to volunteer at an animal shelter."

"Oddly enough, this wasn't what I had in mind, either. I definitely didn't expect to give fifty rescues a bath."

"I'm relieved to hear that. Do you need any help washing them? I can try to figure out how to fit it in."

I grimaced at the thought of being covered in filth for hours. "I think I'll be all right. Only one of us needs to sacrifice our dignity and cleanliness. I've been promised humanity until after a shower. Please tell Gavin thank you, but if I shift before I'm in clean clothes, he dies at my hands."

"You got it. Shout if you need me. I'll check in with you and get the bathed dogs cared for and fed."

"Sounds good. And Chase?"

"What is it?"

"I'll need to be restrained if I meet the mill operators."

"I'll help you hide the bodies," he countered before walking off.

Was I supposed to add 'will help hide the bodies' to the con or pro list? I went with the pro column. It took real dedication to see a murder through to the very end.

THE LAST DOG of the batch cowered in the corner of the playroom and whined. What was left of my bruised and battered heart shattered at the sorry state of the animal.

However accidentally, I'd saved the dirtiest horgi for last, and I had no idea what I'd find under the muck and mats.

I couldn't even tell its gender. Once I cornered the pooch, I crouched. "Hey, baby. I'm not going to hurt you."

I'd lost count of the number of puppies I had needed to coax into cooperating with me since starting my mission to get them all cleaned so Chase and Leah could feed them and settle them into the kennels.

Some rescued dogs cowered, some became aggressive, and others did anything they could to please so they wouldn't be punished. The horgi wagged its tail so hard I worried it would hurt itself. I patted my leg. "Come here, baby."

I tried not to think too hard about what I'd need to touch to get the animal tolerably clean. When I finally coaxed the horgi to me, I discovered it—a she as far as I could tell—weighed far less than I expected.

The premeditated murder of a puppy mill operator wasn't really a crime, was it? If I got a good enough lawyer, could I swing a justifiable homicide conviction? I'd be happy serving years of community service in animal shelters as penance. Caleb would understand. He adored dogs. He'd scold me for taking the route of most violence, and I'd have to explain why he shouldn't kill puppy mill operators, too, but I'd figure something out.

Once the puppy trusted me enough I could pick her up, I carried her to the grooming room and set her in the tub, taking my time soothing her before subjecting us to the tedious process of trying to salvage her fur. She cowered through her bath, which took two bottles of shampoo before I surrendered to the inevitable and got out the clippers.

I hated muzzling her as much as she hated being muzzled, but I'd learned my lesson early: shaving a dog in such a condition hurt, and dogs in pain would bite to defend themselves. The only way to help her heal was to get rid of her matted fur and let it regrow.

Beneath the mats was raw, tender skin, and as I'd been instructed, I put a cup of warm water out with tea bags in them to brew, and once they were ready, I filled the spray bottle marked for tea and spritzed it all over her until Leah could administer the oral antibiotics.

She cried through the whole process, and so did I.

"All right, Miriah. It's time for us to go home. It's nine in the morning," Chase said from somewhere behind me. "A few volunteers made it in despite the storm. They can handle the rest. We've been here all night. Dad brought his SUV over, and he won't mind having it cleaned."

No. I didn't want to leave the horgi to go through the next stage by herself. "I have to cone her and she needs antibiotics. I had to shave her, and she'll get cold if she stays in the kennel."

"Blankets can take care of that, and I can help you get the cone on her. She'll be okay."

I didn't want to let her go, and I petted her head to reassure her. "She'll get cold," I repeated.

"Easy there, karma chameleon. I'll wrap her in my coat. She'll be fine on the walk to reception. Leah can take care of the rest, I promise. There's a displaced three-legged cat I'm taking home to foster so one of the smaller dogs can stay in its cage. If Leah can clear it, I don't mind bringing the puppy home, too. You can hold her in the car, but Leah wanted me to have her microchipped."

I shook her head. "Her skin is too raw. It could get infected. She'll have to be chipped later."

"Miriah, Leah still needs to see the dog."

"Later."

The woman in question laughed. "You're not winning this battle, Chase. That's one tired woman on a mission. What's this I heard about antibiotics?"

"Her skin's bad. I had to shave her."

Leah came over and examined the horgi. "I've got the antibiotics, I see you already treated her with tea. She's right, Chase. The microchip could abscess with her skin in this condition. She'll definitely be better off in a foster situation than trying to keep her warm in the kennel. I'll fill out the form and let the boss know I let a rescue out without a chipping. Take the muzzle with you in case you need it, and get her into a good cone. Don't worry about coming in tonight. I'll find someone to cover your shift. You need to get ready to go home so you can take a shower."

"I deserve a shower and a bath," I muttered.

"Let me take the puppy for a few minutes," Chase said, holding out his hands to take her.

While I grumbled curses, as the puppy didn't seem to object, I handed her over. The horgi tried her best to lick Chase's hand despite the muzzle. I couldn't tell if she wanted affection or was afraid.

"She'll be okay. The vet arrived ten minutes ago, so I'll jump this little lady to the front of the line and make sure she's cleared to leave the shelter. She won't be vaccinated, so you'll need to be aware of that when you're keeping her at your house, Chase. She'll need to come in for her vaccinations as soon as her skin has healed and she's off the antibiotics. Bring the puppy, Chase. Miriah, you're a mess. Hose yourself off. There's a towel by the door that's clean, and you can use the blow dryer."

Chase snorted. "Don't worry about cleaning off, Miriah. Wait till I get you home. Dad needs to clean his SUV anyway. If you hose yourself off, you'll freeze to death walking across the parking lot. I'll ask Dad to help you get ready to go while the vet checks the puppy over, okay?"

It would do. I doubted I could handle hosing myself off in the grooming room anyway. "Okay."

"It won't be long," he promised.

Silly man. Hadn't he ever taken a pet to the vet's before? We'd be waiting an eternity. I looked over my filthy clothes and sighed.

A trash can, some gasoline, and a match would solve the problem, as I doubted I'd ever get my outfit clean enough to wear again.

ELEVEN

If you're not out in twenty
minutes, someone will be
coming in to check on you.

TRUE TO CHASE'S WORD, I got to hold the shaved puppy on the ride to his house. I exchanged her muzzle for a cone, and she flopped on my towel-covered lap and fell asleep without a fuss. I stared out the window and admired the sunshine glistening off the snow. Any other day, the two to three feet covering everything might've annoyed me, but Chase's father handled the SUV like a champion, taking his time navigating the slick roads and sticking to the routes the plows had already cleared.

To keep me from shedding dirt everywhere, I wore a rain poncho over my clothes and sat on a towel. Father and son found my precautions ridiculous, but I'd won the battle with a few sniffles and a refusal to budge until I got my way.

The poncho and towel also kept me from getting dirt on the puppy's skin.

In defiance of Gavin's prediction I'd need to be carried, I

marched to Chase's front door, took my shoes off at the threshold, and set them in the trash can in the entry.

"I'm going to assume you don't believe your shoes are salvageable," Chase said, cradling the sleeping puppy in his arms while his father hauled the cat carrier into the house. "The bathroom is down the hall past the kitchen. Take your time."

While I'd already discovered the bathroom during my explorations, I played dumb and tiptoed across his home so I wouldn't make too much of a mess. Once inside the safety of the bathroom, I shed my clothes, which I immediately wrapped in the poncho and stuffed into the garbage can.

Someone knocked on the door. "Miriah?"

Damn it, I didn't want to deal with Gavin and his curse. "I'm about to take a shower. You're not invited."

"I brought clothing for you, and Chase offered a bathrobe as I forgot to grab yours."

Huh. Miracles could happen. "Thank you. Please crack open the door and leave everything inside. I'm going to take my shower now."

Gavin chuckled. "If you're not out in twenty minutes, someone will be coming in to check on you."

"Can that someone be Chase?" I wouldn't mind if Chase interrupted my shower. I could show off my tramp stamp to a desired audience that wasn't me for a change.

"I'll think about it. By the way, you're so tired you're not thinking before you speak. At all."

The pesky divine capable of reading minds would know. Damn, damn, damn. "I want a bath, but honestly, I'd drown right now."

Gavin sighed. "I'll ask Chase if he'll be a gentleman and

monitor you in a bath. I'll also be a gentleman, and as a reward for your good dog-helping deed, I'll refrain from restoring the curse until you're in your favorite pajamas and have had a chance to watch it snow while sipping hot chocolate. You might even get to have a cat on your lap and a puppy at your feet."

Gavin described my personal heaven, and I wanted it so much I almost cried. "You're being frighteningly nice."

"I'm proud of you for pulling an all-nighter to help those dogs and make them more comfortable and a little happier. Selfless acts deserve reward."

More miracles. Who knew Gavin could be useful in the miracle department? If I asked him for a few on purpose, would he be nice to me? "Thanks."

He chuckled, probably at my thoughts rather than my modest display of gratitude. "You didn't pick a bad man this time, but can you convince him to love you back?"

Wait. To love me back? I blinked. Oh. His comment made sense when I considered how often I thought of Chase as having possession of my heart and needing him to give it back. It made sense that somewhere along the way infatuation had taken a turn into the not-good category of flat out love.

Damn.

"You really are tired. Miriah, I cheat. It's what I do. But I don't cheat in the way you think. When I was with you, I was only with you, just like I was only with the other women I spent time with. I just didn't wait for long before moving on, that's all. That's my nature. I know it's not yours. How do I know? It's always at least a few months before you'll look at another man before you've had your heart broken yet again. It's like I actually pay attention to these things. That's all."

That's all. That was Gavin. I could accept that.

"Hey, you haven't yelled at me yet. That might be the real miracle here. I'll take it. Anyway, I'll tell Chase you could use some help and have him deal with your bath problem. You couldn't lift your arms over your head at this point even if you tried."

I tried and failed, as my shoulders throbbed from the motion. Ouch. "What did I do to deserve this?"

"No good deed goes unpunished. Consider it the price of admission for a shower with your current infatuation."

Love went beyond infatuation, but I'd worry about my love life problems later. Until Chase returned my heart through nefarious deeds and assholery, I was stuck. I'd just have to cope.

"You're something else, Miriah."

LIFE ALWAYS FOUND some way to screw with me. As Gavin always kept his word, I must have gotten into my favorite pajamas and had hot chocolate while watching it snow.

I remembered nothing of my shower, the following bath, if there had been one, or anything else of importance for that matter. While resigned to my frequent stays as a chameleon thanks to my inability to ignore Chase, I resented my inability to remember my hard-earned prize. Tricksy Gavin. No wonder he'd been so cooperative. He likely had known I was an incoherent mess and wouldn't remember anything. I refrained from hissing, snuggling into my warm nest to indulge in a proper sulk.

My nest purred.

Nests weren't supposed to purr.

I opened my eyes to a sea of gray fur. The purring intensified, and the three-legged cat Chase had opted to foster dragged its rough tongue over my nose.

Chase laughed, and he stroked his finger down my head and along the length of my back. "He cried until he could cuddle with you. He came from a household with a lot of lizards, and he was surrendered after his owner's death two years ago. He's six, and it seems his favorite thing in life is to sleep curled around lizards."

Right. No good deed went unpunished, and I was slated to become the pet—or appetizer—of a cat. A three-legged cat. With a lizard fetish.

Chase had picked his new pet well.

I'd have an interesting tombstone, that much was certain.

Chase smiled, and I decided potential death by cuddly three-legged feline was worth the risk.

"Good morning. You slept through most of the day and night. If you can get yourself together, Dad will bring the SUV over and take us to work. I packed a bag for you in case you shift again. I also took the liberty of ordering chicken for you. Dad's picking it up. The cat and dog are also coming into the office with us. They suckered me."

I needed half the luck of the two fostered pets. I foresaw Chase adopting them both in the near future. I stretched and yawned. The gray cat rolled onto his belly and batted me with his front paws. While curious how the cat had lost his back leg, I'd have to wait until I returned to human to ask—

and prepare with a box of tissues, as I'd inevitably cry because the cat was short a leg and I couldn't make it better.

I couldn't blame Chase for being suckered. The trap of an exposed kitty belly couldn't be resisted, not by me. I risked life and limb to pet the belly.

The kitty didn't eat me.

"Miriah? Are you up for going to the office?"

My work wouldn't finish itself, and until I finished my work, I couldn't ensure Chase's company was secure against whomever was trying to financially destroy it from the inside. The sooner I finished, the faster I could forget the little I remembered of my talk with Gavin. One question remained: how was I supposed to convince Chase to love me?

Life sucked sometimes.

SINCE ASSAULT with a glass of ice water and allergens hadn't worked, someone decided a Molotov cocktail tossed from a nearby roof with the help of some magic might do the trick. Instead of smacking into Chase's face, it hung inches away, its flame frozen in time.

When I grew up, I wanted a talent like the one Chase's father packed.

The horgi yipped and circled Chase's leg, tangling in her leash and the jury-rigged sweater meant to keep her bare skin protected from the cold. The cat, contained in his new fleece-lined carrier, hissed.

Chase's father stepped out of an SUV parked on the curb, and it wasn't the same one he'd brought the last time

I'd seen him. Why did crazy rich people insist on having more than one vehicle of the same type? As far as I could tell, the only difference was color, and the bright red blinded when showcased beside sun-touched snow. "You all right?"

"We're fine." Chase stared at the mess of dog and leash wrapped around his legs. "Mostly. I might need a hand with this. I don't want to drop the cat."

Bye-bye, heart. At the rate I kept wishing my poor heart off on its latest journey longing for Chase and his sweet ways, I'd be even more of a mess by the end of the week.

Men who cared about others did wonderful but terrible things to me.

"I'll get you untangled. Hand me Miriah. I'll put her in the house."

No. I liked Chase's shirt. I scrambled deeper into his clothes and hoped I wouldn't be removed from my favored spot.

"She rejects that option. She's fine where she's at. The fucker might try to torch the house with her in it, and she can't get out on her own."

"Quite possible." Convinced my sanctuary would remain mine, I returned to peeking over the collar of Chase's coat. His father pointed at the roof of a townhouse across the street. "They tossed that from over there."

"I don't see anyone. Damn it."

"Probably a toss and run with a bit of magic to help make certain they hit you. You've got a lot of trouble on your hands, boy."

"Mind taking the cat and dog to the car while I call the cops? Maybe we'll get lucky on some fingerprints." Chase eyed the floating Molotov cocktail with a scowl. "Have I ever told you you have one insane magic trick, Dad?"

"That insane magic trick saved you from reconstructive surgery to your face."

Chase muttered curses while his father took the cat to his SUV and then untangled the horgi from around Chase's legs. After twenty minutes of waiting, the cold seeped through Chase's coat, and not even his warmth prevented the lethargy from creeping in. I pressed as close as I could.

Chase's father hooked Chase's coat with a finger and peeked at me. "Take her inside, Chase. The poor thing's turned herself blue. If you don't want to put her in the house, put her in the SUV. I'm freezing my ass off, and I'm not cold-blooded."

Chase grunted, went to the SUV, and pulled me out of his coat, setting on the front passenger seat. "I won't be far," he promised.

The heater helped, and when I roused enough to want to move, I explored the vehicle. The puppy slept on the backseat, and the cat pawed at the mesh door of his carrier. I climbed to him, grabbed the zipper, and wiggled it open enough he could reach through it.

Since I couldn't keep Chase company, I'd play with the kitty. Could anyone blame me for wanting to play with a pretty gray kitty? Whoever blamed me needed to mind their own business. We took turns lightly batting at each other, and the times he won, he never pawed me hard and his claws always remained sheathed.

When the police finally arrived, I climbed on top of the carrier to watch through the window.

Chase's scowl warned me the conversation wasn't going

like he wanted. While they argued, the cops smothered the frozen flames, which involved a damp cloth wrapped around the wick using a pair of tongs. It took a long time for them to extinguish it without touching the rest of the bottle. Once extinguished and safe to handle, the Molotov cocktail went into a bag to serve as evidence.

I wondered if the culprit had expected the volatile bottle to survive long enough to become evidence.

The wait bored me, and when Chase and his father finally returned to the SUV, I scolded them with several hisses.

Chase twisted in his seat, stretched between the seats, and snagged me off the carrier. "Sorry, Miriah. I should've put you in the SUV before you got cold."

With admirable powers of observation, he dumped me on his lap and took the time to nudge the cat's paw back inside the carrier and close the zipper.

"I'm not sure I want to take you to work. They're upping their game from single attacks against Miriah to attempted double homicide. That could have killed both of you."

"I'm aware, but we need to flush them out and catch them in the act. There's not much else we can do. The faster Miriah finds out the source of the thefts, the faster we're clear of this mess."

Great. I couldn't tell if the pressure from trying to meet Chase's expectations or the culprit would kill me first.

Chase's father sighed. "You're a pain in my ass. What happened to her shopping trip with Tiana on Sunday? If you haven't figured this out yet, I'll do you a favor. Do not interfere with a mother shopping for her child on Christmas. It may very well be the last thing you do."

"I'll be going with her. Let's make a day of it. Bring Mom

and tag along. She probably has some shopping she needs to do, and if Mom can't handle any unforeseen circumstances, no one can."

Stunned silence answered Chase's suggestion. I lifted my head and stared at Chase's father. What was so abnormal—or terrifying—about Chase's mother that his father would look like he faced the devil himself?

"You want to bring your mother to the mall on Sunday."

"That's what I said, yes."

"I know you don't like going to the mall, but bringing your mother is excessive. She might flatten the whole place if she has to handle any problems. Have you ever met your mother, boy? She might literally flatten the entire mall. The entire building. Gone." Chase's father snapped his fingers. "Just like that. Boom."

Chase rolled his eyes. "Would you please stop exaggerating? You're going to freak Miriah out. Anyway, Mom wouldn't flatten the entire mall. She'd only relocate the parts that annoyed her, got in her way, or otherwise posed a threat to a place of her choosing."

"Son, I don't want to pay a hundred thousand dollar fine again for any incidents. That's her base fine. You hear me? The base fine is a hundred thousand dollars. You know how much I'll have to pay if she relocates the mall?"

"Nothing unless she doesn't put it back where she found it. It's only when she destroys something she has to pay more fines."

"You're willfully forgetting the per-person fine tacked on to the hundred thousand."

"You can afford it."

"If I keep having to pay her fines, I won't be able to! She'll bankrupt me."

"No sympathy from me. You married her."

Chase's father sighed. "Please, Chase. Don't invite your mother."

"I'm inviting my mother. If you aren't enough to safeguard Miriah's Christmas shopping, I'll use the big guns. In this case, the big guns is my mother. Deal with it."

"You're being a little overbearing."

A little? While I'd heard of teleportation magic, those who possessed it were few and far between, and I'd never heard of anyone capable of relocating entire buildings before. I wondered how far Chase would go to protect my Christmas shopping adventure.

As long as I could find the right puppy, the rest of the shopping I could do online. Did I want to remind him of that? I'd have to put a lot of thought into it. On one hand, online delivery would be safer. On the other hand, I wanted to meet Chase's mother and see if she was half as crazy as his father. How had two insane people produced someone like Chase?

What was his magic trick if he came from two overpowered humans?

Chase glared at his father, and after a few muttered curses, he sighed. "And? It's obviously needed. Maybe I wouldn't need to be overbearing if people stopped trying to kill her."

"There's no need to get hysterical. She's fine. She was playing with the cat while she waited. If she can handle this without having a fit of hysterics, so can you."

"Dad, I'm not having a fit of hysterics. Someone tried to kill her."

"Boy, I helped raise you from the day you were born. You're five minutes from a meltdown and a round in time-out. Settle down. She's fine. Nobody was hurt, and now that we know they're serious, we can take steps to protect her. You've already cut off their main funding source, so it's possible that bottle bomb was meant for you and not her. If you expose or accuse the involved companies for siphoning funds, they'll be in some severe financial trouble. And you will expose them. You're a stickler for fair play and you have a reputation for honesty. Some days, I swear your mom banged an angel on the side."

"Dad, Mom didn't bang an angel or the angel's incubus sidekick."

"Much to her disappointment, I'm sure," Chase's father muttered.

"Complain about me inviting Mom to the mall with us on Sunday, and I'll tell her you think she's disappointed she didn't bang an angel and an incubus."

"You're supposed to be embarrassed, not using my commentary as blackmail."

"Why do you think the Molotov cocktail was aimed at me?"

"I think it was specifically aimed at your head. A person on the roof would've had no idea Miriah was in your coat. Most would have assumed she was in the carrier. No, I think it was aimed at you, and I think whoever lobbed it used a practitioner trick to make sure they didn't miss. You're fortunate my magic is stronger than practitioner trickery."

"I could've handled it."

"Only my son would believe he can handle a Molotov cocktail to the face. Where did I go wrong with you?"

"Why are you being a jackass today?"

"Someone tried to fry my boy with a Molotov cocktail. You tell me."

As I wasn't about to come between Chase and his father, I listened to them argue and feigned disinterest while wondering how my parents would've reacted if I'd been the one almost hit in the face with a flaming bottle.

They'd likely be disappointed the attacker had missed.

A woman who'd lost her last fuck was to be approached with caution.

In the reception of Chase's office, a woman with the face of an angel and the mouth of a devil dressed down an older man in a suit. The suit warned me the old man had been around the block in the business world, but he flinched at every profanity pouring out of the woman's mouth. She seemed young, but I refused to trust my eyes when she faced off against an experienced businessman without a single fuck to give about his pride. I expected she'd been around a lot longer than her cherubic appearance implied.

I added her to my short list of women to automatically respect, since a woman who'd lost her last fuck was to be approached with caution.

"You were given clear instructions," she snapped, and that she'd delivered the line without a single curse rang alarm bells in my head. She likely wound up to deliver an even worse blow—or gave her vocabulary a rest to find more effective curses. Either way, I foresaw trouble. "Explain exactly why you opted to ignore them?"

"Please," her opponent begged. "It's not my fault."

I hoped the poor man survived giving her the absolute worst answer a man could give a woman on the warpath.

Her eyes narrowed, she sucked in a breath, and barked, "Like fucking hell it's not! You're in charge of the entire marketing department. You better damned well start figuring out that every fucking thing that goes wrong in marketing is your fucking fault!"

Chase retrieved me from my safe haven in his shirt and placed me on his shoulder. "There are other words. You don't need to sprinkle fuck in all the time. Add some variety."

I hoped Chase survived his blunder, and I hoped I stayed out of the crossfire. I clutched his jacket, and pondered climbing to a safer location.

The woman sniffed. "I don't want to accidentally summon the devil. If I summon him, it'll be on fucking purpose, and I'll use the phone to call him like a civilized being. Mind your own fucking business."

Without a care in the world, Chase snorted. "It's my company. I am minding my business, thank you."

Brave, foolish Chase. I searched for an easy path of escape but determined I'd have to stay with him and watch the fireworks. How many times would I witness Chase in a life-threatening situation in a single day? I'd reached my quota at two.

"You weren't supposed to remember it's your company now. Why aren't you in your office where you belong? If you were in your office where you belonged, you wouldn't be witnessing this right now."

Considering her volume, Chase would've probably witnessed the opening volley instead of arriving partway through, and I was grateful I couldn't open my mouth and speak my mind.

As though sensing I considered making a run for it, Chase lifted his hand and stroked my back. I'd have to thank Gavin for that part of the curse later. When else would I get so much affection without having to ask for it?

Chase's father cleared his throat. "Someone threw a Molotov cocktail at his face this morning." When Chase scowled at his father, the older man swiped me off his son's shoulder and set me on the woman's head. I grasped her hair so I wouldn't fall, eyeing the floor and the quickest route of escape. "This is Miriah. He gets hysterical whenever she's threatened, so don't threaten her. Her favorite food is fried chicken, and she will bite you if you tease her with her favorite food. Chase has been warned he'll be put in timeout if he can't cool his heels. The cat and dog are fosters because the shelter's full due to a busted puppy mill operation. He couldn't stand seeing them crammed into cages, so he took home two."

The woman reached up and patted me, keeping her touches gentle. "She's a lizard. Chase, darling, have you lost your fucking mind? Are you a moron? You're supposed to date a human—or at least a sentient. Honestly, I won't be picky. If you want a non-human sentient, I'm okay with that."

I snapped my teeth at her hand, and when I missed, I went for the bitch's ear and latched on as hard as I could. She howled and smacked at me with her hands. "Get it off! Get it off!"

"Hit her, and I make no promises Chase won't be earning a fine using his magic," his father warned in a tone so cold I worried the temperature would drop in the room.

The woman spewed more curses, but she didn't hit me. "Just get the fucking thing off!"

Chase sighed, shook his head, set the cat carrier down and grabbed me around my middle. "Let her go, Miriah."

I bit harder.

"Miriah, my mother's very sorry she was uncouth and insulted you. I'll make sure she pays penance later. Please let go."

I obeyed, but I hissed profanities at the woman, and I didn't care if she was his mother. Also, if I looked that young after having a son like Chase, I'd count myself blessed.

Raising a man like Chase must have taken a great deal of work, but one critical fact remained: I'd bite her again. To make it clear I'd bite her again, I showed off my teeth and hissed some more.

"Mom, what are you doing here?"

"Apparently, I'm getting my ear pierced by a lizard and asking you about why you tried to have reconstructive surgery with a Molotov cocktail."

Chase rolled his eyes. "Craig, retreat while you can. We'll be discussing the stolen funds situation as soon as I'm finished here. If you would compile a list of all marketing team members with authorizations to draw from the extra expense account, I'd appreciate it. If you have the information available, a list of everyone who can draw from that account would be useful. Thank you."

The older man fled without looking back. I hissed at him, too.

"Are you finished terrorizing everyone, Mom?"

"I'll think about it. What's this nonsense about the reconstruction of that pretty face with a Molotov cocktail?"

On that, his mother and I were agreed: Chase's pretty face had no business being reconstructed with a Molotov cocktail.

Chase shrugged, settled me on his shoulder, and stroked my back. I considered the gesture an act of defiance, and I participated through strategic nuzzling of his hand to indicate I enjoyed his attention.

Which I did, shamelessly.

Chase gave his mother a few minutes to stew before he shrugged. "Someone took offense to my pretty face. Dad thinks someone is pissed off I cut off their easy way to suck money out of my company."

"What a cretin. Faces should be off limits, especially faces as pretty as yours."

Again, I agreed with her, but that didn't stop me from hissing at her when her attention fell on me again.

"Also, your lizard bit me."

"My 'lizard' is a rather nice woman who has been attacked several times while helping me identify who is behind this mess. Denise tried to kill her in my office. Someone else, the culprit still unknown, tried to hurt her in the spare office a few doors down, too. Using a glass of ice and water."

"It doesn't take much to kill a little lizard like that. Bad aim?"

Chase grunted, and when he made a quiet growling sound in his throat, I patted his cheek to soothe him. "They had bad intel with a little help from a divine curse. The curse makes her pretty durable while a karma chameleon. Her allergy to almonds isn't that severe, which helped a lot," he admitted.

"Caught the woman in the act?" his mother asked.

"Miriah witnessed it while she was hiding in my office when Denise paid her a visit. Dad put her in timeout afterwards until the police arrived. What bothers me is she went right into my office to do it."

"Well, that wasn't very smart of her. So, your lizard is a sentient, then?"

"She's the one who has been analyzing the company reports to find the culprit of the fund discrepancies. As such, yes, Mother, she's a sentient. She's also a single mother of a son. He's twelve, and a pretty nice kid."

Damn straight my little boy was a pretty nice kid, and to make it clear she wasn't going to be saying anything bad about my boy or my single mom status, I hissed at her and changed to my brightest, angriest red.

"She's not your girlfriend?"

"Mother!"

Chase's response I expected, but the interest in his mother's tone earned another hiss, in part due to my inability to claim status as his girlfriend. In the grand scheme of things, I'd do a lot more than earn my way to the top of Santa's naughty list for a chance to claim someone like Chase as my partner in life. At the rate we were going, a partner in crime might be the stronger possibility, since I had the growing need to bite other people for messing up my life, too.

Chase's father cleared his throat again to draw attention to himself. "Let him get his menagerie settled into his office.

The puppy has had a rough time of it lately, and Chase'll get pissy if we stress her more than necessary."

The puppy in question sat quietly at Chase's feet, wagging her tail with no sign the conversation bothered her at all.

To keep Chase's father from adding me to the menagerie, I crawled into Chase's coat and hissed at the older man.

Chase laughed, snagged the collar of his coat with a finger, and made more room for me. "You don't have to hide, Miriah. Really. Mom's crazy, but she's not that crazy."

"What have I told you about calling me crazy?"

"Before I turned eighteen, you kept threatening something about cleaning my mouth out with soap, but honestly, your threats lost their effectiveness because you loved me too much to put soap in my mouth. After I turned eighteen, you kicked me out of your house for doing it and told me to get a life, which I did."

If Chase taught Caleb to be even half as smug, I'd have a lot of trouble on my hands.

"What did I do to deserve you for my son?"

"You decided to have sex with Dad. To me, it sounds like you got exactly what you deserved. You wanted a kid. Dad can't take any of the credit; I've heard the story enough times to be well aware he was a hapless, seduced husband wanting to keep the home happy." Chase laughed, snagged the cat's carrier, and hauled it towards his office. "Hey, Dad? Mind getting the rest of the supplies while I get everyone settled?"

Chase's father sighed. "Keep an eye on our son while I'm gone. He's nothing but trouble."

"He's been that way since he insisted on putting up a thirty-two hour fuss about his eviction from my womb. Thirty-two hours, you ungrateful little snot!"

Chase snickered and herded the puppy while carrying the cat down the hall. "Love you, Mom. Please don't traumatize Miriah. She's had a rough time of it lately."

"Worse than thirty-two hours of son eviction?"

"Well, she bathed fifty shit-covered rescue dogs in an all-nighter the other day. How does that rank?"

"Since she's only twelve years into her solo parent adventure, I'll let her win this one. What happened to the dogs?"

Chase set the cat carrier down long enough to untangle the horgi from his legs, who insisted on keeping close and whipping him with her tail. "Puppy mill got busted. Miriah started to cry after shaving this poor girl, so I agreed to foster her. She's unvaccinated because of her skin issues," he warned. "She needs to heal first, but hopefully it'll only be a few weeks before she can go in for her shots."

"What's her name?"

"Don't know yet. I'll have Miriah name her. The cat's name is Stumpy, but I don't like it, so I'm renaming him. I haven't decided what yet."

Yep, Chase had adopted a dog and a cat and didn't know it yet.

"Why is the cat named Stumpy?"

"He only has three legs."

"Well, that makes sense. How about Shùdūn?"

"I'm not naming him Stump in Mandarin."

"Fine. Be that way." His mother followed us into Chase's office. "No grandbabies for me yet?"

While I rather liked the idea of having another child and wouldn't have any objections to testing my luck with Chase in bed, I gaped at her bold question.

"Have I brought home a woman yet for Thanksgiving,

Christmas, or any other holiday for that matter? No, I haven't."

"Don't be unreasonable. You took a single mother home with you. Sure, she's a little cursed, but she comes prepackaged with a grandchild for me to spoil. I can work with a prepackaged grandchild to spoil. Is he cute?"

"Mom, you don't get any say in this."

"But I want a grandchild to spoil."

Me, too, but I estimated I had at least another ten to twenty years of patiently waiting to get one, and in the meantime, I wouldn't object to a second child. If that meant providing Chase's mother with a prepackaged grandchild to spoil in the meantime, I'd be okay with that.

I needed to put my ovaries in timeout before they got any additional ideas. For some reason, I doubted Chase's father would help me out even if I asked. He'd probably lead the army seeking a grandchild. He seemed like the type.

"I'm sorry, Miriah. Please feel free to ignore her."

I wiggled out of his coat, waited for Chase to reach his office, and pointed at his computer. After his mother closed the door, he freed the cat from the carrier and unclipped the horgi's leash before unlocking the system for my use and opening his word processor.

I asked if she babysat for free as part of the spoiling package.

Chase laughed so hard he slumped over his desk and beat the polished surface with his fist.

"What's so funny?" his mother demanded.

While he attempted to splutter something, he ultimately pointed at his monitor. With a puzzled expression, his mother joined us and read the screen.

Then she joined her son in helpless laughter. "I'm retired, Miriah. It's in the handbook. Retired grandmothers offer free spoiling of grandchildren, and temporary accommodations are included in the package. I take it you have problems finding a babysitter?"

I could find a babysitter easily enough, but Tiana couldn't teleport parts of buildings or put people in timeout. I bobbed my head.

Tiana would forgive me after I told her about Chase's parents and their excessive magical abilities.

"I remember those days. Tell Chase if you need a sitter, especially if you want to plan a date. Dating's hard without kids. With? Surely impossible."

What was dating? I tapped out a message indicating I'd consider giving Caleb away some weeks for a single hour in a bubble bath without interruption.

"You poor thing. Chase, darling, do arrange for her baby boy to come over every now and then. Moms need uninterrupted bubble bath time. It's a law of the universe."

Chase groaned his laughter and oozed to the floor.

"It's really not that funny."

Chase certainly thought so. Shaking my head at the man's absurd behavior, I skittered across his desk to my computer and went to work.

WITH CHASE and his parents on guard, I enjoyed a full day of work without interruption. To my delight, the cat wanted to cuddle while I navigated the murky waters of corporate reporting. He kept me warm, sported a perpetual purring motor, and hissed whenever Chase edged in on his turf.

Add in a breakfast and lunch of fried chicken, and I could get used to life as an inconvenienced lounge lizard. Gavin's curse could kiss my ass. Who needed to blend in when I could have fun, get my work done, and keep company with a cool cat?

Since being good hadn't gotten me anywhere, I'd have to try something new. But what?

I'd spent so long trying to be a good mother I wasn't sure how to go about changing my colors and having fun despite Gavin's curse. Silently laughing whenever Chase was thwarted by a three-legged cat counted, I hoped. Sometime after I lost count of Chase versus Cat incidents, I crawled across the desk, borrowed Chase's computer, and notified him he should name the cat Goliath. As Chase's name wasn't David, he'd be stuck losing to the cat. And, as I was working hard on earning coal for Christmas, I told Chase he wouldn't make a very good David in general.

I returned to my computer to finish working, hoping to find the solution to Chase's mystery sooner than later.

"That isn't fair," Chase complained. "I buy you chicken. Goliath doesn't."

The newly dubbed Goliath returned to his nap while I prepared a list of companies likely involved in the effort to siphon an extra ten percent out of Chase, a relatively easy task when I compared current financial data with historic performance and isolated dives in the figures.

It took me most of the day to determine when the scheme had begun, but I emerged the victor.

Satisfied with my effort, I emailed Chase the list and thumped his desk to get his attention.

"She's pretty demanding, isn't she?" Chase's mother asked from her post as a couch warmer. Chase's father snored from his side of the couch.

"She's not being demanding. She's telling me there's something that needs my attention." I suspected Chase had some form of telepathy as he checked his email without me needing to go to his computer and tell him to. "She's made a list of companies likely involved, and I can link most of them to one parent company. This simplifies things a lot—and gives me a good way to put a permanent end to this. Wake Dad and guard the hallway for a few minutes, please."

"And what about Miriah?"

"Miriah stays with me, of course."

On a scale of one to ten, Chase was approaching twelve on the dominant alpha male controlling chart. I missed having eyebrows, as I wanted to raise one at his statement.

Obviously, I needed to take lessons on being naughty from Chase, and I'd sign up for clothing-free sessions if he insisted on displaying protective tendencies.

As long as he kept his protective tendencies reasonable.

Keeping me close and safe counted.

Yep, I had more issues than I knew how to fix, and I wasn't sure if I wanted to fix them. It'd be tough raising a son while stuck as a chameleon most of the time.

Chase's mother sighed. "You're going to skin some other CEO aren't you?"

"Something like that."

"Have fun. Try not to burn down too many bridges today."

Chase arched a brow. "I left the Molotov cocktail with the police. It seems I'm out of matches, too. I'm sure I'll be able to manage without burning any bridges."

His mother scowled, heaved a sigh, and woke his father. "We're being evicted by the brat. He wants to make a phone call. You should go check on your gorgon while I guard the door."

For two people who didn't have any specific reason to stay in Chase's office, they took a long time leaving.

Chase leaned back in his chair and chuckled the instant they were gone. "I might have to hire you away from Alex. Did you know most of these companies were under the umbrella of one larger corporation?"

I shook my head.

"Well, they are, and I wouldn't be surprised if the company's main shareholders were in on it. They're greedy bastards—the type of people I don't want investing in my business at all. We'll find out soon enough. The owner of the main company is Mitchel Ganarn, and he's transparent without realizing it. If he acts surprised, he's in on it. He's quiet when he learns something new, and then he acts surprised. There's a little hesitancy when he's taken by surprise."

Interesting. I wondered what Chase thought of me. Was I as transparent?

I abandoned my computer and crawled across his desk to sit near the phone. Goliath yawned, stretched, and shot Chase a dirty glare before resuming his nap.

I wanted to take Chase's new cat home with me. Would Chase accept applications to live in his house so I could spend time with his cat? I could live with chilling out at Chase's house while a chameleon, assuming I could figure out how to handle Caleb's care. Talking to Gavin about putting more duties on his fatherly shoulders might do the trick. I could handle once a week chilling with Goliath and his pet human Chase.

Chase reached for his phone, detoured long enough to give my back a brisk rub, and dialed a number. He enabled speakerphone with the press of a button.

"It's not like you to call me on a Friday, Chase. What can I do for you?"

Something about the man's voice, carrying a hint of sarcasm and a sharp edge I didn't like, annoyed me so much I had to fight the urge to hiss at the phone.

I succeeded, barely.

"Were you aware someone in marketing at your companies is skimming up to ten percent of the advertising invoices issued to my company?"

I understood what Chase had meant about the man's behavior; there was a hint of silence before the other CEO replied, "Did you just say someone has been skimming up to ten percent off my advertising invoices?"

"Yes, I did. Also, someone tossed a Molotov cocktail at my face this morning because I cut off the extra expenses fund, which is where the increased percentages were being paid out from. Assuming you know nothing about this, you're likely missing a hefty chunk of change, too. One of those responsible has a magical ability capable of disguising their activities. It seems I've developed a resistance to it due to exposure."

"I think you're not the only one. I have noticed there's been something fishy about my numbers across the board, but I haven't been able to figure out what."

"Well, I've mostly figured it out for you." Chase read off the names of most of the companies on the list. "From what I can tell, the magic in use alters perceptions of the statistics reports and redirects attention elsewhere. I have someone in my employment who is immune to this redirection."

"And you said they're skimming ten percent?"

"Roughly. That used to be the wiggle room I'd allow for campaigns for additional expenses. That wiggle room is now gone. Your numbers will show change effective today, but I expect more problems unless we can identify who is siphoning the money and using the magic to hide the theft. The why is easy enough. It's a lot of money. We've been working together for a long time, Mitchel, but I can't allow a ten percent theft to slide. We need to cut this off at the source, and I'm willing and eager to renegotiate a new contract once the culprits in both of our firms are identified. Unfortunately, to make sure we both don't continue to take losses, I'm going to implement the out clause for all our advertising contracts. I'll be terminating all employees found guilty of this theft and pressing charges as able. Once you've done the same, we'll talk about how to expand our operations using that extra ten percent we've been losing."

Mitchel chuckled. "I can accept a full loss right now for a ten percent expansion after the dust is settled. I'll call you back in a few hours if I find any information. If I don't, I'll send you a message as soon as I find something out."

"Sounds good." Chase hung up. "And that, Miriah, is how to light a fire under someone's ass. He wasn't aware that the funds were being siphoned, but he was aware something was up—so I don't think he would've pocketed the ten percent or even part of it himself. He's been after a contract expansion for a while, too. This could benefit us both in the long term. Now, to make him squirm a little more." Chase pressed a button on his phone, and a woman answered. "Rachel, I have a job for you."

"What can I do for you, sir?"

"I'm executing the ten-day out clause on all companies belonging to Mitchel Ganarn. Please pull copies of the contracts, send them to our lawyer, and have them prepared for signing by the end of the day. I also want a list of all employees with any involvement in those contracts. I don't care what department they're in."

"Yes, sir. Effective when?"

Chase checked his cell. "The ten day timer starts now. I've already notified Mitchel."

"The contracts should be ready for you for signing within the next two hours. Do you need anything else?"

"A vacation and possibly a stiff drink. Thanks, Rachel," he replied before hanging up. "Want to make a bet on how long it is before someone tries to kill us again?"

I shook my head.

"We could bet chicken. No one's going to target you anymore because I just painted 'target me' on my forehead with my decision to sever those contracts. They're going to forget all about you when they find out they just lost their jobs and their monthly illegal bonus. I hope they saved some, because they're about to find out that crime doesn't pay."

An angry Chase seemed to throw caution to the four winds, and I had a feeling it would bite us both in the ass before everything was said and done. While landing us in hot water belonged on the con list, I wanted to watch the fireworks and help him make the most of a bad situation.

Forget my damned heart. I needed my common sense back.

THIRTEEN

Are you going to die of
embarrassment if you're seen
wearing pajamas in my office?

As soon as the call ended, Chase summoned his parents back to discuss methods of ensuring no one could siphon funds again in the future. With the primary issues identified, Chase no longer needed me, and we both knew it. It took me several hours to work up the nerve to ask him if he needed me for anything else.

I wanted him to say yes.

"I'll make something up for you to do on Monday. Until I know, for certain, who is behind this, you're staying with me. They've tried violence to stop us, they'll probably feel no compunctions about revenge, and while I'm the primary target, you're safer with me."

I liked the way he thought. Longer with him gave me longer to figure out how to earn a coal mine from Santa and ditch Gavin's pesky curse. I had only one idea on how to ditch the pesky curse.

Using his computer, I suggested he propose a stay of

curse to Gavin as the culprits weren't above attempting murder, and it would be much easier to protect myself as a woman than as a chameleon.

"That's probably a good idea." Chase retrieved his cell and thumbed through his contacts before holding it to his ear. "Gavin, I have a favor to ask of you. It's about Miriah. The situation has become serious enough that I can't guarantee her safety if she stays a chameleon. We're getting close; someone tossed at Molotov cocktail at us this morning. Yes, she's fine. My father froze it, and the police took it as evidence. I'm sure you have your—"

Chase blinked, and his mouth dropped open. "Well, now that I'm aware of the situation, yes, I'm definitely interested. That aside, her safety comes first."

Gavin said something that made Chase roll his eyes. "Miriah, are you going to die of embarrassment if you're seen wearing pajamas in my office?"

I'd be perfectly fine wearing nothing at all in his office, and I'd ignore any humiliation associated with anyone other than Chase seeing me naked, meaning his parents, both of whom were lounging on the couch. I shook my head so hard I rattled my brain in my lizard skull.

"She's about to give herself whiplash. I'm fairly confident she wishes to talk in English without requiring the assistance of a computer."

Truer words had never been spoken. Before I could draw a breath, I snapped back to human, clipped my head on the edge of Chase's desk on the way to the floor, and barely missed landing on the puppy, who pounced with excited yips. I fended her off with an arm, which left me easy prey for Goliath, who invaded my lap.

A lap full of cat and puppy with Chase for company all while I was a human seemed like a Christmas miracle to me.

"Thank you, Gavin. I'll keep you in the loop on how we're progressing on identifying everyone involved. I'll let her know." He hung up. "Gavin changed the terms of your curse, as he claims it's too much of a bother to fully remove it. So, as long as you don't book plane tickets, wear a bikini outside while it's snowing, jam out to heavy metal in a library or a church, or buy chicken for yourself, you'll remain human."

I was fully behind all the conditions until he reached the chicken part. I could live with everything except that last, critical condition. "I can't buy chicken for myself?"

"He said the instant you reach for any method of payment, you'll become a chameleon. Also, you can't pay anyone back for buying you chicken. If you try to ask for chicken, you'll also turn into a chameleon."

Chase's parents stopped paying attention to their phones long enough to laugh at me.

"I can't even ask for chicken?" I wailed.

"He had to make the conditions equivalent, and it seems I underestimated your adoration for fried chicken. You're now at the mercy of those who know you for your next hit of chicken."

I needed to figure out how to get revenge on Gavin. Death wouldn't do. Oh, no. Death would limit his suffering. I scowled and stroked the animals vying for space on my lap. "He will pay for this."

"It's not that bad, but if it makes you feel better, I'll help you make him suffer for limiting your access to your favorite food. In good news, there's still chicken left over from this morning."

Leftovers would help some. "I feel like I've been tricked."

Chase grinned. "Being a chameleon was easier knowing you could ask for chicken?"

"Now if I ever ask for chicken again, I'll have to do it as a chameleon, and I'll have to hope my wallet doesn't transform with me. Knowing Gavin, it will. With my wretched luck, I'll never have chicken again."

I blamed the stress of people trying to kill me for my overreaction, but I gave myself credit for realizing I overreacted. A normal person wouldn't get so upset over losing fried chicken, would they?

Then again, I was cursed by a divine for refusing to marry him. That eliminated me from the pool of normal people.

"Well, I wouldn't worry much about your chicken problems. I think you'll find your chicken supply safe despite your new inability to ask for it at your whim."

I considered his words and the implication he'd provide me with chicken. Yep, my odds of locating my lost heart and restoring my common sense deteriorated by the minute. I'd cope, and while I coped, I'd look for some new goals in life, including ditching my tendency to blend in even when human. "Do you think killing Gavin will put me on Santa's naughty list?"

A coal mine would make me a fortune in the long run, wouldn't it?

"Don't limit yourself to murder, Miriah. The suffering lasts longer if you leave him alive."

Who needed a heart or common sense when a partner-in-crime could be had? Not me. "What do you think would maximize his suffering?"

Chase's grin promised trouble for someone. "Well, it's obvious he likes you, so you should date others and think about how much you're really enjoying your dates with other men. Since he's a telepath, you'll drive him loony. You might even teach him to stop listening in on your thoughts. With a little work, you can make him uncomfortable *and* jealous."

I knew one way I could make Gavin jealous. "Like thinking about the location of my tramp stamp?"

"Yes, but it's a tattoo. It's not a tramp stamp if you're not a tramp. You're not a tramp."

"Why do people keep telling me this?"

"Because you're too sweet and loyal to be a tramp. I thought this was obvious."

I hoped my heart and common sense enjoyed their vacation together, probably visiting somewhere with better weather. "Do I have to charge to be a good tramp? Is it the sweet or loyal part that's a problem? I don't see how I'd make a poor tramp, thank you. I'd make a good tramp if I tried, I'm sure of it."

"Tramp, Miriah. Not prostitute."

"There's a distinction?"

"Prostitutes are paid."

I narrowed my eyes and considered that. "Ask Gavin if prostituting for chicken is off the list."

"It's off the list. You'd still be asking for it."

Judging from the sounds coming from Chase's couch, his parents might die from trying not to laugh. I sighed and bowed my head. A double count of accidental murder would put me on Santa's list and likely land me in prison. In court, would they believe me if I blamed Chase for their demise?

"That came out wrong. I'm sorry," Chase muttered.

His parents laughed harder.

The glare he leveled at his parents would've killed lesser mortals. "Are you two children?"

"Body of an old woman, mind of a teenager," his mother reported.

"I never matured beyond age eight or so. I was an early bloomer," his father added.

Chase grunted. "Want a pair of parents? I'll sell them cheap."

Chase's parents seemed like an upgrade over mine. "If I take them, you have to take my prejudiced devout Catholic parents off my hands."

"I sense family drama worse than mine on the horizon."

"I'll give them to you for free."

Chase eyed his parents. "Your parents can't be that bad, can they? Do you spend any of the holidays with them?"

"Christmas Eve Mass. Otherwise, no."

Chase's smirk, a reflection of his father's when he meant to cause trouble, worried me. "Want to have some fun with them?"

I really needed my common sense back. "What do you propose?"

I'd accept any offer of marriage, possibly participation in parental shaming, or anything else that might land me on Santa's list—or admittance into mandatory community service and possibly prison.

"Invite me to the Christmas Eve service along with the troublemakers on the couch. We'll have a great time. Go for broke and invite Gavin, too."

The thought of Gavin, a non-Christian divine, attending

a Christian holiday service was enough to make me giggle. "May I borrow your phone?"

Chase handed it over, and I called Gavin.

"Hello, Miriah," he answered, confirming the pesky divine continued to snoop in my business. "What can I do for you?"

"Please ask Caleb if he wants you to go to Mass with him this year."

"Your parents are Catholic, Miriah."

I smiled at the utter disbelief in his tone. "I'm aware."

"You want me, a divine with zero affiliation with the Christian religion, to go to Midnight Mass, arguably one of the Christian faith's most important religious ceremonies?"

"Yes. That's exactly what I'm asking of you."

"But why?"

I grinned, unable to contain my good humor. "I'm going to be so bad for Christmas this year Santa will give me a coal mine."

"And here I thought you were preparing to kill me for the curse condition."

"Death is too good and kind a fate for the likes of you, Gavin. Also, thank you for the heavy metal in church idea. I may use it at Mass."

"Are you feeling okay?"

I rolled my eyes. "Obviously, this is psychosis triggered by the new curse conditions. Hey, am I allowed to prostitute for chicken?"

Chase sighed, his parents snickered, and Gavin laughed. "No, you're not. Also, it's a case of equivalent exchange. I hope he's worth it."

It annoyed me he considered my adoration of chicken to be on par with my crush on Chase. "I'm not that petty!"

"No, you just love that chicken that much. Equivalent exchange. You're a smart woman. You'll figure it out. Eventually. Maybe. Honestly, I'm not so sure anymore. This is your beloved chicken we're talking about here."

"Why would you ban jamming to heavy metal in a church, anyway? I've never jammed to heavy metal in a church."

"I want to see a karma chameleon rock it out in a church. We'll be there. Anything else you need?"

I thought about it and had to admit it seemed more like a benefit than a disadvantage to me. "Are the new curse conditions permanent?"

"That depends on you. Anyway, I need to fetch Caleb from school."

As my son would always come first, even when I fixated on a potential father figure for him, I took the hint with grace. "Okay. Thanks, Gavin."

"I think you'll find I've only minorly inconvenienced you for the rest of your life."

I scowled. Minorly? Minorly? My love of chicken was *not* minor. "Our son better be the happiest child on Earth this Christmas, or I'll majorly inconvenience you for the rest of my life. I'll also talk Caleb into majorly inconveniencing you for the rest of his life. I'll make your misery a family tradition."

"Simmer down there, Miriah. I think everything will work out to your satisfaction."

Gavin hung up on me, and I returned Chase's phone. "Thank you."

"What did he say?"

"Want to go to Midnight Mass with me? I'm going to do my best to earn a coal mine for Christmas this year."

"I wouldn't miss it for the world."

AS CHASE WANTED to draw fire to himself, he kicked me off investigating the reporting issues, had the active contracts for all advertising firms brought into his office, and put me to work going through them. I sat on his floor in my pajamas and navigated through a sea of paperwork.

The puppy, still requiring a name, slept with her head on my foot. Goliath owned my lap, and he refused to stop purring.

At least one of us was happy with the current situation. Gavin had his moments of utter assholery, but to make me choose between Chase and chicken?

I'd miss getting chicken whenever I wanted.

Chase chuckled, leaned over, and arched a brow. "Would it help if I promised to pick up chicken for dinner on our way home tonight?"

Chicken always helped. Chicken was the miracle cure over all miracle cures. I nodded, and because I wasn't quite on par with the devil himself for earning my way onto Santa's naughty list, I opted to ignore Chase's cackling parents. "I bet Goliath likes chicken, too."

"And how about the pupper? Think she'll like chicken, too? Have you picked a name for her yet?"

"We could just call her Pupper. That's cute. Just like her."

"No. I'm vetoing that. We aren't calling the puppy Pupper. Pick a proper name."

I scoffed at the idea Pupper wasn't a good name for a puppy. "Pupperina. It's like ballerina but cuter."

Chase's brows hiked towards his hairline. "You want to name her Pupperina?'

"Want is a strong word." I patted the closest stack of contracts. "I've used up all of my words reading these. Pupperina is a leftover word not yet stolen by these papers."

Chase peeked into the chicken bucket on his desk, which I'd learned, after one brief foray as a chameleon, was devoid of chicken. "I better get two buckets. Are you two gluttons following us home tonight?"

"Yes," his parents chorused.

Joy. We had adult supervision, and we were adultier adults than the adults attempting to supervise us.

"Why?" Chase's expression turned suspicious. I assumed this was due to his status as an excellent man with many functioning brain cells.

Chase's father raised his hand. "I can freeze time around your house and catch anyone trying something stupid."

His mother smiled. "I can relocate the interior of your house at my leisure."

According to Chase's pained sigh, he regretted being an adultier adult than the adults attempting to supervise us. "No. Well, you can do the time-freeze trap, Dad. Mom, you can't move the interior of my house."

"You're being rude," his mother grumbled.

"I better get three buckets. Would you like anything for dessert, Miriah?"

"Tiramisu?" I whispered with wide eyes.

"Mother, I'll reconsider your request to relocate the interior of my home in case of emergency if you go forth and tiramisu."

"Tiramisu is not a verb."

"It is now. You can even stay the night in my guest bedroom should you go forth and tiramisu."

"And where is—" his mother blinked. "Oh. Right. I'm going to go forth and tiramisu now. I'll meet you at your place in around two hours."

"Thank you, Mom."

His mother left in a hurry, pausing long enough to snatch her purse and give Chase's father a kiss.

His father waited until she was gone to snicker. "She forgot you have two guest bedrooms."

"That seems to be the case," Chase agreed. "Miriah can pick where she wants to sleep."

In his bed would be nice. "Maybe we should name the puppy Tiramisu."

"That's almost as bad as Pupperina."

"Coffee would be a little mean—and weird," I confessed.

"How about something dignified? How about Angel?"

"While she's the dog equivalent of an angel, she's part husky. They're naughty."

"True. She's going to grow to be rather energetic. And trouble. She's definitely going to cause a great deal of trouble."

I grinned. "How about Mrs. Pawsworth?"

"You know what? Pupperina is a perfect name. Let's go with that."

Laughing, I went to work stacking contracts in organized piles so we could leave sometime tonight. "I should be sorry, but I'm really not."

"I'm so glad dogs can't speak English. She'd kill us in our sleep for daring to name her Pupperina."

"No kidding."

The newly dubbed Pupperina slept on.

CHASE CALLED in an order for three buckets of chicken while I sorted through the contracts and finished setting aside the ones I'd deemed weird. With his blessing, I packed them into a box to go over in the evening. I'd use Chase and his parents to help determine if any obscuring magic had been used on the documents.

What seemed weird to me might appear normal to them thanks to the manipulative magic wreaking havoc in Chase's company.

It would make me a target again, but I'd cope. I hoped Chase wouldn't realize I'd lined myself up for more trouble. Then again, he likely knew but believed he could keep unwanted attention off of me through his actions.

We left the office with Chase's father, and to keep Chase happy, I stayed in the SUV with the animals while he retrieved our dinner.

"He's going to make a fool out of himself," Chase's father announced as soon as his son entered the restaurant.

"I have no issues with him joining my club. I invited a non-Christian deity to celebrate Christmas Eve with a bunch of devout Catholics."

"But he's the father of your son."

"That really didn't go over well with my very, very devout Catholic parents. I figure I'll help that general train wreck along. My parents remain blissfully unaware I was cursed by a divine outside of the scope of *their* religion."

"And you're planning on jamming to heavy metal during their Christmas Eve celebrations so you become a chameleon."

"Chase is welcome to join my special club of fools. It's exclusive."

"Well, he's definitely joined your fried chicken cult."

As I'd sacrificed most of my dignity already, I pretended I still had some left, lifting my chin and faking a delicate sniff. "It's good chicken."

"It really is. I can easily understand your reaction to the changed curse conditions. I'd be upset, too."

"I'll survive."

Maybe.

"You don't sound convinced."

"It'll be a challenge." I foresaw many incidents of becoming a chameleon, and I worried my grocery shopping would become complicated.

Chase's father chuckled. "I recommend you add a chicken clause to any relationship you enter."

I wish. "I'd get cursed trying. Trust me on this one. Gavin can be ruthless."

"He seemed nice enough."

Damned Gavin and his ability to charm people. "If he wasn't at least somewhat nice, I wouldn't let him run off with Caleb whenever he's in town."

"That's understandable, and that's a good point. I can't see you being okay with him taking your son without fuss if he wasn't nice. And ruthless isn't necessarily a disadvantage when it comes to protecting your boy, is it?"

"It's not," I confirmed.

"Beyond chicken and tiramisu, what do you like?"

I didn't get a chance to answer, as Chase emerged from the restaurant burdened with three buckets of glorious chicken, and he was a sight almost as delicious as my dinner. With a smirk, he deposited the entire load onto my lap for the trip to his house. The smell made me drool, which I swallowed so I wouldn't humiliate myself further.

"For the record, son, you better count yourself as lucky. Your mother never made it easy to figure out what she really wanted."

"That's because you don't know how to listen. When a woman tries to take my finger off because I withheld her chicken, it's obvious she really likes chicken. Through the art of careful observation, I've deduced she puts her boy first, which is why she's trying really hard to hide that she adores my cat while valiantly attempting to adore my dog to the same esteemed level."

"I see fostering has resulted in adoption."

"If I have the cat and the dog, Miriah has reasons to visit and stay with me often."

I raised a brow at that. I needed another reason other than a hopeless crush and his continued acceptance of my presence? If he wanted to encourage me, I wasn't going to argue.

"I raised a smart boy. Carry on. Don't forget to use an assortment of bribes to hold her attention."

"She named the cat and the dog. Doesn't that count?"

"I was thinking more like a weekly bribe of chicken for life offered along with an engagement ring."

While I'd never admit it to anyone, Chase's father had earned himself a permanent spot as the best prospective father-in-law to walk the Earth.

"Dad, if you want a wedding, renew your vows with Mom."

"But I want to go to *your* wedding, and I've determined there's a really nice young lady in the back perfect for you. Your cat and dog already love her, too. It's important to pick a partner that your pets like."

"You're already planning a wedding, aren't you?"

I could live without planning a wedding myself, but I'd slide Chase's father a note for special requests, one of which would include an entire table burdened with tiramisu since I couldn't ask for fried chicken without becoming a chameleon. With a little luck, he'd figure it out.

"Wedding photos in a church with a chameleon wearing a wedding veil would be amazing."

The details of a potential wedding forgotten, I stared at Chase's father with my mouth hanging open. "What?"

"All it'd take is some good heavy metal. It'll be fun. Despite appearances, Chase is a good catch."

I'd figured that part out for myself. "You want to take wedding photos while I'm a chameleon wearing a wedding veil?"

"Exactly so. You'll have the best wedding photographs of the year without contest."

"Miriah, please feel free to ignore his ramblings. Please," Chase begged in a strained voice.

"But Chase, she's willing to put up with you."

"Dad!"

Since being greedy fit in well with my plans to earn a coal mine, I smiled and asked, "Is your father paying for the wedding? Can I charge him fifty grand per chameleon incident he induces? I have a college fund to fill."

I loved the sound of stunned silence.

I squirmed on my seat and adjusted how I held the chicken on my lap, lifting my hand to examine my bare left ring finger. "I like colored stones, especially opals and sapphires. I don't see a need for a very expensive ring if it uses opals; opals are fragile. It'll break and need to be replaced. Don't ask me about the chicken," I added in a whisper. "Please."

I'd had enough chameleon incidents for one week.

"I won't," he promised. "Opal, huh?"

"I also like unusual stones. Anything with color and meaning. I'm not very picky." If he wanted my ring size, he'd need to use clever tactics to get it or ask. "Colored diamonds are okay. The clear ones are boring."

"I'll pay for the wedding and all chameleon incidents at a rate of fifty thousand per incident," Chase's father announced.

"I want that in writing. Legally binding writing."

Chase's father twisted to face me, scowled, and redirected his displeasure at his son. "She's ruthless."

"I'm confused," Chase admitted, and he turned to face me although he kept a close watch on his father. "How did this turn into wedding planning?"

Good question, although I had an answer I liked. "You have my cat and my son's dog, and as I'm trying to earn an entire coal mine from Santa, I'm being a gold digger. Also, I have three buckets of chicken on my lap right now. I like this math. For once in my life, I win."

Best of all, I got to keep Chase, the perfect end to a long week.

FOURTEEN

Don't you even think about
contaminating dinner.

SOMEONE DROPPED a bag of almond flour off Chase's roof, and it smacked into the top of my head. A cloud of white powder erupted around me, and the instant it touched my skin, I itched. I itched so much I unleashed my vilest curses.

Goliath howled his complaints from his carrier. Luck alone spared him from being dropped, and I set him down so he wouldn't be hurt. I could deal with people targeting me, but almond flour to the head was just rude. It amazed me the one-pound bag hadn't done more than rattle my brain around in my skull and give me a mild headache to go with my allergic reaction.

I found one silver lining in the storm cloud of my evening: Chase's father carried the chicken, thus sparing it from a fate worse than death.

"Miriah!" Chase joined me in cursing, slipped on his way up his walkway, and landed on his ass on the sidewalk.

After a close encounter of the almond flour kind, I would

need at least a bucket and a half of chicken. "Don't even think about freezing me," I growled out through clenched teeth. "And don't you even *think* about contaminating dinner."

I shot a glare at the father and son duo. Once certain they weren't going to impede me, I unlocked the door following a brief but intense disagreement with Chase's keys and grabbed Goliath's carrier and set it inside before entering the house while Chase and his father wrangled dinner and the dog. Pupperina took advantage of Chase's prone position and washed his face with her tongue.

The cat hissed.

"Soon," I promised. "Chase will release you after he's inside. I'm going to take a shower."

A shower wouldn't stop the itching, but at least it would get the damned flour off. If the past was any indication, I'd be a miserable mess of itchiness for the next day or two. Antihistamines would help—if I didn't mind being reduced to a semi-comatose state for a minimum of eight hours.

I made it to the bathroom before Chase, burdened with a wiggling, excited puppy, caught up with me. "Are you all right?"

"I was bonked in the head with a bag of flour. Almond flour. I itch. I'm just telling you now, if I find out who bonked my head with a bag of almond flour, I may very well require you to help Gavin care for my son, because there will be a murder. Or at least a violent assault. I can probably live with a violent assault. I'm borrowing your bathroom. And burning my favorite pajamas."

"You don't need to burn them. They can be cleaned. I'll take care of it. I'll have Mom do it. She salvaged clothes from my childhood, so I'm sure she can get all the almond flour out."

I'd appreciate that after I stopped itching. "Okay. Thank you. I'll dump them by the door. I won't touch them after I get this rinsed off."

"I'll come detox the bathroom, just keep the shower door closed. Let's not have you have another reaction because the flour wasn't cleaned up."

I'd definitely appreciate that. "Thank you."

"Dad's calling the police now. He didn't see the asshole who did it, so he couldn't freeze them. His tricks only work if he knows where to strike or can see his target. I'm sorry."

"I'm grateful I wasn't frozen because I don't want to itch while paralyzed."

"You're not going to have any breathing troubles or anything like that?"

"It only makes me itch. No other reactions," I promised.

"I'll take care of the cops until you're done your shower. If they give me any trouble about you washing away evidence, I'll make it clear I'll file a case for willful injury. Your allergy is documented with your doctor?"

"Yes. I can call for the testing record if needed."

"Good. Leave your pajamas by the door, and I'll make sure they're bagged and that Mom knows they might classify as evidence, and if they don't, to have them cleaned. If they can't be cleaned, I'll replace them with the same ones. I'll check your bag for something you can wear, but you're welcome to my bathrobe in the meantime."

I loved being a bad, bad woman. "Your bathrobe is now my bathrobe."

Chase arched a brow. "You're feistier than I expected for this situation."

"Point me in the direction of the bitch who tossed a glass at me. I'll show you feisty. And the almond flour? If I find out who dropped a bag of almond flour on my head, I will arm myself with a spoon and start digging for the bastard's heart."

"I'm going to chalk this one up as you're madder than hell and have a headache."

I forced a smile. "Don't tell the cops I'm feeling murderous right now, please."

"That makes two of us. Shout if you need anything, okay? I'm going to call in a favor and have someone bring you antihistamines. I don't have any allergies, so I don't keep any around."

"I'll be fine. I'll just be a little cranky. I'll just go ahead and apologize in advance for that. I'm sorry."

"You're going to have to work a little harder if you want to earn your coal mine. Be a little less sorry, be a little more feisty and cranky. Feel free to sprinkle in some extra curses to add extra points towards your coal mine. I'd say go steal some chicken, but I'd rather have the cranky, feisty woman around than the hissing, angry karma chameleon. Either way, you'll get chicken, so don't stress yourself over it. Dad promised none of the flour got into it. He put the chicken in time out to make certain."

The chicken in time out beat me in time out. "Thank him for not putting me in time out, please."

"Will do. Seriously, shout if you need anything."

I could think of a few things which involved a removal of clothes and someone helpfully making sure I got all the almond flour out of my hair. Fortune favored the bold, and I needed to practice being bold. I pointed at my hair. "I'm going to need help with this in the shower. Flour in the hair is hard to get out."

Chase raised both brows. "You want me to come into the shower with you and help you get the flour out of your hair?"

"While you're at it, you can inform me if I have an appropriate tramp stamp. You can certify it. Maybe tell the cops to go away first. And your parents. They're not invited for the tramp stamp certification, but I'll accept any edible gifts they might want to leave for our enjoyment. Is that sufficient to earn some credits towards my coal mine?"

"It's a good start. Excuse me for a few minutes. I have some cops to attend to and parents to redirect and otherwise evict."

"If you have a basement, lock them in there. That might keep them out of trouble."

"They'd use their tricks to escape."

"How rude of them." As the cops wouldn't leave until they questioned me, I'd settle for a basic shower first. "I'm going to get most of this flour out and wear your towel if the police have any questions for me. Towels are probably easier to clean than bathrobes."

"They are, but do you really want the police seeing you in a towel?"

"Do I lose or gain points towards my coal mine if I wear a towel in front of the police?"

"You lose points. You definitely lose points. I'll bring you a change of clothes, and it can join what my mother will have to clean later. I'm sure she won't mind."

I had no doubts Chase's mother minded but loved her

son too much to say anything. I would earn a few points towards my coal mine by neglecting to inform him I could wash my clothes to safe wearing levels without issue.

I respected his willingness to put in the effort—and foist the job on his mother.

"I'll be in the living room. Let me know if you need anything."

Him naked in the shower would've been nice, but I'd work on adding more points towards my coal mine later, preferably after the itching stopped.

THE ALMOND FLOUR caked in my hair, which made removing it interesting. The itching leveled out at a full-body nuisance, and I cursed my traitorous body for its immediate and unreasonable reaction. After three rounds of using Chase's shampoo, I still wasn't convinced I'd gotten it all. According to my scalp, I'd be bald by morning even if I managed to resist the urge to claw at my irritated skin.

While it wouldn't get better for a while, I deemed I'd survive, grabbed the fluffiest towel I could find, and wrapped it around myself to limit showing too much skin to the wrong people. After I dealt with the police and their questioning, I'd begin stage two of my plan to earn my coal mine.

A pair of cops, the same ones who'd come to deal with the Molotov cocktail incident, waited in the living room while talking with Chase and his parents.

"Your tiramisu is in the fridge," his mother told me. "I'm concerned I didn't get enough; I wasn't expecting you to be assaulted with a bag of almond flour. I'll handle disciplining the boys for their inability to prevent it."

I looked Chase over and raised a brow. "What if I want to handle disciplining the younger one?"

"Save me some tiramisu and you can do whatever you want to him. The punk's mooched off me for long enough. Make certain he signs his new ownership papers before you give him access to your bank account."

Hello, coal mine. How could I say no to owning a man like Chase? "I told the older one he had to pay for the wedding *and* fifty thousand for all chameleon incidents he is responsible for. I've got a kid to put through college."

"I'll have signed paperwork confirming that to you by tomorrow," she promised, starring at Chase's father. "Isn't that right?"

"I have misjudged how ruthless the karma chameleon can be," Chase's father muttered.

The cops stared at each other.

I graced them with my best smile. "I'm sorry. I've completely forgotten your names, sirs."

"I'm Officer Calrig, and my partner is Officer Yamos," the older of the two replied, and I wondered what had caused the thin scars crossing his cheek to halt near his mouth. I was willing to bet the incident had contributed to several streaks of gray in his brown hair. "We were informed you were showering due to allergies?"

I showed him my arm, which had escaped the worst of the exposure. "This is close to my normal skin color." To illustrate the reaction, I splayed my reddening hand on my skin. "My hands were exposed. The red in my cheeks, I promise, wasn't from the heat."

"How would you rate the severity of your allergies?"

"The itching will go away in a day or two, but I'll be miserable until then. I don't typically have any breathing problems, but it's definitely uncomfortable. The last time I was exposed, I had to wear mittens to keep from scratching myself bloody," I confessed.

Chase's mother hopped to her feet. "And I'm off to get the antihistamines and some mittens. Do you want anything while I'm out?"

"Are you going to your pharmacy on Broadway?"

My brows went up at that. What sort of idiot went to Broadway to go to the pharmacy?

"Maybe."

"If you go to the one down the street, there is a pet store on the same block. You can spoil your grandpuppy and grandcat."

"You just want me out of your hair," she complained.

Chase grinned. "Take Dad with you. And while you're at it, perhaps see if the boutique down the street is open. Miriah needs some new pajamas. You can grab the ones from the bathroom to get the size and figure it out, I'm sure."

"You're a wicked child." His mother grinned and skipped in the direction of the bathroom. Moments later, she returned with my pajamas tucked under an arm. "Don't forget to spray the hall and floor with water and wipe it up so you get up all the almond flour. I'll make sure these are cleaned, too."

"Was she wearing those?" Officer Calrig asked.

Chase's mother scowled. "You're going to claim it as evidence, aren't you?"

"Unfortunately. We might be able to get information from the flour samples."

Huffing, his mother checked the tags. "Get a bag so this doesn't shed all over the house and get the poor woman sicker."

Officer Yamos walked out the front door and returned a few minutes later with a clear plastic bag. To keep from shedding more flour in the house, they took it outside to bag. Within five minutes, Chase's parents left, and the cops watched my every move.

As I expected them to grill me, I lifted my chin and told them everything that had happened from the moment we'd left Chase's work until the moment I'd gotten hit in the head with the bag. I declined their offer to call for an ambulance, they tried to convince me to go in for testing as additional evidence, and Chase's eyes narrowed as he considered the argument.

"What are the odds that going in and having an examination done will help the case?"

"Considering she's turning redder than a lobster fresh from the pot, I'd say it'd be good evidence of intent to harm," Officer Calrig replied. "Properly documenting the allergy will be useful in court, and it'll make sure they can provide proper treatment. With something like this, it shouldn't be too much of a time sink, as we'll call it in as part of an investigation."

"Can we skip the ambulance and drive in?"

"We can escort you, yes," the cop confirmed. "I'd be more comfortable if this reaction was handled officially, and it will ensure the investigation isn't impeded."

"Sorry, Miriah. Did you get enough of the flour out of your hair to be all right for a while?"

I wanted to curse over the delays, but I sighed and nodded. "You're going to owe me for this."

"You really want that coal mine, don't you?"

As I'd already lost most of my dignity, what was acting like a fool in front of a pair of cops? "Yes, I do. I'm looking forward to properly disciplining you later."

"I'll go crate the puppy while we're gone and text my parents to come puppy sit while we're at the hospital." Chase smirked, and shooed me off. "Go get changed. The faster we're out of here, the sooner we get back home."

Fortune truly did favor the bold, and I hunted for my clothes, grabbed the first outfit I could find that didn't clash, and changed in his bedroom so I wouldn't run the risk of exposing myself to more of the pesky flour. Within five minutes, I declared myself prepared to raise my insurance premiums to all new highs. In good news, I'd hit my insurance cap for the year.

It always helped when I looked on the bright side of things.

FIFTEEN

I'm not sure what the windshield
did to you, and I'm afraid to ask.

IF CHASE ASKED if I was all right one more time, I'd snap. I'd snap so hard they'd hear my frustrated wailing in Jersey. I doubted auditioning for a gig as a banshee would help me accomplish anything beyond potentially helping Chase crash his luxury family car, which had no business on snowy roads.

To make it clear I wasn't impressed with the effort, I flipped my middle finger at the windshield.

"I'm not sure what the windshield did to you, and I'm afraid to ask."

"The snow. I'm flipping off the snow."

"Being itchy makes you grouchy, doesn't it?"

I gave up any hope of maintaining my dignity and howled my disgust over my situation. "After I'm done clawing off my flesh, I'm going for them! I swear, I'm going to flay the flesh from their bones and sew myself a hat."

Chase pressed a button on his steering wheel. "Call Gavin," he ordered.

His car obeyed, and a moment later, his speakers rang.

"Hello, Chase. How can I help you?" Gavin chuckled. "Miriah."

"You're a cheating bastard of a divine," I grumbled.

"Someone dropped a bag of almond flour on her head. She's very itchy. I wanted to ask you how concerned I should be if she wants to flay the flesh from someone's bones and sew herself a hat."

"Well, I recommend you don't give her a knife and an excuse," my former-lover and father of my son replied. "An hour following exposure, you'll need to put mittens on her hands, Chase, or she'll claw herself bloody. If you give her anything for the allergies, you'll need to put her to bed within about five to ten minutes. It doesn't really hurt her, but she'll be uncomfortable and grumpy until the reaction stops. How badly did you get hit, Miriah?"

"A pound bag to the head, and it exploded in a cloud of flour. In good news, dinner wasn't ruined. In bad news, I haven't gotten any. His mother bought me tiramisu." The bright side had great things, including chicken and tiramisu. "But because someone did it on purpose, I have to go to the hospital so they can tell me what I already know. Guess what? I'm allergic to almonds, I'm turning redder by the minute, and the fucking police claimed my favorite pajamas as evidence."

While I liked to think of myself as a rational woman, I really would snap if Chase asked if I was all right one more time.

"A piece of advice, if I may?"

I grunted, and Chase arched a brow before asking, "What?"

"She'll be fine. If you want her to be happy with you, instead of asking if she's all right, tell her you're going to tuck her into that chair she likes near the fireplace, give her some hot chocolate, and put that cat you adopted on her lap. If you insist on having the hospital treat the developing rashes, be prepared to care for a zombie. In good news, she's not actually a zombie. She just does a really good impression of one. I wish you the best of luck convincing her to take anything for her allergies."

"As I control the chicken *and* tiramisu supplies, anyone who is having an allergic reaction in my presence gets to take medication to limit the damage it causes, but I'm sure I can arrange some chair time, hot chocolate, and a cat." Chase chuckled and shook his head. "Anything else I should know?"

Gavin chuckled. "Sunday is sacred because she's shopping for Caleb. If anyone screws with her Sunday, she really might go off the deep end. If you value your life, you'll make Sunday perfect. Also, I have adjusted the terms of her curse temporarily to allow for her to enjoy her Sunday. It would be cruel of me for you to spend all of Sunday as a karma chameleon, however amusing it might be. I'm taking Caleb out for the weekend, so don't be surprised if you get some excited phone calls either tomorrow or Sunday night. He's packing for the trip right now, so I'll be very surprised if he remembers to call you."

I wondered if Caleb's tendency to forget about the world around him—and his mother while on visits with his father—came from Gavin's genetic contributions. "Tell him I love him, and I'd prefer if you didn't tell him about the flour, please. He'll obsess."

"That's my fault. Sorry, Miriah. He'll be fine. He just needs to learn how to better control that part of his personality. I'll work with him on it. Once he has some direction and finds his passion and purpose in life, he won't drive you as crazy organizing things to his liking. It's just a matter of focus."

"Focus? You mean he needs a hobby?"

"He needs a specialty. I'd say it's a bit more than a mere hobby. I'll help him explore his options. And don't beat yourself over it like you usually do. Caleb doesn't need to be fixed because he isn't broken, so you haven't failed him in any fashion. He is how he is because I am as I am."

Jerk, jerk, jerk. Not only had he been poking around in my thoughts—long term—he'd blabbed right in front of Chase. "Go ahead, Gavin. Come near me while I'm still itching. I'll flay your flesh from your bones and sew myself a hat."

Gavin laughed. "I was giving Chase a fair warning of what he has in store for should he decide to stick around."

"Considering my mother is probably screaming at my father over formally legalizing a verbal agreement to pay for a wedding *and* compensate Miriah fifty grand per chameleon incident he induces to pay for Caleb's education, I'm feeling confident I'll be sticking around. She's already whipped both my parents, and I'm waiting for my turn."

Gavin sighed. "You're supposed to whip him first, Miriah. After you've finished whipping him, that's when you're supposed to manipulate his parents. You're doing this backwards."

"Do you know how much weddings in New York cost?" I demanded.

"I have a rough idea. And as you refuse to go into debt for anything other than our son, it comes as no surprise you'd find some way to either skip the ceremony or just not get married. I suspect an opportunity knocked, and as you're a skinflint with the objective of putting our son above all else, you wanted to secure everything you were worried you can't provide. In this case, your real goal was Caleb's college fund since you conveniently forgot I'm a divine and am perfectly capable of putting our son through college."

I scowled at the irritation in Gavin's tone. "You've never offered."

"You never asked."

"Fuck you, you egotistical sex demon on steroids!" I howled. My face burned to go along with my head-to-toe itching. "Sorry."

"That's definitely a contribution to your coal mine," Chase informed me. "But you're not supposed to apologize when you start the tirade. Try again, but with a little more cursing and a little more description of the standards I need to live up to. The sex demon on steroids portion of this conversation is a little concerning, but I'm game to do my best and work on improvement."

"Are you after a coal mine, too?" I muttered.

"If I wanted a coal mine, I'd just buy one, but I'm not sure what I'd do with it, so I can't say I'm after a coal mine. All that said, watching you do your best to earn one is the most entertaining thing I've done in my adult life, and I can't wait to see what you do next."

Gavin chuckled. "What I find absolutely fascinating about

this is he's telling the complete truth. I never thought I'd see the day you actually had good taste in a man."

To dodge my wrath, the bastard hung up. "Can I flay him?"

"No; he's responsible for Caleb when we want to go out of town just the two of us, and trust me when I say you don't want to recruit my parents as extended babysitters. We'd return to the world's most spoiled child with no hope of taming the beast afterwards."

"That's a part of the spoiling package," I reminded him. "We get a babysitter, but we come back to a spoiled child."

"But if anyone can watch a child, it's a divine."

"This is true."

"If we have children, think he'd watch over them, too?"

"Call the fucker back. Let's find out."

Laughing, Chase pressed the button on his steering wheel again. "Call Gavin."

"You're not going to let me escape, are you?"

"No. If we have children, are you going to agree to babysit them when you take care of Caleb? Should you agree, I won't flay your flesh from your bones and sew myself a hat." I thought my offer was a reasonable one.

Gavin erupted into laughter, which took him several minutes to contain. "Okay, Miriah. Sure. Should you have more children, I'll babysit them for you when you go out of town. I'll even be generous and watch the pets, too. I expect you'll have a lot of them for some reason. You should be careful about that, Chase. She's got a soft heart for the furry ones."

Chase's chuckles rumbled in his chest. "That's because she's a nice woman who cares for others. It's a price I'm willing to pay as required, although I hope she's willing to accept there is a limited number of space for new animals in the house."

"You're going to need a bigger house," Gavin predicted. "I wish you luck with that. Caleb's done packing, so if you'll excuse me?"

"Thank you, Gavin." Before I had a chance to add anything, Chase hung up. "I'm going to win the medications at the hospital argument, but I'll make it up to you with something a little better than time to sit in a chair and drink hot chocolate. You've been twitching since you got in the car, and you've put lobsters to shame. I'm worried you might develop blisters, and those can take a long time to heal and are painful. I don't think it's worth having an argument over. You don't deserve to be uncomfortable, and if you're a zombie tomorrow, I can live with that. Caring for zombies is easy."

"It is?"

"Sure. I'll tuck you, my zombie, into your new favorite chair, put Goliath on your lap, and feed you chicken and hot chocolate all day. See, I'm already ahead of Gavin. I didn't forget your chicken. Honestly, he must be an idiot for not suggesting chicken be a part of the bribe. That said, if you want something other than chicken for dinner, I make a mean steak. I also know how to make lasagna from scratch. I even make the noodles myself. From scratch."

My eyes widened. "You know how to make lasagna from scratch?"

"Since tending to a zombie isn't typically time consuming, I can make it for you tomorrow and feed you light snacks of fried chicken so you don't ruin your dinner."

Who the hell needed common sense or a heart anyway? "I will take any medications the doctors decide to shove down my throat even if it turns me into a zombie."

"I'll still make sure you get fried chicken at least once a week, remember this: Gavin didn't bar you from asking for your favorite food. Nothing in his rules says I can't explore the world and find you a food you love even more than your chicken. I heard him very clearly. His curse covers your chicken. If I find you a new favorite food, that curse won't be so bad, will it? And yes, I'll even put it in writing; I'll provide your favorite fried chicken, barring unforeseen circumstances, at least once a week. I might even beg the restaurant to teach me how to make it."

"You'd need one hell of a bribe to get that recipe out of their hands," I muttered. "I've tried."

"I bet you have. But I'll try, even if they laugh me out of town."

"It's not fair," I complained.

"What's not fair? I mean, beyond the almond assault, someone throwing a glass at you, and the other crap you've been put through lately?"

"You're perfect, and that's just not fair. In comparison, I'm a hot mess. I'm such a hot mess I've been trying to earn a coal mine because every time I try to be good, it blows up in my face. Tiana's going to hear about this on Sunday, and she might laugh herself to death. Don't underestimate Tiana. She will find out. She'll make me blurt it out. I'll humiliate myself in public, too. Just you wait and see. I hope you don't have any secrets. She'll learn them, and she'll make sure you suffer."

"Yet you're friends with her."

"Well, yeah. She's fun, and she's willing to babysit, and when she's done with Caleb, he isn't a little demon. She's just a little evil sometimes."

"Did it occur to you she might have tips on how you can earn a coal mine?"

I thought about that for a while. "No, but I can make some guesses what she'd suggest."

"Do tell."

I laughed, as her solution to my life's problems might land me in hell for all eternity. "She'd just tell me to keep walking in on you while you're in the shower until I verified my tramp stamp. I only got the damned thing because it'd annoy Gavin. He kept bothering me and asking me to marry him."

"Well, I promise I won't be bothered if you ask me to marry you. It seems somewhat important I inform you of that. I'm also taking this as a hint not to bother you with repeated requests unless you tell me otherwise."

"Stop being so damned perfect," I complained, grabbing handfuls of my hair and tugging. "You're driving me crazy."

"No, I'm driving you to the hospital. We're even being tailed by the cops, but for once in my life, I'm not worried about being pulled over. Honestly, it's creeping me out a little. The only times cops follow me is when they're waiting for me to speed. I don't even know why I drive this car. It makes cops want to pull me over for speeding all the time. When I got this car, I thought I was picking a model that wouldn't get me the attention of the police because it's technically not a sports car!"

"You shouldn't have picked 'make it go faster' as your color choice. That was a mistake."

"But 'make it go faster' is such a pretty color."

"Next time, I recommend a classy silver."

"They called the silver one 'makes it go so fast you'll be cited before you leave the parking lot.' It didn't seem like a good idea. I saw it and wanted to test the engine."

I laughed. "You need a new car, one that isn't an open invitation to be ticketed."

"I really thought I was picking a family car to avoid that," he mumbled.

"It looks like you're driving a million dollars, and honestly, it's comfy enough to be worth it. This is a really nice car."

"I could repaint it. Think that'd help?"

"Maybe? I don't know. I've never had a car like this before. Don't even look at my car. It's sad."

"I'm thinking we're going car shopping immediately following marriage. There's more rust than paint on yours, and it makes me worry for your safety just looking at it."

"It's not that bad!"

"I nudged the wheel well and part of your car flaked off. Sure, the rest of the body is sound, but there's a lot of issues around the undercarriage."

I frowned. "You were poking around my car?"

"Tiana showed it to me on one of my visits to the office. She really wanted you to work with me so you'd have a backup plan if you were fired. Initially, Alex wanted to bring her in for checking the base marketing issues, but she suggested you because you have a knack for the reporting and an understanding of how marketing works so you'd be in a better position to evaluate what was going on at my company. She was right, too. How do you feel about being poached?"

"You want to poach me?" I blurted.

"I was going to offer you being poached as a Christmas present, but I came up with a better idea."

Chase wanted to hire me? "That breaks every company policy I've ever heard of regarding fraternization in the office."

"My company has a history. Mom was Dad's assistant from early on. Officially, she was his executive secretary, but in reality, she was his partner. We're capable of sharing space working for more than an hour without either one of us wanting to attempt murder, and I'll allow you to bring pets to the office as long as you clean up after them. Call it a hiring perk. But marriage may very well be a hiring condition."

"Have you lost your mind?"

"No, but I might lose my life when Alex finds out, but he'll forgive me if I marry you as part of the deal. He'd probably have to fire you due to potential for becoming a corporate spy. I'm just sparing you from being fired. I'm trying to be generous here, but I honestly never believed I'd use Dad's tactic."

"This seems to be a case of 'if it isn't broken, don't fix it.' Your father's already foolishly agreed to pay for a New York wedding. Your mother's on board. And Caleb's college fund should be covered; I only need him to pay out twice."

"You've been saving up for his college since the day he was born, haven't you?"

"You kidding? I started the day I found out I was pregnant. I've been scraping pennies since I couldn't nickel and dime it to death. I didn't want him to be unable to pick the school he wants because of money."

"And you'd rather pull your own teeth than ask Gavin, I take it?"

I shrugged. "He pays child support. I put as much of the check as possible in the college fund. Caleb might want to live in the dorms, and that's more expensive—or he might want his own apartment. I don't want him to have to work through school."

"How many pennies have you scraped together?"

I reached down, grabbed my phone, and logged into my banking app to check. "Three hundred thousand. Do you think that's enough for his college education? If he gets a good school? What if he wants to become a doctor?"

Chase opened his mouth, closed it, cleared his throat, and tried again without making a sound.

"What's wrong?"

"Your son isn't even in high school yet and you've squirreled away three hundred thousand for his college fund?"

"Well, yes."

"Tiana keeps complaining how you're utterly convinced you have no money. But you have three hundred thousand for his college fund."

"That's his college fund! I can't touch that."

"Miriah."

"What?"

"On average, it costs less than a hundred thousand for four years at a good university. For three hundred, you could send him to the best school in the world for eight years and have money left over."

I stared at him, and my mouth dropped open. "What?"

"We need to have a long talk about the definition of reasonable penny pinching, Miriah. In good news, should there be a second child, you won't have to do much to the college fund. If you don't mind me asking, most came from the child support check?"

"Divines are asked to pay a lot per month because they might disappear at any time. I was warned most divines only pay for a few months before they lose track of time. I've been told Gavin's an exception. So I started saving as much as possible expecting him to vanish, but he never did."

"There's nothing wrong with planning ahead, and there's nothing wrong with living within the means you know you can afford if the child support dries up. However, that said, you'll enjoy a raise when you're working for my company, I pay bonuses, and while there are days I'm sure you'll want to quit because I annoy you, I'm your lifeline to your fried chicken supply, so you'll put up with me on the bad days."

I gave credit where credit was due: Chase locked onto my weaknesses and took advantage of it. "What other benefits do I get for working for you?"

"I'll make you tea in the morning because I can't function without tea. I can even be talked into contaminating the house with coffee."

"Do you pick up wayward children from school?"

"I can as needed. No one is dumb enough to tell the CEO he can't leave work to pick up wayward children from school, although you might have to do it if I have a critical meeting. And if we can't, I come prepackaged with two almost responsible parents capable of picking up any number of children from school. It's part of the grandparent spoiling package I keep hearing about. And if it isn't a part of the package, it is now."

"Two week vacation?"

"That's default for those in their first year for the company. I'll give you three weeks because I'm spoiled and don't want my wife working while I'm on vacation. That said, work tends to follow me around, but the company tries to only bump the critical stuff my way."

"I can work with that, but I get mad if my boss slacks off at work."

"Would you like a whip to keep with you at work?"

"Do I get to hit you with it if I catch you goofing off?"

Chase thought about it for a while, his eyes narrowing while he drove. The signs for the hospital directed us to the ER lot, and we had to circle the lot twice before finding a spot. The cops parked near the entry and waited for us.

"Those cops are cheaters," I muttered, waiting until he killed the engine to unbuckle my seatbelt.

"That they are. To answer your question, yes, you may, but I will expect you to kiss it and make it better after work."

"I accept your terms."

SIXTEEN

I nominated Chase to
handle any applications.

WE WASTED five hours in the hospital, and it would've been a lot longer without the police tapping their feet and otherwise encouraging the hospital staff to tend to me sooner than later. The ER nurse took one look at me, called for a doctor, and began the tedious process of poking and prodding to determine how severe my reaction was.

The speed of my reaction put me in the 'not good' category, but the nature of my reaction reassured me—and the ER doctor—I wasn't going to keel over dead. I could breathe and would continue to do so unless something unexpected happened. Unfortunately for me but fortunately for the police's case, the doctor believed I'd develop allergic contact dermatitis by morning, and to mitigate the risk of scarring, they gave me a list of three prescriptions and a shampoo to spare my scalp from lasting damage. One of the prescriptions would reduce me to a mostly comatose state until Sunday morning, one would ensure I felt no pain if I needed it, and the third, a dainty bottle of cream, would require a second pair of hands to make sure it got everywhere required.

I nominated Chase to handle any applications, and I'd refuse to take the first prescription until he finished his sacred duty as cream applicator.

He'd find out about his nomination after we returned to his house. If his parents were there after running errands, I'd be forced to kick them out. Taking over Chase's home as a base of my operations might earn me points for my coal mine, too.

The thought helped me get through the annoying process of filling out insurance forms, giving yet another statement to the police, and filling my prescriptions.

At the end of the day, and right through until Sunday morning, life served me an important reminder about the nature of plans. While I got to evict Chase's parents, Chase insisted I take the cursed allergy medicine before he'd even think about helping apply cream anywhere. Exactly as warned, the little pill packed a big punch, and within ten minutes, I couldn't remember my own name let alone enjoy Chase's help preventing my skin from filing its pink slip and turning into a blistered mess.

I missed most of Saturday, and when Sunday morning rolled around, I staggered around Chase's house in search of coffee to revive me from the dreary lethargy induced by the stupid little pill the doctor insisted would stop the reaction in its tracks. While I no longer itched, my skin remained redder than I liked, but I couldn't spot a single blister.

A plate with a piece of fried chicken hovered in front of

my face. I blinked, staring at it while trying to figure out where it'd come from and why it was floating in front of me.

"Take your chicken, sit down, and eat it before you melt all over the kitchen floor," Chase ordered, pointing at his dining room table. "Mom brought over a coffee maker, and I'm pleased to inform you she even showed me how to use it. I didn't know it took so long to brew coffee, however. Eat while I get it finished. What do you want in it?"

I took the plate, changed directions, and sat down, answering him with a grunt.

"If you don't tell me how you like it, I'm going to experiment with it," he warned.

I lifted my chicken, stuffed as much of it in my mouth as I could, and grunted again.

"If I kill your taste buds, I'm not responsible. I'm going to make three cups for you. One will be black, one will be white with hints of coffee flavor and loaded with sugar, and the other one will be somewhere between the two. I will observe your reactions and use this as a guideline for how I make your coffee in the future."

Three coffees sounded better than one coffee, so I turned my attention to my chicken.

Someone knocked at the door, and Chase strolled over to answer it. Within moments, Tiana bounced into the room. "Good morning!"

I grunted at her, too, since I wasn't quite ready to tell her she could shove her good morning right up her ass.

"She seems to be suffering from medicine-induced lethargy this morning. I've been told she should perk up after I give her some coffee."

"Why are you pouring three cups of coffee?"

"When I asked her how she wanted it, she grunted at me. I'm improvising."

Tiana laughed and sat beside me. Goliath jumped onto the table, and I stared at the three-legged cat, wondering how he'd gotten up there with a missing hind leg. I didn't bother with a grunt; it hadn't been effective on Chase or Tiana, so I saved my breath.

Chase ferried over the coffee, and I redirected my attention to the closest one, snatching it and pouring it down my throat as fast as I could without choking. It was like a sugar factory exploded next to a creamery with a faint hint of something that someone might consider coffee in a dire emergency.

Had I been paying more attention to the cat than the beverage thinly disguised as coffee, I wouldn't have lost my chicken to him. He stole the piece right out of my hand, turned tail, and ran off with it.

Empty coffee mug in hand and bereft of my chicken, I alternated between staring at where the cat had fled and my plate, which no longer held any chicken.

The second piece was going on an adventure into Tiana's stomach.

Resigned to my fate, I grabbed my second cup of coffee, which proved to have no sugar or cream to smooth out the brew's bite. If I drank it fast enough, I wouldn't have to taste it, so I went to work, puzzling how I'd get more chicken without violating Gavin's new curse conditions.

"If she asks for chicken, she'll turn into the karma chameleon," Chase announced.

"That's harsh," my friend replied, and because she loved tormenting me, she gnawed on her freshly stolen piece with a few lip smacks added for good measure. "So terribly harsh. Man, that chicken is good though, isn't it?"

"It sure is." Chase chuckled and went around the table. "Goliath certainly thinks so."

Man and cat waged a brief but fierce war over my stolen piece of chicken, and once Chase took it from the cat, he shredded the meat off the bones and offered it to the thieving feline.

Revenge would be sweet, and I'd need to spend some quality time coming up with something appropriate. Chase and Tiana would face the brunt of my revenge. I would need to do some serious thinking on if it was possible to obtain revenge on a cat for the theft of my breakfast.

"You three suck," I announced, reaching for the third mug. To ensure Chase would have to invest more effort to figure out what kind of coffee I liked, I treated it like the first two, guzzling it as soon as it cooled enough so he'd be given no clues to my preference.

"For the record, she just outplayed you in the coffee game, Chase. Good luck with that."

"So I see." Chase sighed, retrieved an entire bucket of chicken from the fridge, and set it beside me. "Try to save her a few pieces, Tiana. Caring for a zombie is hard work, and despite her seemingly undead state, she does need food to get through our holiday shopping adventure."

"What's our budget for the squirt today?" Tiana asked.

I flipped my middle finger in her direction and grabbed a piece of chicken. To ensure no one stole it, I kept both hands on it at all times and wasted no time chewing and swallowing.

"She might be upset; I reviewed part of her finances Friday night."

"Figured out she lives like she's destitute but has a college fund for the squirt some might kill for?"

"Yeah. You knew?"

"The squirt knows, too. I'm pretty sure part of his charming issues with perfectionism come from the inherent understanding his mother obsessively saves for his college education. The two simply can't handle the thought of disappointing each other. Whatever your intended budget for Caleb is, add two hundred to it, Miriah. Despite your conditioning to believe you can't afford it, you totally can."

I took another bite of my chicken and glared at her. "We haven't even left for the mall and you're starting already?"

"It's my sacred duty as your best friend to start poking you early. He's also old enough you can get him the laptop he wants. He's going to need it if you want your plans of him being the best educated brat on Earth to succeed. Your desktop is a piece of shit, plus you only have one of them."

"How does computer shopping sound to you?" Chase asked.

"That's a great idea. I'm so impressed you came up with it. Hey, Miriah? Did you already transfer a disgusting amount of the child support check for this month into your savings account? Also, you can withdraw at least four times each month from the account without penalty. Despite your belief, that account is not a black hole. View the computer as an advance to further your college plans for the ultra-organized demon you call your son."

I swallowed my chicken and muttered, "You went to my apartment and touched the tree, didn't you?"

"It was one ornament. I liked it better in its new spot. Ye holy gods, the temper tantrum. I didn't measure it before placing it. How was I supposed to know a glass ball couldn't be within four inches of another glass ball?"

"Welcome to my life." I devoured every scrap of meat I could from my piece of chicken and snatched another before the bucket wandered off. "How much are you expecting me to spend on this laptop?"

"Coherency is returning!" Tiana reached over and grabbed another piece of chicken. "A grand should get him a good system. If you dump down two grand, you won't need to replace it for a few years unless it breaks. If you go with a grand on the laptop and a grand on his own desktop, he'll be set for a while. The desktops are bigger. But kids nowadays use laptops in school for their classwork."

"I'm getting him a puppy for Christmas, Tiana. We went over this."

"You're getting him a laptop, too. It's a good investment."

Why was I friends with Tiana? I sighed and stared at my chicken, wondering what I'd done in life to deserve this headache so early in the morning. "You're pure evil."

"Nah, I'm only a little crooked. Someone with my hair can't be evil. This hair? This hair is everything."

As she expected me to admire her curly hair, which she'd somehow contained to actually fall to her shoulders rather than stick up in a fro. "Hey, it's not a fro today."

"This hair is *magnificent*. This hair also cost me several hundred dollars plus the sanity of my stylist."

"How long will it last?"

"We estimate approximately forty-eight hours. I wanted to make myself pretty for you on our shopping day. I also didn't want to disgust Chase too much. The fro might've been too much for his delicate sensibilities."

"My delicate sensibilities can survive your fro, I assure you." Chase deposited another piece of chicken onto my plate and returned the bucket to the fridge. "If you ladies would get ready, we can go on our quest to procure Christmas presents for the young child named Caleb. So far, we have to go to a computer store, a pet store for puppy supplies, and, may someone have mercy on our souls, a mall."

Tiana beamed. "This is going to be so much fun. I brought nerf swords with me in case we need to wage war to navigate the mall."

We were going to get arrested. Tiana armed with a nerf sword in a mall would somehow lead to our arrest. "We need to go to the shelter and find a puppy. I was supposed to spend a lot of time at the shelter working with the puppies to find the perfect puppy. I couldn't go yesterday," I complained. "And Chase adopted Pupperina."

He'd gone sometime while I'd been dozing off to finalize the paperwork for both the cat and the dog, making them officially his. If I wanted to visit them, I'd have to stage invasions.

"And Goliath," Chase announced proudly. "He's such a good three-legged cat."

"He jumped on the table and stole my breakfast," I wailed.

"You should have defended it better. He's a fierce hunter, and you lowered your guard." Chase smirked. To make it clear I'd lost the war, he bent over and picked up Goliath. "Aren't you a good little kitty?"

"We need to go to a place that cuts keys," I announced.

Tiana blinked and stared at me. "But why?"

"I'm stealing his keys, making a copy for myself, and invading whenever I want to visit my cat."

"She's working very hard to earn herself a coal mine for Christmas. So far, she's dipped her toes in through careful conning of my parents, she's going to flay the flesh off the bones of the individual who hit her with a bag of almond flour, which she'll use to sew herself a hat, and I'm sure she's scheming some other things."

"Wow. How hard were you hit? That's so not your style."

"What is my style, then?"

"You blend in. That's your gig. You're a good little karma chameleon who blends in because you hate drawing attention to yourself. Or, you know, you're worried you'll get fired again because you have this transformation issue whenever you get anywhere near someone you like."

I sometimes hated my frenemy while also loving her too much for my own good.

"She wants an opal or a colored stone in her engagement and wedding band, my father has to pay a ridiculous amount of money if he induces any of her transformations, and he's also paying for the wedding. I'm thinking I'll lure her into a jewelry store and just buy the first ring she falls in love with. Is that a good plan, Tiana?"

"I know just the place, but don't let her get an opal. It'll break. Get her a necklace with an opal so she can wear it to special occasions. As for the waiting until she falls in love with one idea? Smart move. She'll be stuck with it for life, so you definitely want to make certain she likes it. And Miriah, if you're going to marry him, just give Caleb Pupperina for Christmas along with a cool step-dad. He'll love it."

Chase scowled. "But she's my dog."

"She could be a family dog."

"But I'm getting Caleb a dog for Christmas," I protested.

"Then I guess you're just going to have to adopt a second dog," my best frenemy announced. "You best get enough puppy supplies for two dogs."

"But I already have supplies for Pupperina," Chase protested.

"She needs more supplies. She obviously does not have nearly enough dog toys. I didn't step on a single one coming into the dining room. Go get dressed, Miriah, while I teach this dastardly fellow the errors of his ways."

Sometimes, I questioned what I'd done to deserve Tiana as a friend. The rest of the time, I wondered how I could possibly live without her.

I SHOULD'VE KNOWN shopping on a Sunday right before Christmas would turn into a living hell. Tiana did her best to drive me up a wall, but the damned woman found ways to make me laugh despite wanting to wrap my hands around her throat and throttle her. Every time I contemplated doing it, she knew.

She knew, and because she knew, she grinned and reminded me I'd miss her if I killed her.

To add to the chaos of my day, Chase's parents insisted on joining us, and I couldn't help but feel guilty as Pupperina had whined when Chase had put her in her crate while we were gone. When we'd left, Goliath had been keeping her company, reaching towards her with his paw.

I had wanted to stay and watch them. Chase had ultimately wrapped his arm around my waist and dragged me out of his house while I complained over his cruelty. I sulked over the entire lot of them forcing poor Pupperina to stay in her crate while we were gone.

Tiana and Chase worked together to force me into the computer store, and once there, they had a freak out over the selection of computers. I pinched the bridge of my nose watching them flail about trying to decide which system would be best for my son.

Chase's father patted my shoulder. "I'm sorry. He gets excited sometimes, especially when a computer is involved. If it's too expensive, say so. You do not have to listen to them about the computer. Buy the one you think your boy will like best."

"So you can go behind my back and buy a better one?" I muttered.

"You caught on to that really quickly."

I pointed at Chase, who was singing the praise of a system while Tiana argued with him over the same exact one but in a different color. "I've been told I'm an unreasonable person and don't need to put anything in my child's college fund because I've covered it twice over. They're going to coerce me into getting whatever one they think is best."

"And they won't agree on it, ultimately forcing you to pick. And I'll still uphold my agreement for all chameleon incidents even though you've been a very good mother in terms of planning for your son's future. You might have other kids down the road. You're spry and young enough if you want them."

"You just want two grandchildren to spoil instead of just the loaner."

"This is a factor, yes."

At least I knew where Chase's father stood in the grand scheme of things. "Fine. You'll get your karma chameleon in a wedding veil picture, assuming you can convince him to ask me because I'm not asking him; plus, you pay for the computers, plus the fifty grand for the incident to go into the care and upbringing of one of my children. Even if I only have just the one."

"You have a deal." Chase's father skipped off to hunt for an employee.

Chase's mother took his place, shook her head, and laughed. "You're a cunning one, that's for certain. I take it you intend on saying yes should Chase ask?"

"I gave up fried chicken for him."

"Well, technically, you gave up the willful acquisition of fried chicken, relying on someone else to provide it for you, but that's close enough. You're trusting him with your fried chicken supply."

"He makes lasagna. From scratch. I'm pretty sure he said he was making it yesterday, but I don't remember if he did."

"You were mostly asleep when you were eating it, but you seemed to really enjoy it. By that, he tried to take your empty plate away and got snapped at. You hadn't licked it sufficiently."

I foresaw a lifetime of embarrassing myself over food. "I should apologize for that when I get a chance."

"Don't worry about it. He gave you another piece and you got teary eyed because you liked it so much. While we understand the medications are mostly to blame, I think he took it as the compliment it is. Ask him to make turkey for you sometime. He learned that one from his grandmother, and if you're lucky, he'll be the one cooking dinner this year."

"Turkey? He makes turkey?"

"It's not chicken, so you can ask for it whenever you want. And, if he's feeling up for a challenge, he'll deep-fry it for you. He's not above taking a few risks for a good dinner."

"He's probably a better cook than I am."

"That'll make him happy. He likes pulling his own weight in everything he does. Expect some posturing when it comes to your boy, as Chase will try to compete with a divine." Chase's mother rolled her eyes. "I'd be more upset over this, but at least he's being stubborn for a good cause."

As my son's happiness was the best cause I could think of, I nodded. "I can work with that, but I draw the line at them actively fighting over it."

"That's a reasonable line to draw. You realize you made a mistake, right?"

"I did? What mistake?"

"You didn't specify the number of computers my husband is to buy."

"But I did. A laptop and a desktop. We spent how long talking about them?"

"Ah, but you didn't specify how many of each." Chase's mother pointed at me, and then she pointed at Chase. "My husband is not a reasonable man. In the future, specify. You can thank me later."

What had I gotten myself into?

SEVENTEEN

The worst he could do was say no.

I SURVIVED THE SHOPPING EXPEDITION, and I even managed to buy my son several presents without the interference of Tiana, Chase, or his family. I'd avoided gaming consoles mostly due to their costs, but I spent some of the money I'd been squirreling away to get him a portable system and a few games to start him off. I even picked one game destined to occupy his time more than I liked.

Collecting things in a game meant he wouldn't be collecting things in the apartment, and I thought everyone won as he could indulge in his OCD tendencies without driving me insane in the process.

Add in a fortune of puppy supplies, which I would wrap individually and organize so he'd open them in the order I wanted, and I thought I'd do okay on giving Caleb the best present possible.

The lie I'd told to Chase's mother would be exposed soon enough. If Chase didn't ask, I would, and I meant to give

Caleb something even better than a puppy: a second father to fill the spaces when Gavin couldn't be around. Chase wouldn't replace Gavin, and I'd make certain my son knew it, but whenever he needed a father figure in his life, he'd have one. On the big events, I'd make sure he had two.

I'd give Chase until Christmas to take the initiative, and if he didn't, I had some red string with his name on it. It'd only take a few minutes for me to braid it into something vaguely ring shaped. While I wouldn't win any awards for creativity or investments, I thought I'd be able to get the point across with my choice.

The worst he could do was say no.

A mountain of bags and boxes occupied the SUV, and everyone except Chase's father had to hold something on their lap. To make it clear I'd been had, Chase's father made me carry the bag containing multiple laptops, and he'd had them gift wrapped at the store so I couldn't investigate.

Instead of taking out my share of the presents, Chase's parents evicted me from the vehicle upon arrival and ordered me to go away.

"But I need to wrap those!"

"You can wrap another day. Have Chase bring you over sometime during the week. I'll even feed you your favorite," Chase's mother replied.

I couldn't win with his family. I waved my fist at Chase. "This is your fault."

"It really is. I've been told they were perfectly reasonable people before I was born, then I came around and made a mess of everything." Chase grinned at me, put his hands on my shoulders, and pushed me towards his house.

I wasn't the only one to look up to make certain no one

was about to drop another bag of almond flour on my head. With no evidence of impending assault, Chase unlocked his door. His father joined us on the porch and peeked inside the house.

Chase frowned, stepped inside, and headed for the living room where we'd left Pupperina crated.

The excited puppy yips I expected didn't come, and neither did the three-legged purr machine determined to make everyone happy. "Chase?"

"Dad? You need to come see this."

I followed Chase's father into the living room to discover Pupperina's crate open and empty with a note taped to the cage's door.

"Someone stole them?" My voice rose an octave. "Are you fucking serious?"

"And they want you in exchange for them."

Someone was going to die a brutal and terrible death at my hands, and I'd do so with a smile plastered on my face. "Someone stole my cat?"

"Someone broke into the house and stole both of them," Chase replied, and he pulled his phone out. "Don't touch anything. The police might be able to get evidence."

While I'd gotten angry over someone trying to kill me multiple times, the idea that someone would hurt the animals Chase had rescued from the shelter stoked a fury so intense heat washed through me. I clenched my teeth. "Why the fuck would anyone take two animals to get to *me*?"

"Your sight is a pretty amazing ability," Chase said, turning to face me. His eyes widened, and he pointed at me. "Hey, Miriah?"

"What?" I snapped. I grunted, shook my head, and took a deep breath. "Sorry. I shouldn't have snapped at you."

"You have literal smoke rolling out of your ears."

Chase's father faced me. "Huh. You really do."

Both men snapped pictures of me with their phones.

"Could you stop that? Someone took Goliath and Pupperina!"

"Dad? You want to handle calling the police? I'll call Gavin."

Chase wanted to call Gavin? I frowned. "Why?"

"Miriah, you have literal smoke pouring out of your ears. I mean, I knew you were probably packing a bit of a temper under that cool temperament, but if anyone would know why you're blowing smoke out your ears, it's that divine." Chase tapped his foot, thumbed through his contacts, and called Gavin. "Hey, Gavin? Would you happen to know why Miriah might have smoke pouring out of her ears?"

Chase blinked and stared at me. "Oh."

To my surprise, he held out the phone to me.

Careful to keep my temper from fraying completely, I took his phone and held it to my ear, which did feel warmer than usual. "Gavin?"

"What happened to get your temper up?"

"Someone stole Goliath and Pupperina."

"And that would do it." The divine sighed. "Are you all right?"

"I'm fine, but my cat might not be! And my puppy. She's just a puppy. She's been terrorized enough. Those fucking bastards left a note."

"What does it say?"

"Give me a sec." I went to the crate to read the piece of paper taped to the door. "If Chase wants to see the cat and dog again, he'll deliver me to them. The note doesn't say where, though."

"They'd probably call him later from an untraceable line. That's what crooks like this do. Does anything else look disturbed?"

"No, not that I can tell."

"That's something. Wash your clothes just in case they added some almond flour to inconvenience you. Cool your heels. You can't do anything right now."

"Like hell I can't. You're a divine. Tell me where I can find my cat and dog!"

"My cat and dog," Chase muttered.

"Mine," I howled at him.

"Just order him to marry you so you can both have equal ownership of the pets, Miriah," Gavin said, his tone resigned.

I pointed Chase's phone at him. "My cat, my dog, and you can marry me and pretend you have joint ownership. But they're mine." I returned the phone to my ear. "Like that?"

"Close enough."

"It doesn't work like that, Miriah," Chase replied.

"Like hell it doesn't! It does now. You're now under orders to marry me so you can pretend they're your cat and dog. They're actually mine, I'm just letting them live with you until I can ferry my stuff over here and refuse to leave. I have copies of the keys now."

Granted, I only had copies of the key because Chase's father had given me his.

"Thanks, Dad."

Chase's father shrugged, and nothing about his expression seemed repentant. "It saved us a stop while we were out, and I recognize when a woman is going to get what she wants. Just roll over and agree to her terms. She's a little riled up right now, though. I'd tread with care. Just give her what she wants. Anyway, don't even try to tell me this isn't the result you want. I saw you checking out jewelry stores when we were shopping. The only reason you didn't drag her in was because Tiana saw that gaming store and suggested a gaming system for Caleb."

"I want the address so I can rescue my cat and dog, and I want it now, Gavin," I hissed.

"67 West Street, first floor," he replied. "It's abandoned because of problems with the landlord and him being unable to sell, so it's been infested with squatters. The current infestation of squatters has your cat and dog. They're fine, although you may wish to bring gloves and clothes you're not afraid of ruining when you go. I also recommend you go armed. And Miriah?"

"What?"

"You officially can't say I don't cheat on your behalf now. You can thank me on Christmas Eve when I bring Caleb to that service."

"I'll thank you by not strangling you."

He laughed. "Please be careful."

"I'm probably going to need bail or an alibi," I confessed.

"I'll come up with something," he promised before hanging up.

I handed Chase his phone. "Goliath and Pupperina are at 67 West Street."

"He actually told you?"

"Yes, he did. Please excuse me a moment."

Chase and his father stared at me, with Chase's father returning to his call with the police. I began my search in the kitchen, pulling out his largest chef knife in case I couldn't find a more potent weapon. When the kitchen proved to be a bust, I expanded my search to his bedroom.

I struck gold in his nightstand, discovering a Glock hidden under a few magazines in the drawer. I checked the weapon, pleased to discover it was unloaded. Then I checked again, frowning at its unclean state. A brief blitz through his closet found a gun-cleaning kit, and I hauled it and the weapon to the dining room table. Huffing my annoyance over the state of the weapon, I dismantled it and went to work caring for the weapon. "This does you no good if you leave it just sitting in a drawer without taking proper care of it," I announced.

"You know how to handle a gun?" Chase blurted.

"If I catch you treating a good gun like this again, I'm taking you to a range and beating gun safety into you. After I'm done, I'm going to make you practice until you lose feeling in both of your hands. This is not how you care for a good gun. This is a crime against guns. Why do you even have it?"

"Apparently, I have it so you can have an opportunity to correctly tear into my ass for mishandling a firearm."

"Do you even have a carry permit?"

"No, but I did legally acquire the weapon."

"You do not store your gun in your night stand. It belongs in a gun safe. You will get a gun safe for this, am I clear?"

"I am now."

I shot another glare at him before returning to my work. I was hard at work reassembling the gun when the police arrived. As I expected them to jump on me for having a firearm out, I retrieved my purse, slapped my conceal carry permit onto the table, and went through my final checks of the weapon.

Chase, his mother, and his father stared at the carry permit with their mouths hanging open.

"Single mother of a child living in New York," I stated, raising a brow. "Do you really think I wouldn't have a gun around if I needed to protect him? I don't usually carry a gun, but you better believe I have one and will use it if someone fucks with my kid."

"I'm never going to think of your purse as harmless ever again," Chase admitted. "On the other hand, I have no problems with you being able to protect yourself. I'm just impressed you were able to get the permit. They're not easy to get here."

"Single mother of a divine's child. Add in my lack of significant magical abilities, and I was bumped into a special queue to get training and the permit. My permit is valid for New York, New Jersey, Delaware, and Maryland."

"Please don't shoot me."

"Are you going to hurt Caleb?"

"No."

"Then I have no reason to shoot you."

"You probably shouldn't be saying that in front of the police, Miriah."

I jabbed my finger at my permit. "You hurt my baby boy, and I'll use this and shove it right up your ass!"

Chase grinned at me. "All right there, little lady. Gavin's with your baby boy, so he's fine. I'm certainly not going to do anything to him, and I'm certain the police won't, either. I know a secret that'll make you feel a little better."

I glared. "What sort of secret could you possibly know that'll make me feel better?"

"Your grandfather on your mother's side is a djinn, and you were blowing steam out of your ears, not smoke. You can enjoy tormenting your mother over the holidays for her mixed heritage. Djinn are not Catholic by nature."

"Djinn? Like a genie?"

"Your mother's literally the wish child of a human and a djinn. Gavin thought I might be able to use this to keep your temper directed at someone other than me."

"That bitch! She bitched at me and crucified me about sleeping with Gavin when she's only half human?"

"Yes, she did."

"And you believe Gavin?"

"Well, he explained why your ears were steaming, and since he had a logical and immediate explanation for it, I see no reason to believe he's lying about it."

"You know that Christmas Eve service we're going to?"

"Yes. What about it?"

"We're bringing my kitty and my puppy, and you're going to be packing some death metal on your phone. She who throws rocks at me best not stand near windows, and I'm going to enjoy earning my fucking coal mine."

"Should I be concerned?"

"Only if you get in my way."

Chase shook his head, laughed, and returned to answering the cops' questions. With a murderous smile fixed into place, I waved at Officer Calrig. "Long time no see, sir."

"That gun will do you a lot more good if it's loaded," he replied before returning to questioning Chase and the disappearance of Goliath and Pupperina.

"See, Chase? Officer Calrig knows his stuff. Listen to him. So, where do you keep your ammunition?"

Chase sighed. "Shoe box in the back of my bedroom closet. It's the one with the red sticker."

"I'm buying you a gun safe tomorrow. Merry early Christmas."

IT TOOK an hour for the cops to leave, and I bit my tongue so I wouldn't lose my temper over the delays. The instant they drove away, I turned to Chase and said, "We're going."

"You're really going to need bail, aren't you?"

"When I get my hands on the fucker who stole my kitty and my puppy, you better fucking believe I'm going to need bail. But they're definitely getting a fucking smackdown for daring to touch my kitty."

"All right, all right. All I'm promising is we'll check the place out. If it looks dangerous, we're calling the police and letting them handle it. Deal?"

"That's not even fair."

"It is completely fair, and it's safest for us, for Goliath and Pupperina, and for the police, too. I'm taking you to check the place out only because if I don't, you might beat me with my own gun. I'll probably deserve it for provoking you, but I'd rather let you blow off steam on someone other than me."

"Load your father into the car. Your mother stays home and guards the fridge."

"Mom? Can you go get a fresh bucket of chicken and some tiramisu while I take Dad on a drive?"

"Bring him back intact, please. Anything else?"

Chase grinned at me. "Don't be shy, Miriah. The future grandmother spoiling package includes spoiling the mother of the child."

"A vacation."

Chase tossed his head back and laughed. "And since you can't book a flight without turning into a chameleon, that's a pretty smart request. Hey, Mom? I think she wants a vacation for Christmas."

"I'll come up with something. In the meantime, anything I can get you?"

"I could go for a cupcake."

"Now that I can handle. I know just the place. Go bring my grandkitty and grandpuppy back safe and sound. And Chase?"

"Yes, Mom?"

"I recommend if anyone gives her a reason to shoot your gun, you get out of the way."

"I'll keep that in mind. Let's get the SUV unloaded first. The last thing we need is the presents being ruined because we're in a rush. I don't savor the thought of trying to repeat Christmas shopping so close to the wire," Chase admitted.

"What he said."

I could only hope Goliath and Pupperina would be all right.

THE INSTANT I got within sniffing distance of 67 West Street, my temper crested, and I gnashed my teeth. "Do you smell that?"

Chase parked his father's SUV in the first free spot he found, lowered his window, and sniffed. "Yes, I do. Dad?"

"That smells like rotting dog shit but worse," his father complained.

I'd smelled something equally worse once, and the rank fumes would haunt me for eternity: before her bath, Pupperina had smelled similar. "Why the fuck hasn't someone reported that fucking stench?"

"Because we're in a shit part of town no one cares about. The warehouses here are rotting, and people expect it to be a dumping ground," Chase replied, killing the engine and tossing the keys to his father. "Dad, if anyone even looks at Miriah wrong, freeze them."

"Is that all I am to you? A living time stopper?"

"Yes," I said, as did Chase.

"While I understand her being mean due to her interest in earning a coal mine for Christmas, is that any way to treat your father?"

"Yes," we chorused again.

"I demand you marry her immediately."

"While she technically has ordered me to marry her, we're not actually engaged, Dad."

"Fix that immediately."

Chase rolled his eyes. "Now is not the time. That smell is very similar to what the puppies fresh from the puppy mill smelled like at the shelter. So, let me repeat myself. Now is not the time."

"Like hell it's not. She searched your house, found your

gun, cleaned it defiantly, scolded you for not taking care of it properly, and essentially coerced us into raiding a warehouse to rescue her pets. You just don't let a woman like that get away. I'm doing this as a loving father."

I rolled my eyes. "Take this seriously, please."

"I am. I'm also taking my son's happily married life seriously, too."

"Goliath and Pupperina first, delusions later. Move it!"

"You lied to me, son. You told me you'd found a nice, sweet, and gentle woman through work. Does she look like a nice, sweet, and gentle woman to you?"

"She looks like a pissed off mother who has had her territory violated. Also, be quiet, Dad. If that's a puppy mill like it smells like, we're going to have to keep her from killing somebody. If we get between her and rescuing any puppies in distress, the somebody might be us."

"While I've encouraged you to take a few more risks in your life, I never once meant for you to literally risk your life. I just thought it was important to mention that. I meant financial risks with a few forays into having a love life."

"You're going to get me killed, Dad."

"No, you're going to get yourself killed, especially if your nice, sweet, and gentle woman doesn't have patience with an inexperienced virgin." Chase's father sighed and got out of the SUV. "Move it, kids. We don't have all night, and if that *is* a puppy mill like you two think, we're going to be here all night because she's going to want to rescue those dogs."

I grimaced, but as he was right, I shrugged. "I'd say I'm sorry, but I'm really not."

"I recognize when there's a fight I can't win." Chase stared at the decaying warehouse and shook his head. "Who knows? Maybe we'll get lucky and there'll be no one inside."

"Don't ask for miracles, Chase. That way, you're not disappointed when they don't happen," his father muttered.

I had to give the older man some credit. He gave sound advice.

EIGHTEEN

Just get me into that building.

THE REEK from the warehouse made my eyes water. The block and a half to the building confirmed my fears. Even with the doors and windows closed, the sounds of whimpering puppies reached the sidewalk. Murder seemed too good of a fate for those behind the puppy mill, and when I got my hands on them, I'd earn every minute of my prison sentence.

Fuck bail. I'd deserve it, and I'd serve my time with a smile—or in community service, which was more likely due to my status as a single mother.

"Try to keep your cool, Miriah. You're steaming again," Chase whispered in my ear.

"Just get me into that building," I hissed.

While I would've broken a window and climbed in that way, Chase checked the knob, and to my utter astonishment, the door opened. The sounds of whining dogs intensified right along with my urge to beat someone senseless for being cruel to innocent animals.

"Miriah? While I'm not going to stop you if you try to beat anyone we find here for mistreating these dogs, I will stop you if you try to kill them," Chase whispered. "I can justify some violence on behalf of distressed puppies. It's a lot harder to convince a judge to give you community service if you actually kill someone."

"I can beat, but I can't murder? How is that even fair?"

"Please try to be reasonable in here."

Chase's father snorted and slipped into the warehouse. "Why is breathing necessary? I thought it couldn't get worse. I was wrong."

"Yeah. It smelled about this bad at the shelter when Miriah bathed all those poor dogs. You're going to be bathing dogs again tonight, aren't you?"

"Assuming I can get the dogs somewhere safe without being arrested, yes. Honestly, I'm expecting to be arrested tonight. Please do any parenting duties in my stead until I'm released from prison."

"Just go with it," Chase's father muttered.

"I think I can manage that. Remember what I said. No killing anyone. If you stick to no killing anyone, I'll pretend you're not beating them for a few minutes, because honestly, you're less likely to kill the fuckers than I am. I probably hit harder."

He probably did. "Good plan. I'll take care of the beating, you'll take care of the bail."

Chase sighed. "What could possibly go wrong?"

I pushed Chase's father out of the way, retrieved Chase's handgun from my purse, and checked to make sure the safety was engaged before marching deeper into the warehouse. The entry consisted of several hallways before I spotted a set of open double doors leading directly to a huge collections of cages piled on each other, most of them occupied by one or two beagles.

I halted, my eyes widening. "Beagles?"

Chase paused next to me, shaking his head. "My bet is that these are illegal medical testing lab animals. Beagles are the preferred breed for the legal labs, but the legal labs would never treat their test animals like this. While they're used for medical testing, they're treated well. No, this is probably an illegal testing lab supplier."

"How do you even know that?"

"I did some research after we helped those animals from the puppy mill. There's a huge business in illegal drug testing, as the CDC and other various government organizations don't approve a lot of new drugs and medication. They have some pretty strict controls in place, so some pharmaceuticals take the cheap route, get their animals from puppy mill operators who breed only beagles, and cut their spending down because they don't have to worry about the cruelty to animals legislations when they're working secret labs. So they keep the mandatory number of well-treated dogs for their public trials and do the equivalent of running the illegal labs in the basement. It's a huge business."

"How huge of a business?"

Chase scowled, looking over the warehouse and shaking his head. "Multi-million dollar type of business. The labs will pay hundreds to thousands for dogs of all ages. That's as far as I got with the research before I hit a roadblock."

"What sort of roadblock?"

"Locations of labs, who the buyers are, how much a single lab can move in a month with a supply of dogs, and how many dogs are sold a month. I did find out that beagles were the breed of choice, though. Beagles have a long history of being used in medical research."

"But why?"

"They're loving, dependable dogs, and once they give their loyalty, they don't change their mind. They're really good dogs."

"You can keep Pupperina, but you're rescuing one of these dogs for Caleb."

"We might have to negotiate on one dog per person in the household."

"Sold." I lifted my chin and stepped into the warehouse, searching for someone to take my temper out on. The nearest dogs cringed at our approach, which stoked my anger into a living flame writhing beneath my skin.

Chase tapped my shoulder and pointed across the dimly illuminated space to a table where someone worked bent over a table.

Perfect.

The whining dogs hid the sounds of my footsteps, and I unloaded the gun, made sure the chamber was cleared, and firmed my grip on the weapon.

Going to hell, and prison, would be worth the few minutes of satisfaction I'd get from beating the shit out of someone willing to hurt puppies to save pharmaceutical labs money and effort.

I hoped launching a sneak attack would earn me a few extra points towards my coal mine, and I wound up and smacked the asshole as hard as I could upside his head. He cried out, clutching his skull where I'd hit him. It took me three more solid blows to knock him to the floor.

Since killing him was out but kicking him wasn't, I cracked my foot into his ribs, planted my foot against his side, and rolled the fucker over so I could get a better look at him.

I recognized the older man who'd tried to go up against Chase's mother and failed. My eyes widened. "Uh, Chase? You might want to come look at this."

He hurried over, halted beside me, and his mouth dropped open. Chase turned to his father and said, "Dad? You might want to come look at this."

"It's like an echo chamber in here. What's going on?"

Chase's father took one look at the man sprawled at my feet, cursed, and snapped his fingers, pointing at my gun. "Give it to me. I'll kill the fucker myself."

Well aware it was unloaded, I handed it over. Chase's father disengaged the safety, aimed, and pulled the trigger. When the gun clicked but did nothing else, he scowled. "You unloaded the gun?"

"It's a rule of gun safety. When you hit someone with your gun, you unload it first and clear the chamber. If I can't kill him, neither can you. Same with you, Chase."

"That lying son of a bitch," Chase snarled. "I trusted him!"

"So did I," Chase's father confessed.

"Your mom sure didn't. She wanted to flay him with words alone. It seems she had good reason to even though she didn't know it." I clenched my hands into fists but forced myself to relax. "You better call the cops, and when they get here, I'll tell them I hit him with the gun. I didn't kill him, so it's not going to land me in prison for long, right?"

"I'll be very surprised if you're not released on bail right away, but all three of us are going to have to deal with breaking and entering charges and trespassing." Chase shrugged. "What's one more count of a minor misdemeanor to my list?"

"They'll just tack on a day to mine because why bother? I'll be a hundred years in the grave before I get through all the community service I've been assigned. But, to make sure he doesn't actually die, I've put him in timeout. That will probably land me an extra three or four days and another fine. But at least this time I can say I'm doing it for a good cause, right?"

"Sure, Dad. Whatever you say."

"Go find Miriah's kitty and her puppy before the cops get here. I'll take care of calling them. I'm sure Officer Calrig will be *so* happy to see us again tonight. We should've just brought him with us."

I shook my head. "No."

"Why not?"

"I wouldn't have been able to hit the fucker if the cops were here."

"True, true. Go find your kitty. I'll hold down the fort."

I FOUND Goliath and Pupperina sharing a cage tucked away in a corner, and I considered going back and killing Chase's employee for daring to steal my cat and traumatize my puppy. I handed Pupperina to Chase and buried my face in Goliath's fur. As always, he purred when I held him.

The cops arrived shortly later, although Officer Calrig

wasn't among them. The questioning session started before I even had a chance to introduce myself, and when one of the officers tried to take Goliath from me, I clutched my cat and snarled curses.

"Sorry, sir. He's our cat, and he was stolen from my house," Chase explained. "She's really fond of him. His name's Goliath. Anyway, we were out shopping when someone came and stole our pets. Officer Calrig and Officer Yamos are in charge of the investigation. We were told someone here might have information on our missing pets, so we came here to find out what we could. We didn't think we'd find this."

Goliath, as though sensing the police wanted to take him away, shoved his head under my chin and intensified his purr, clutching me with his paws.

"They're your pets? They were stolen?" the cops exchanged looks, and after a few minutes of debate, one of them got the brilliant idea to confirm our claim with the pair of cops who knew us. Once confirmed, we were ordered to wait nearby without touching anything.

"Want to make bets on how long this takes?" Chase whispered.

"No. Why am I saying no? Because there are hundreds of poor dogs in here needing baths. Hundreds of them. This place is awful."

"They'll be okay. The police will make sure they're placed with a shelter and are taken care of."

"They better."

Chase laughed. "You're just ready to take heads as trophies tonight. Did the shopping get under your skin that much? I'm sorry. If I'd known it would stress you out so much, we could've lounged on the couch and ordered stuff online and planned for an unChristmas to take place as soon as the packages arrived."

"He broke into your house, stole pets he believed belonged to you, in exchange for me. That's just awful."

"And I had no idea he was even involved. First Denise, then Craig? I'm going to have to take a close look at the employee list and see who else is involved. I don't like my suspicions. My CFO may be involved, but I'm not certain; he's never gotten on that well with Craig, but a lot of my marketing department work closely with him. What I want to know is why he'd be working on the side somewhere like here while also siphoning millions of dollars from my company. To make things worse, considering the dynamics at the office, I'll have to take a closer look at ten other upper management employees. This goes beyond simple embezzlement. Pharmaceutical companies and labs would've paid a lot for these dogs."

"I'm sorry."

Chase shot me a look, and I couldn't tell if he was annoyed with me or not. "Don't be sorry for something you didn't do. I asked you to come into my company and help me. You have. I'll still need those eyes of yours for a while, but I meant everything I said about how I want you involved with my business. Eventually, if you're game, our business. We can even work on a plan to lure Tiana over to the dark side. Alex might forgive me, especially when he finds out about Craig's activities. I'm going to need a strong marketer, and he's always trying to bring up fresh blood. I can probably cut him some form of deal where he'll let me hire Tiana out from under him without holding it against me for long.

I'll probably have to let him borrow you every now and then."

"I don't mind helping him if I get poached."

"I figured you wouldn't. You like helping people. Animals, too." Chase made a thoughtful sound in his throat. "Wait here a second."

He went to talk to the police, and on his way over, he handed Pupperina to his father along with a stern warning not to lose her. Within a few minutes, he returned, a pleased, smug expression on his face.

"What did you do?"

"I lowered the police's dog relocation problem by two. We'll have to wait for some paperwork, plus we'll have to swing by the station because someone—you, to be specific—needs to acknowledge you're being released without holding and bail and promise to show up for a hearing where you'll be assigned some form of community service. We're old hats at this, especially Dad. You can thank Dad later for smoothing the way on that one."

"Theft of a pet equates to provocation. Add in the animal abuse laws and the horror show this place is, and any reasonable animal lover would snap when spotting a potential culprit. Slap on the wrist," his father confirmed. "How are you helping with the dog relocation problem?"

"I'm going to take Goliath. Miriah is going to look around the cages and pick two puppies to take home with us. I'll call an emergency clinic, and we'll drop them off along with rescues in critical need of care while on route to the police station. We'll go back after we've dealt with the legalities. I already got approval from the cops to do it, too."

I handed Goliath over before turning in a slow circle,

taking in the numerous cages and the dogs trapped within. Given my way, I would've taken them all and tried to love them like they deserved. Being able to pick only two hurt. Was I better off picking young puppies? Older dogs? One of each?

How was I supposed to pick only two?

I explored the warehouse, watching the animals and approaching each cage to watch the occupant—or occupants. Most were older, but down one of the narrow pathways between cages, I found a trio of puppies alone that looked too young to be separated from their mother.

I crouched, open the cage, and picked up the first, who whined and wiggled in my hand.

As I meant to earn a coal mine, I would begin with changing the number of animals I'd rescue from two to three. I scooped up the other puppies, cradled them in my arm, and returned to Chase. "I have a new way of counting," I announced.

"Do tell," Chase replied, arching a brow and counting the puppies I held.

"One, more than one. These are more than one, and they don't have a mother. They're too young to be without a mother."

"I can't win this one, so we'll go with one, more than one math in this instance. I'll be right back and inform the police that I've helped relocate an extra unexpectedly."

Chase's father chuckled. "Found them together in the same cage?"

I nodded.

"It couldn't be helped. Don't worry. Chase likes dogs, and if four dogs becomes too much to handle, I'll talk the wife into taking one of them. She won't mind. This little girl might come home with me so the litter isn't separated if that's the case. She's weird but cute."

"Like hell you'll take one of my dogs," I muttered. "And you're not allowed to take my cat, either."

"I see four dogs is not going to become too much to handle, will it?"

"Over my dead body."

"Good to know."

I huffed, lifted my chin, and strode to Chase, who worked to secure approval for me to rescue the trio of puppies I couldn't bear to leave behind.

THE EMERGENCY CLINIC receptionist took one look at my three puppies and the steady stream of crates Chase and his father hauled in, called for the vet immediately, and confiscated my puppies with a promise they'd be ready for us to pick up in a few hours. The other dogs would stay longer, but the woman assured me they'd worked with the police before and would take care of everything. They weren't the only puppies to join the fray, as the police brought over crates of the ones worse off for emergency treatments. Chase gave them his payment information, paid the basic examination fee before we left, and drove us to the police station for the next stage of our night.

Goliath and Pupperina tolerated the activity better than I thought, although Chase bought two carriers at the vets to ensure they wouldn't get lost in the chaos.

Two hours after arrival, which involved three questioning sessions, more forms than I cared to think about, and a list of charges I'd face at my hearing in a few days. The cops seemed convinced I'd face some form of community service and no permanent mark on my record.

Nobody liked animal abusers, and the puppy mill operation broke Federal law.

"They'll give her thirty days of community service, and my bets are with a restriction to shelters and animal services," Chase's father predicted. "They'll slap me with a few days out of pure spite with no limitations on what I do. You? You'll walk away without anything because you're a brat."

Chase grinned. "They'll give me thirty days hoping she'll teach me better manners and ethics, and they'll tie my community service work with hers. Look on the bright side, Dad. You didn't have to pay any bail tonight, and as the most responsible adult currently present, that job would've fallen to you."

"You think he's responsible?" I blurted.

"I also think he dropped me on my head a few times when I was a baby, but what can I say? He is my father, and I try to give him some credit from time to time. It makes him feel important."

"I need to feel important at least once a day. If I don't, I whine."

I gave up. "Do whatever you want. Can we leave yet? We have to rescue the puppies from the vet."

Chase laughed, confirmed with the police we could leave, and drove us back to the vets, who'd given the three beagles a bath, checked them over, and determined they were somewhere between two to four weeks old, but thanks to malnutrition, the vet wasn't certain. They still needed milk, which would require an emergency trip to the store to get some as the clinic didn't have enough in stock with the other puppies in need of care.

Through it all, Pupperina and Goliath dozed in their new carriers while waiting for us to take them home.

After paying for everything, Chase looked me in the eyes and announced, "You're not naming them."

I laughed. "So I guess Latte, Tiramisu, and Lasagna are out?"

"For names of these puppies, yes. For dinner tomorrow, no."

I could work with that.

NINETEEN

I loved my best frenemy.

UNSATISFIED WITH CRAIG'S ARREST, which led to Timothy's arrest following the first questioning session, Chase threw himself into his work, convinced someone else working within his company was still involved with the puppy mill operation and the siphoning of his funds. Worse, he worried the funds might've been used to subsidize the puppy mill, something that infuriated him to the breaking point.

I found it amusing Chase's frantic work routine involved drinking so much tea he might float away and a tendency to mutter curses under his breath. Each day, from the moment he woke up to the moment he fell asleep, often on his couch still working, he focused on ferreting out the guilty. Sometimes he went to the office, and when he did, the entire circus went with him, and I was given the job of caring for puppies and keeping a close eye on my cat.

Two days after we'd rescued the three puppies, I coerced Chase into taking the entire circus to my apartment so I could retrieve my regular firearm. While there, I looked Chase in the eyes while I packed my things, including my old desktop, filling every spare inch of space in his car.

It took three trips to transfer enough of my things to satisfy myself that Chase had no doubt I'd staged a takeover of his home. In a bid to play almost hard to get, I took over a guest bedroom. I'd stage my invasion of his bedroom immediately following the Christmas Eve service, and I'd recruited Tiana to pick me up something a lot slutty with a bow and a collar customized to read 'Ho, Ho, Ho.'

I'd even talked her into picking up a matching leash. She'd found the whole idea hilarious, and she promised she'd show up at the service with a wrapped present for me so I wouldn't scandalize my son.

To sweeten the deal, she even planned to think about the purchase a lot to make Gavin uncomfortable.

I loved my best frenemy.

Four days before Christmas, I determined if I wanted Chase to stop working in my lifetime, I'd have to solve the mystery for him since he wasn't having any luck solving it himself. I began with Timothy Gaithers; with his higher position within Chase's company, I suspected all roads led to him in one fashion or another. Chase kept his search to evidence within his company.

I looked for motive, and I doubted it would be found within Chase's business.

What would drive a man into trying to kill someone to protect a money source? Why join forces with so many in a reeking warehouse full of abused dogs? No sane man would. At last count, the police had apprehended fifty-three accomplices, seven of whom had worked for Chase.

I believed something drove Timothy into a dive into the deep end. But what?

Snooping around in Chase's files after he went to bed classified me as a bad person, but I swore to ignore my guilty conscious and snooped into the former employee's personal life. On paper, he had everything. His parents, both over a hundred years old, still ran an investment firm, although a note in Chase's files indicated the pair would retire sometime soon.

Timothy was second in line to inherit the role of CEO.

As Chase had wasted a week on dead leads within his company, I decided to give Gaithers Mutual Funds and Investments a thorough looking over. Of all the reasons I might dive off the deep end, family came in number one. While I liked to pretend I was a decent human being, I'd do a lot more than beg, cheat, and steal to protect Caleb.

I'd raised Caleb to put family first. I'd caught him lying to protect me more than once, although I tried to contain his fibbing to the white lies meant to make people feel better than crueler deceptions. Some days, I wondered how well I succeeded.

Within twenty minutes of starting my search, I uncovered that Gaithers Mutual Funds and Investments had laid off a quarter of its staff several years ago. Since then, the publicly traded company had suffered from falling stock figures, although it'd stabilized to something I might consider healthy comparatively.

Frowning, I dug out the reports revealing how much money Chase had lost. If a struggling investment firm needed to pay out portfolios and had run out of money, I could see someone siphoning funds from somewhere else to keep the business afloat long enough for there to be a recovery—or a change of management.

No one wanted to inherit a sinking ship, and I could see numerous ways an enterprising individual might stage a buyout, especially if he believed he could turn the sinking ship into a thriving business.

The police had already confirmed Timothy had the talent required to mask the truth in the reports, a talent my eyes could see through.

No wonder the asshole had wanted me out of the way. He could've gotten away with it for months—maybe even years —longer if not for me. The puppy mill operation bothered me, but I suspected Chase had been onto something.

A little research implied each dog could be worth up to several thousand dollars on the illegal market, and a large-scale pharmaceutical firm would need hundreds of dogs to do their tests. The age of the dog mattered, too. Some firms might need younger dogs, some might need older dogs, and the firms didn't necessarily need healthy dogs.

In fact, I suspected some of the firms might want sickly dogs to test cures on them for a variety of ailments.

On the legal market, a single dog might earn a breeder even more than the illegal dogs, but the requirements for a dog to be suitable for medical testing boggled my mind. The government's requirements for ethical treatment ensured the animals had a dedicated caretaker, they were given the best conditions possible in a lab setting, and underwent constant evaluations to ensure they were treated in a humane fashion.

The dogs that survived the trials underwent extensive treatments to ensure the rest of their lives were spent happy and healthy, and they were put up for adoption. The ones who weren't so lucky were given humane deaths, and their bodies went to schools for education purposes.

They helped teach doctors and nurses about the diseases humans suffered, and some helped train veterinarians so they could help pets live happy lives.

I could accept that. I couldn't accept what I'd seen in the puppy mill.

If I ever got Timothy alone in a dark alley, one of us wouldn't be leaving alive, and I'd do my damnedest to make sure his next home was the cemetery. If opportunity allowed, I'd bury him in a pet cemetery so the spirits of the furry dead could torment him for all eternity.

Fortunately for Timothy, the last time I'd checked, he'd been denied bail along with Craig and Denise. The initial trial would begin sometime after Christmas, and I expected both would be slapped on the wrist and given community service for the majority of their punishment.

The prison time for any attempted murder charges would be partially covered during their wait in holding for their trial's completion, which could take a year or longer depending on how complicated the case became. The reality of the situation annoyed Chase far more than it annoyed me.

No amount of prison time would undo their crimes, and I rather liked the idea of some rich, old fart of a goon being forced to serve others as punishment.

He'd hate it, and that was good enough for me.

To gather as much information as I could on Timothy and his family's business, I made a pot of coffee, tip-toed around the dozing Chase, who kept all five animals company on the couch, and did my best to give him a miracle.

My reasons were purely selfish in nature, as I'd have no chance of verifying my tramp stamp if Chase worked himself into an early grave.

In the morning, hopefully after I figured out the missing pieces of the puzzle, he'd be able to do something other than work and sleep for a change.

AT SIX IN THE MORNING, I found several lawsuits buried in the court system accusing Gaithers Mutual Funds and Investments of stealing funds from investment accounts to pay off withdraws and maintain the appearance of being a thriving company. What happened to the funds I couldn't guess, but I suspected it had something to do with the Gaithers and their excessive family homes with excessive price tags of several million apiece.

Stealing Chase's money would allow them to maintain the ruse long enough to survive the court investigation—maybe.

I suspected Timothy used the money to replenish the money stolen from various accounts at his parents' firm to cover up the losses while the company was investigated.

If the numbers matched and they claimed the portfolios hadn't performed well, a lazy investigator might be fooled.

When I estimated the value of the dogs and the amount Chase's business had lost, it made a lot of sense to me. I emailed Chase a copy of the court filings, linked to the performance history of Gaithers Mutual Funds and Investments, and called it a night. A glance at the clock promised I wouldn't have time to catch a nap, so I made a new cup of coffee and started tea for the morning zombie.

To my amusement, Chase and his companions all fought waking up, although I had an easier time coaxing the puppies and my kitty to cooperate. Goliath moved like a bat out of hell the instant I opened his can of wet food, and Pupperina barreled over hot on his heels. The trio of babies needed more care from me, and Chase finally got on the move while I had all three on my lap drinking warmed replacer milk from a bottle.

"You're too awake for this early in the morning," he complained on his way to the kitchen. A few grunts, what I suspected was a mumbled thanks, and some slurps later, he returned to the living room. "Why are you still in your clothes from last night?"

I pointed at his laptop. "Merry Christmas."

"Christmas isn't for a few more days."

"I'm bored of watching you work so I finished your work for you. Merry Christmas."

Chase narrowed his eyes. "You did what? How?"

"I followed the money." As my answer would likely drive him crazy, I smiled. "That's what I do. I talk to the numbers, and they talk back. We had a delightful conversation last night while you were sleeping on the couch. Were you aware you have a bed in this house? I'm sure the puppies wouldn't mind sleeping there, too. You don't have to sleep on the couch to keep the zoo company."

"You followed the money? How?" Chase sat on the couch, set his tea aside, and grabbed his laptop. It amazed me the computer survived through Chase's careless handling of it. Then again, I rescued it the nights he didn't find his way to bed. My rescuing likely had a lot to do with his laptop still working. "What did you send me? This is timestamped at six in the morning, Miriah."

"Well, it took me until six in the morning to figure it out. I just wanted to know why Timothy would need all that money and need even more money after taking so much from you. Honestly, I'd started with medical research using dogs as my starting point to figure out how much the poor puppies were worth."

"What'd you figure out?"

"The puppies are worth around two grand, and the older dogs can be worth up to five grand, roughly. Maybe more if the dog has a specific ailment they're looking to treat." The thought of why Timothy and his accomplices would abuse animals annoyed me into grunting and hunting down another cup of coffee so I wouldn't take my agitation out on Chase. "The CDC had a page reporting the most they'd found was seven thousand for a specific animal with a specific ailment. Then the pharmaceuticals save tens of thousands because the animal treatment laws require medical testing animals to be treated with upmost care. From my understanding of what I read, it can cost them upwards of thirty to forty thousand in extra expenses per dog for caring for them during testing and afterwards if they survive, and they're not allowed to kill the dogs if they survive through testing for autopsy. They have to be treated and placed in a good home."

"They pay some asshole a few thousand to save themselves a fortune? That's disgusting."

"So, the lawsuits I sent you accuse Gaithers Mutual Funds and Investments of mishandling funds. It looks like Timothy was working to replenish the accounts in his parents' company *or* working to ensure he fully inherited the business. Maybe both. If I add the puppy mill operation profits and what was stolen from your company, it's the type of money that might be able to hide the thefts in the Gaithers operations."

"Add in some bribes to the right people, and I could see a business dodging the full brunt of their scam in the courts. I'd been so busy trying to root out any other participants I failed to look for additional information," he admitted.

"I'm just tired of watching you work day in and day out. It's almost Christmas, and you are done doing overtime because of that piece of shit."

Chase arched a brow. "I see you have opinions you wish to share with me."

"No more overtime until January at the absolute earliest. Non-negotiable."

"I see you find overtime offensive."

"Overtime would be easier to deal with if you weren't exhausting yourself. I had time to claim an entire room for Caleb and set it up. I'm still working on how to get out of my lease with my landlord, as I have decided I'll be staging a permanent invasion as a Christmas present to myself."

"Well, you certainly seem to know what you want for Christmas."

"Think that's worth a few points towards my coal mine?"

"Definitely. All right. The office is closed until after the holidays, so I do have to do some stuff to make sure this is taken care of. I'll forward your emails to Dad and have him do his fair share of the work, too."

"What about your mother?"

"You're joking, right? Mom's probably ready to kill my father for working overtime, too. And I'm not even realistically paying him for it, either."

"Wrote in a clause he'd only be paid when present in the office?" I guessed.

Chase grinned. "As a matter of fact, yes."

"Well done. Did you get his agreement to pay for any future weddings and fifty thousand per chameleon incident notarized?"

"I have the paperwork. I locked it up at a bank, I had three certified copies made, and I've hidden them in safe locations. My father looked rather miffed about my precautions, but I enjoyed reminding him New York weddings are serious business. I'd be worried, by the way."

"Why?"

"He's informed me he's sneaking in several hats sized for chameleons into the Christmas Eve service."

"What kinds of hats?"

"A Christmas hat and a wedding veil at a minimum. He was trying to have one of those little lady's hats made, but he's discovered they are rather complicated to create in miniature."

"Get an amendment added to that documentation. It's going to cost him ten grand for every hat after the first one."

Chase laughed. "You have yourself a deal. Since it seems I've been cruelly forced to take time off work, what do you recommend we do until Christmas?"

I didn't need to think about it for long. "Work at the shelter! Those puppies need love."

"The puppies are spread all over the city, Miriah. We can't love all of the puppies."

"We can spend several days loving puppies, even if we can't love them all."

Chase sighed, grabbed his phone, and tapped the screen before putting it to his ear. "Hey, Dad? I need a pet sitter during the days until Christmas Eve. You will have four puppies and one cat to protect with your life. Should you fail to do so, Miriah will kill us both. It seems I've been ordered to go love puppies in need of love until Christmas Eve. She's giving me the look Mom gives you when you do something incredibly stupid and is thinking of the best way to punish you. As I'm smarter and better looking than you are, I'm giving her what she wants. Also, I'm forwarding you a few emails. You can look into it while I go with Miriah to give puppies in need of love their fair share of attention."

Pleased with my victory, I sought out my cat, picked him up, and cuddled with him, burying my face in his fur. "Who is the best kitty? Yes, you are, Goliath. The absolute best kitty."

As Goliath always did when anyone even looked at him, he began to purr.

"And she's showering Goliath with her affection, although this is not unusual. Ah, yes. I've been informed we have to add an amendment to the contract. For every hat you put on Miriah's head when she's a chameleon, you must add ten thousand to her payment."

While I'd ordered him to make it for every hat after the first, I wasn't going to complain.

"Yes, Dad. Also, as one of the puppies will be Caleb's, I need you and Mom to pretend my animals are yours for the Christmas Eve service. What? Of course we're taking them

to the service. We're not going to leave them home so—"
Chase blinked. "Okay. Let me ask Miriah."

"If it involves leaving my babies unattended, the answer is no."

"Mother would like to put them in a safe place using her magic for the duration of the service. They'll be at their house, which is what we need for Christmas morning anyway. It'll make things easier Christmas morning and help make sure Caleb's puppy is a surprise. Have you decided which one you're giving to him?"

"The boy." That left me and Chase with the two girls and Pupperina. The horgi stuck to Chase like glue, which left us to accept the inevitable: she was his dog.

"Okay. Dad? We're giving him the boy beagle, so when you're preparing them for Christmas morning, make sure he goes to Caleb. I'll email you with their feeding instructions for the night and morning until we get a chance to come over. Yes, Dad. I'll make the turkey, just make sure you have all the ingredients I emailed you the other day."

He hung up, shaking his head. "They'll be around in half an hour if traffic doesn't delay them."

I set Goliath down and headed for the bathroom to take a much needed shower and change my clothes so I could catch up on doing time at the shelter.

TWENTY

You will learn the powers of a child's disappointment, Chase.

I OVERDOSED on puppies and kittens and bunnies and other small animals at the shelter and dealt with the shortest hearing in the history of hearings, resulting in thirty days of community service working in a pet shelter. Although confused if I was being punished or rewarded, I wisely kept my mouth shut.

Opening my mouth might make them change their mind, and I left the courthouse with a skip in my step.

When Christmas Eve finally rolled around, I spent the entire day wrapping presents for Caleb. After several hours of watching me work, Chase laughed and said, "I'm not sure Caleb's obsessive compulsive behaviors are solely Gavin's fault. That's insanity, Miriah."

"If they aren't wrapped just right, you will learn the powers of a child's disappointment, Chase. He will give me the look, the one that means I have failed in my sacred duty as a mother to make Christmas perfect. Then, he'll try to fix it because he can't handle the sight of imperfect wrapping paper. He measures everything, Chase. Everything. His obsessive need for perfection is definitely from his father."

"His father is far from perfection."

I rolled my eyes. "You know that, I know that, but he hasn't figured that out yet."

"Maybe you should have put all the dog toys in a single box rather than wrap them individually?"

"You will learn the value of an excited child busy opening presents tomorrow. It's the one time a year I'm guaranteed a chance to drink my coffee without having to do anything other than observe, smile at the appropriate intervals, and otherwise enjoy just doing absolutely nothing."

"Obviously, we're going to have to make sure you get a few extra quiet mornings each year moving forward."

"Lying is bad and will earn you coal for Christmas, Mr. Butler."

"I'm genuinely surprised you haven't started lying to increase your odds of acquiring a coal mine."

I laughed, added the finishing touches to Caleb's latest present, and added it to the growing pile waiting to be delivered to Chase's parents along with the menagerie. "I have to have some standards."

"I suppose maintaining some standards is a good reason."

"I think I'll have to invest at least an entire year to earn that coal mine, so I figure I'll start earning it seriously on Christmas." With only a few presents left to wrap, I'd have time to take a shower and get dressed and still leave on time to deliver Caleb's hoard, get the animals settled, and make it to the church in time for the service.

I had made a special trip, unsupervised in the middle of

the night through the clever thieving of Chase's keys and borrowing of his car, to return to my apartment long enough to pick up my little black dress and its matching heels. The real trick would be changing into my new lingerie without Chase discovering I was up to something early.

My first step in acquiring my coal mine would involve a thorough validation of my tramp stamp, and I'd put my fingers in my ears, sing gibberish, and otherwise ignore anyone's attempts to tell me I failed at acting like an actual tramp.

"Should I be worried?"

"You'll probably survive. You're useless to me dead."

Chase laughed. "Have I told you that you're nowhere near as restrained as I was led to believe? You're hardly shy, you're rather opinionated, and you're definitely assertive."

Before Chase, I hadn't been. "Thank you."

"Just how bad of a temper tantrum does he have if his presents are poorly wrapped?"

"He doesn't. He just oozes disappointment and heaves these horrible sighs making it perfectly clear I have failed as a mother. He particularly hates when I force him to cope with his perfectionism and his tendencies to obsess over it in public settings, and Christmas with family counts. He hates it, but I can't shelter him forever. No one else will in life. He needs to be able to function, and he can, but it's a challenge."

"Would it help if I told him he doesn't have to have the present instead? I can do that."

I chuckled. "That's why he limits his disappointment to horrible sighs. The first time he had a tantrum because of an improperly wrapped present, I took the present away and made him wait two weeks to get it. I informed him he could sigh and only sigh, and for every time he displayed other forms of tantrums, he'd have to wait an additional week to get it."

"Gave him an allowed outlet so he wouldn't have a complete meltdown?"

"He was four, and yes. It worked, fortunately. It's been a while since he's had a complete meltdown."

Chase eyed one of the remaining presents. "Come on. Just one. It'll be spectacular."

I joined him in a staring contest with an inanimate object, a leash and collar for Caleb's puppy. "That's the first dog-related present he gets to open, and if the meltdown isn't spectacular, I'm going to be very disappointed yet proud. It's been a while since I've tested his coping mechanisms."

"What's his least favorite color?"

"He doesn't really have one, but he hates glitter. It's impossible to get out of things."

"Ah, yes. The herpes of the craft world. I do believe I have some jarred herpes of the craft world available from another prank."

Uh oh. The confession he pranked with glitter would likely cause me trouble in the future, but it would keep Caleb occupied in his new room for at least three weeks if any got on the floor. "I can promise you a few weeks of silence and sour glares broken by the occasional disappointed sigh if you do the glitter wrapping in his bedroom and get some in the carpet."

"That is definitely earning you points towards your coal mine. Anything else?"

"If you have string or yarn, knotting it at random intervals and tying it around the present beneath the wrapping paper should drive him wild."

Chase chuckled, grabbed the leash and collar, and headed for the other room. "This will take me a while, so if you want to finish your meticulous wrapping and take a shower, I should be done by the time you're finished."

As Chase intended to drive my son absolutely wild with his wrapping job, I combined his final presents into one larger box, and I kept the wrapping neat but didn't spend the time to measure anything. I spent the extra minutes on my makeup and hair, something I rarely did.

The little black dress took a lot of wiggling to squeeze into, but it did a good job of reminding me I was a woman in addition to being a mother.

It'd been a long time since I'd dressed up for anyone. Then again, the curse had done a good job of making certain I couldn't.

While waiting for Chase to finish wrapping my son's worst nightmare for Christmas, I ferried presents to the car, giggling when I ran out of the room, resulting in me calling Chase's parents to ask for help transferring the presents.

They arrived when Chase emerged from Caleb's new bedroom. "Ack. What are you two doing here?" A few moments later, he noticed me in my dress, and he took his time admiring me. "I have no idea where you've been hiding that dress, but Merry Christmas to me. I've decided I don't actually need any presents at all this year. It seems I've been a very good boy. That dress is stunning on you."

He had no idea how right he was, and I fully intended to make it clear he'd be having a very good Christmas after the service. "Thank you. I loaded the car while you were taking care of that present, but I ran out of space, so I took the liberty of asking your parents for help moving the rest. There isn't enough room in your car for the pets and the presents."

"We really need to go retrieve your car soon," Chase muttered. "I'm also tempted to light that car on fire."

"You're not lighting my car on fire. If you light my car on fire, I'll need to get a new car, and if I need to get a new car, I'll need its trade-in value to help with the down payment."

"That's so practical it's painful," Chase complained.

"There's a reason I figured out your problems so efficiently. Being practical helps."

Chase pouted, sniffed, and captured Goliath and cuddled with him before coaxing my cat into his carrier. "For that, I'm confiscating my cat for the near future. My cat, Miriah. Mine."

I scowled as Goliath's adoption papers did list Chase as his owner. I viewed his statement as a declaration of war, one I'd win through use of my feminine charms by Christmas morning. "Keep telling yourself that, Mr. Butler."

Chase's parents cackled.

MY PARENTS likely hoped Midnight Mass would magically transform me into a proper Catholic woman. Previous years, I'd amused myself watching the other attendees and struggling to remember when I was supposed to kneel, stand, or do whatever it was they expected me to do.

Caleb and Gavin had beaten us to the church, and while

Gavin was many things, he'd taken his fatherly duties seriously, bothering to put on a suit almost as nice as Chase's for the event. I'd have to ask the secret for getting Caleb to dress up, as he wore a suit that matched his father's.

"You're late," Caleb declared, tapping his watch and giving me a dose of the death glare.

"Has the service started?" I demanded, arching a brow. Gavin shook hands with Chase and wisely dodged responsibility for our son's plucky attitude.

"Well, no."

"Then I'm not late. I didn't promise when I'd show up, just that I'd be here. I'm here. That only works when the other party is aware of the time you've decided is late, squirt. That's one confession for you for being bossy to your mother, and you can ask your grandparents to take you in for a good cleansing of your soul. It seems you need it."

Caleb gulped. "Sorry, Mom."

"That's better. And how has your trip with your father been?"

"Good! We went on a long drive, and we got to stay in a bunch of hotels." Caleb adjusted his suit and then showed it off, turning in a circle. "We got matching suits!"

"Your suit looks very nice. Don't forget to remind your father we'll be doing Christmas morning with Chase's family this year, all right?"

Caleb's brows furrowed, the first sign of trouble on the horizon as I disrupted his routines. "I don't understand why."

"It's more fun with more people, and they have space so if your grandparents want to come, they can. Have they arrived yet?"

"They're inside waiting," he mumbled.

Ah. Realization annoyed me into sighing. "They're upset you arrived before I did, aren't they?"

"Yep."

"Well, that's not for you to worry about. Go on in and ask if they'll be accepting the Butler family's invitation. We'll be in shortly."

Caleb bounced forward, grabbed me in a hug, and with the energy of someone who'd likely been given copious amounts of sugar, ran inside the church. As I was a terrible daughter and a worse Catholic, I'd enjoy watching the Midnight Mass mayhem about to unfold. "Dare I ask what sugary substance you fed him?"

"Oh, my sweet Miriah, you assume I used only sugar," Gavin replied.

"Please tell me you didn't give him coffee."

"Two cups. He'll be wired all through Midnight Mass, make it through the reception after, and pass out the instant I get him into the car."

"Clever," I conceded. "Has Tiana arrived?"

"She's inside annoying civility back into your parents because good Catholics don't show their prejudices while in church." Gavin smirked and nodded in the direction of the church's ornate double doors. "It's been a long time since I've enjoyed such entertainment."

"That's only because it takes a real idiot to invite a deity from a different pantheon to a holy day. Think they'll ask me to come to Midnight Mass next year?"

"From my understanding of the situation, I'll be surprised if they want to see you ever again after this," my former lover muttered.

I laughed. "They'd demand I return every year as a form

of penance for my bad behavior."

"Also a strong possibility. I don't think you're winning this one."

"I'll just have to be so poorly behaved tonight I'm banned from attending services again." I lifted my chin, huffed, and strode towards the double doors to begin my mission of naughtiness.

Chase matched my stride and offered me his arm. "If you come in with a man on each arm, you'll send the wrong impression."

I laughed and linked my arm with his. "You'll be scandalous enough, I'm certain. It'll be scandalous enough bringing Gavin into the church where he can potentially seduce proper Catholic girls. He has a reputation."

"It's not a good one," Gavin muttered.

Chase laughed and glanced over his shoulder at the divine. "You only have yourself to blame for that."

"It's okay, Chase. Within the next five minutes, I'm going to ruin your reputation, too. It takes skill to ruin a divine's reputation." I laughed and pulled Chase along with me. "Have you been to Midnight Mass before?"

"I think I went to church once when I was five because my grandparents took me. I'm not sure why. Honestly, I'm more impressed you got my parents to agree to come. With the way they act, they have allergies to organized religion."

"High potential for amusement," Chase's father replied.

"Well, there are some rules you should pretend to know. When we're ambushed by the nice greeters, take the papers they give you. It's an instruction manual for surviving Midnight Mass. Just look like you know what you're doing, don't be shy about singing, as frankly, half the congregation couldn't carry a tune in a bucket if their lives depended on it, so you're not going to hurt anything that way. I'm pretty sure a few of the older folks compete to see who can sing the worst and the loudest at the same time."

Chase grimaced. "It's a singalong?"

"It's only an hour and a half. You'll survive. There's food afterwards as a consolation prize for surviving. When it's time to take communion, just sit tight, and if you get suckered into joining the line, cross your hands over your heart. That's the respectful way of refusing the communion but still getting the blessing."

"How often do you get suckered into joining the line?"

"If by suckered you mean forcibly dragged, every year. Caleb will throw the fit to end all fits if he can't get his blessing. Sorry, Gavin. He's going to drag you up there."

Gavin stared at me with his mouth hanging open. "I have to get blessed by another religion's priest?"

"Remember what I said about making our son cry?"

"With unfortunate clarity."

"I have my gun in my purse, and I will shove it up your lanky white ass and fire if you put up a fight or refuse the blessing. You will play nice with the clergy of the opposing faith. Understood?"

"Yes, ma'am."

"Good. Now get in there and look excited," I ordered.

Chase bowed his head and laughed. "You amaze me."

"This is what happens when a woman gets tired of blending in, Chase," I announced. "For once in my life, I'm going to get exactly what I want. Right now, that's making sure Caleb gets his Midnight Mass. You're also not allowed to escape."

"I'm all right with this as long as you don't shove your gun up my ass and pull the trigger."

"You're safe. I have other plans for you, plans I can't complete if did such a thing. Anyway, Gavin's a divine. It'd probably tickle if I did snap and do that."

"Good to know."

Inside, chaos waited for me, and my parents leveled their worst glares in my direction. To prevent World War III from breaking out in my pew, I sat between my mother and Caleb, and in an asshole move I wouldn't forgive any time soon, they had positioned themselves so Chase, his parents, Tiana, and Gavin were stuck in the row behind us. Had my parents been thinking, they would've kept the troublemakers close at hand.

Midnight Mass started off well enough, but within five minutes, the back two pews turned into my living hell.

If Gavin blew in my ear one more time, I'd crawl over the pew and beat him senseless. To complicate matters, Chase found the whole thing amusing, and between the standing, the kneeling, the standing, the sitting, and the off-tune singing bound to give anyone with functional hearing a migraine, I'd be amazed if I survived until midnight.

Every time we stood to sing, a troublemaker behind me would start something, usually Gavin with his tendency to try to annoy me into killing him.

I made it through Silent Night without trying to kill someone, but my serenity didn't last. I had no idea where Chase's father had found a death metal version of Joy to the World, but the bastard stuck an earbud in my ear, cranked the volume, and before I comprehended what he was doing or why, I was tapping my toes and bobbing my head to the beat.

I smacked onto the pew as a chameleon, and before I could escape, Chase's father snatched me around the middle and held me up while singing at the top of his lungs.

Hissing and biting the man did nothing to free me from my predicament.

My mother screamed and fainted, my father gaped, and Chase howled with laughter.

"Oops," Gavin announced as the entire church fell silent. "Sorry about that."

Chase's father continued to belt out Joy to the World while waving me in the air.

To add to my humiliation, Chase's mother placed a Santa hat on my head and took a picture of me. "I never knew church could be so much fun."

We were going to hell.

I expected my son to have the meltdown to end all meltdowns, but instead of screaming that I'd ruined Midnight Mass for him, he hopped onto the pew, and said, "Forgive us, Father, for we have sinned."

Chase took me from his father and whispered to me, "When we get home, I know what you should do."

I stared at him quizzically.

A slow smile spread across his lips and brightened his eyes. Then, once certain he had my attention, he murmured, "You should confess. I can't wait to hear you say, 'Sorry, Daddy. I've been naughty.'"

Ho, ho, ho, and a Merry Christmas to me.

SOMEHOW, we weren't evicted from Midnight Mass, which I considered a miracle. With a little help from Gavin, my mother recovered from fainting, and he confessed in front of the entire church he was a jealous divine and had cursed me because I'd refused to marry him due to his lecherous ways. I would've been okay with it if he'd stopped there, but the divine went on and on about my better qualities.

Then, in typical Gavin fashion, he tossed Chase right under the bus and declared him the better man in front of everyone.

The benefit of being a chameleon involved changing colors and hiding. The damned red and white hat betrayed me, and I grabbed it and did my best to beat Gavin to death with it.

Chase had no trouble restraining me.

Midnight Mass resumed, the troublemakers behaved, and Gavin returned me to my seat and my human form. Since he had no shame and a love of humor, the hat transformed with me, and he used his divine magic to ensure it wasn't going anywhere without his permission.

"Death is too good of a fate for you," I hissed at him in a lull between the sitting, the standing, and the kneeling.

Since one divine wasn't sufficient to turn Midnight Mass into a circus no one would forget, an angel made an appearance, and he sat on the end of the pew next to Gavin.

Rather than smiting the interloping divine, the two chatted like old friends.

I worried the poor priest trying to lead Midnight Mass might suffer from a heart attack before the end of it.

When communion finally came around, Caleb grabbed hold of my hand twisted around in his pew, and snatched his father's hand, too. He cast a desperate look at Chase, and I fought my urge to laugh.

Chase chuckled, rose, and ruffled my son's hair. "Your mother taught me how to fend off the priest, so I should survive this."

I clamped my lips together so I wouldn't giggle.

Either to keep us out of trouble or help with the blessings, the angel tagged along, and no one faced eternal damnation by the time the priest welcomed Christmas at the stroke of midnight.

The instant Midnight Mass ended, I fled the church. Caleb laughed, grabbed my hand, and dug in his heels. "We can't leave yet, Mom!"

Like hell I couldn't. I shot Gavin a glare and mouthed a fate worse than death and eternal damnation on him if he didn't free me.

"Caleb, you get me for the reception tonight. Your mother needs to go home and make sure everything is ready for tomorrow. She's had a long day. You're not going to miss the reception, but your mother would appreciate the few extra minutes to make things perfect for tomorrow morning."

Gavin would survive until tomorrow morning if Caleb cooperated.

My son narrowed his eyes. "And you're not going to try to get out of presents tomorrow?"

"Of course not. Have I ever tried to get out of presents?" I wrinkled my nose at my son. "Your presents are safe. Unless you have a meltdown. You know the rule."

Caleb crossed his heart. "I'll be good, promise."

"Stay with your father and don't cause any trouble, okay?"

"I will. You sure you don't want to come? They might have chicken."

I admired my son's ruthlessness. "I'll survive the night without chicken."

Gavin faked a swoon.

"And you promise there will be presents tomorrow?"

"I promise there will be presents tomorrow."

"Okay. If you need to go to bed early because you're tired, it's okay. Dad promised me he'd handle the reception."

Gavin smirked at me. "Go home and get some sleep, Miriah."

The divine kept smirking, and I had no doubt the bastard knew what I had in mind—or had heard Chase's comment. I bet on both. "Have a good night. I'll see you in the morning, Caleb." I paused long enough to kiss my son's cheek before retreating to Chase's car.

Tiana intercepted me, thrusting a gift bag into my hand. Leaning close, she whispered, "Merry Christmas. Have a great time and try to get a few hours of sleep, although I expect Caleb will forgive you if you're a zombie. Chase invited me, so I'll see you in the morning. I think he wanted some adult supervision at this party."

"You're both the best and the worst friend I could possibly have."

"You can suck up tomorrow with presents. Make them good." Tiana left, and I dove for the car before someone else stopped me.

Chase unlocked the door so I could get in, and he laughed.

I waited for him to close his door before announcing, "Was that a close enough glimpse into the depths of hell for you?"

"I had no idea Midnight Mass could be so much fun. Think they'll let us come back next year?"

"I hope not. That was a nightmare."

"Hey, think about it this way. You only had to wear one hat tonight. That's something, right? It's really cute on you, too."

Chase must have hit his head sometime during Midnight Mass, as there was nothing cute about a little black dress partnered with a Santa hat. "Please take us home before I try to burn the church down."

"You wouldn't burn the church down with Caleb inside."

"I could come back later and torch it."

Chase laughed. "All right. Obviously, I need to take you home before you begin a blazing career as an arsonist."

"You're going to hell for that. I just thought you'd like to know."

"But it'll be with good company."

I couldn't argue with that, so I didn't.

The short drive felt like an eternity, and I fidgeted, careful to avoid drawing attention to Tiana's present. When he parked, I flung my belt off and slid out of the car.

"Ants up your skirt?" Chase asked, arching a brow.

"I have to use the bathroom before I explode," I lied, twisting around to snatch the bag as though I'd almost forgotten it. "Can I talk you into making me a tea, please?"

"Tea? Not hot chocolate?"

"One for each hand?"

He laughed. "I can make you one for each hand, sure."

I bailed for the house, let myself in, and bolted for the bathroom. Getting out of the little black dress took even more wiggling than getting into it, and I hopped on one foot while attempting to kick off my heels to speed up the process of stripping so I could maintain the illusion I only needed to use the bathroom.

In my hurry to escape the dress's confines, I tore it. I hissed a curse, gave up trying to salvage the damned thing, and ripped it over my head. I gave it a defiant kick before digging into Tiana's present of lingerie.

Just as I'd asked, she'd gotten something red, lacy, and barely there, which would do the trick of getting Chase's attention. A matching red collar and leash, reading 'Ho, Ho, Ho' as I'd wanted, waited at the bottom of the bag.

As an unexpected bonus, she'd included two pairs of fuzzy white cuffs.

I snatched Chase's bathrobe, shrugged into it, and made sure to cover the collar so I wouldn't expose my change of attire too soon. Emerging from the bathroom, I checked to make certain he was in the kitchen.

He was.

Excellent.

I tiptoed behind him, leaned against the door frame, and cleared my throat so he'd know I was behind him.

"You weren't kidding about being ready to explode, were you?"

"No, I wasn't." I allowed myself a smile. "I'm not."

He turned to face me, and his eyes widened as he realized I no longer wore the little black dress he liked so much. Straightening, I allowed the bathrobe to fall open. I twirled one of the handcuffs around one finger and dangled the red leash with the other. "Sorry, Daddy. I've been naughty."

He chuckled, and his eyes narrowed while he admired the little scraps of fabric I'd decided counted as lingerie. "Yes, yes you have been. Shall we go have a very Merry Christmas?"

"Please."

TWENTY-ONE

I wanted to surprise you.

I'D NEED MORE than coffee to make it through Christmas. Despite Chase's usual zombie-like state in the morning, he beat me out of bed and managed to make me coffee before I'd managed to slither into his bathrobe and flop onto the floor. In all my calculations, I'd forgotten to account for our enthusiasm keeping us up the wee hours.

Why had I thought it was a good idea to launch my seduction project the night we needed to be up at dark thirty to go to his parents place to cook dinner for the masses?

Chase chuckled, shaking his head and watching me from the doorway. "You're so tired."

"It's your fault."

"My fault? You were the one who ran into the bathroom so you could tear out of your dress. I found it on the floor. In pieces. I would've been happy to wait. You didn't have to ruin your pretty dress."

"I wanted to surprise you."

"You certainly did. I recommend you get yourself put together so we don't have to explain to Caleb why you're incapable of walking without wincing. For the record, I had no idea you were that flexible."

I hadn't, either. "You owe me a warm bath and a massage sometime in the near future."

"That's the sort of demand I can meet without complaint. Come get your coffee, get dressed, and let's head over to my parents' place. You can curl up with Goliath on the couch and take a nap until it's time to unwrap presents. If anyone asks, I'll just say you've run yourself ragged working in the animal shelters and underestimated how much sleep you actually need. Of course, that won't protect you from my parents nosing about in our business, but it is what it is. At least they'll keep their nosing about when Caleb's not around."

Since getting up and walking seemed like too much work, I crawled to Chase and used his foot as a pillow. I even wrapped my arms around his leg so he couldn't escape me. "I'm good here."

"I'll pull you into the kitchen if you don't get up."

I tightened my hold. "I'm ready. Pull me. That seems easier than crawling to my coffee."

He laughed, bent over, and stroked my hair. "I'm not sorry I tired you out, but I am sorry you're having a rough morning. I'll bring the throw blanket off the couch since you like that one."

"Please take me to the coffee."

He took me to the couch instead, and he helped me crawl onto it before bringing a steaming mug. While I tried to remember how to drink without spilling it on myself, he wandered off and returned with clothes. "I took the liberty of picking the clothes I like best, and I'm considering it a Christmas present to myself."

"Seems fair. You spared me from having to figure out how clothes work."

"In good news, you'll get to catch a nap on the drive over to my parents." Chase set my clothes beside me and retrieved his phone, checking it for messages. "I've been informed that the tree is appropriately surrounded with a mountain of presents. Actually, according to the picture, the tree is barely visible. I think my parents may have gone overboard shopping."

"I went overboard shopping."

"I ordered more things online than I probably should have, and I made my poor parents wrap it for me so my secrets would not be revealed."

I laughed. "Next year, I'm planning earlier and making use of the internet to simplify my life."

"Sounds like a plan. Drink enough of your coffee so you're functional, get dressed, and grab anything you need for today. The sooner we're off, the sooner you can go back to sleep."

"Why are we heading over at dark thirty?" I whined.

"Because I foolishly agreed to feed turkey to a bazillion people. It's my fault. I'm sure you can correct me later. Does this mean you'll move out of my guest bedroom and into my bedroom where you can reign supreme?"

"As I'm too old to be bothered with sneaking across the house to come visit you, yes. But you'll have to move my stuff. I'm too tired to move my stuff." I batted my lashes at him. "Please move my stuff?"

"I view moving your stuff as a small price to pay for convenience and the chance to share my bed with you every night. I'll even remember you're incapable of functioning after only three hours of sleep."

"Midnight Mass didn't help. Just be glad we didn't stay for the reception."

"I'm exceptionally grateful I didn't stay for that. Honestly, I'm surprised the police didn't call me to pick up my parents. They mostly behaved, which I find shocking."

"Except your Dad. Where the hell did he find a death metal version of Joy to the World?"

"I don't know, but I'm torn between smacking him and thanking him. That definitely spiced things up."

I thought about it. "You should thank him. It gave me a good excuse to run away and seduce you."

"You had that all planned out, did you?"

"Well, I certainly didn't have time to go pick up all those things. Tiana helped." Sometime next week, after I fully recovered from the holidays, I'd have to thank her properly. "The handcuffs were her contribution. The rest was all me."

"If I told you we're leaving at dark thirty because my parents relocated the party to out in the country, which is a disgustingly long drive from here, will you get upset?"

"I'm sleeping in the car, and whenever you stop for gas, I'm expecting to be fed coffee and pointed in the direction of the nearest bathroom."

"It's only two hours."

"My condition remains unchanged."

"Noted. I will endeavor to stop at places with tolerable bathrooms. Honestly, I have a ban on gas station bathrooms."

"One too many traumas?"

"I'm potentially scarred for life."

I laughed. "I'll probably manage for two hours without needing a stop, but I appreciate your concern for my trips to the bathroom."

"You really don't mind?"

"Not at all. And Caleb won't, either. It's a few extra hours with his dad."

"I'll get gas down the street, so if you'd care to have your first bathroom stop here, that'd be for the best. I'll fill a travel mug for you with coffee while you get dressed."

I eyed my clothes and contemplated if I had the energy to get dressed. Since getting dressed was mandatory to ensure Caleb's Christmas was perfect, I dragged myself to the bathroom to pull myself together long enough to reach Chase's car. It took a cold shower to wake up enough to get into the car, but even then, I conked out the instant I buckled in.

It took Chase several minutes to wake me up, and I blinked blearily at him.

"We're here," he announced.

I squinted and stared out the window at the snowy road leading beyond a metal gate. "We're at a metal gate. This isn't a house?"

"Well, we'll get to the house portion of the trip eventually. Wait here a second." Chase killed the engine, took his keys, and unlocked the gate, shoving it open before bringing the padlock back with him. "Getting this plowed was a bit of a bitch, but worth it."

"What is this place?"

"You'll see," he promised, starting his car and easing it down the access road. The snow crunched under the tires, and after twisting through the thick forest, the road opened to a giant pit flanked by a huge building I recognized as part of a mine. Construction vehicles and supply pallets littered the ground.

"This is a mine?" I pointed at the building. "Why are we at a mine?"

"Well, I regret to inform you that New York seems to have a sad lack of coal mines, so you're getting a played-out sandstone mine for Christmas. But since giving you a mine is dull and boring, I added a twist. Come on. Follow me."

I waited for him to shut the car off before I unbuckled my seatbelt, my brows furrowing. "You got me a mine? For Christmas?"

"You were working so hard to earn a coal mine, and honestly, it was pretty obvious you were struggling to be sufficiently bad to earn one. I'm hoping you don't mind the substitution. There's a catch, but you'll see once we're inside. Don't worry. The place is heated, the electricity is working, *and* there's a generator in case the power goes out."

"You got me an actual mine for Christmas?"

Chase laughed, came around the car, and planted his hands on my shoulder, bumping my door closed with his hip before pushing me along. "You'll see, you'll see," he promised.

He guided me to the door, unlocked it, and opened it.

Somewhere in the building, I heard puppies—a lot of puppies. With wide eyes, I stepped inside. On the outside, the place looked like a dead-end mining operation, but on the inside, I smelled fresh paint and cleaners. The entry had an empty desk, and Chase pointed me to a door across the room. I went over, grabbed the knob, and cracked it open.

I'd been in pet shelters enough times to recognize one when I saw it, and the new, metal cages were full of squirming beagles, many of them puppies, but some of them older dogs, their coats growing back from being shaved recently. I sucked in a breath. "Chase? Are these the animals from the puppy mill?"

"There were so many dogs the New York City shelters couldn't handle them all. They were going to be euthanized, but I cut a deal with the state to buy them some time. I told them I'd pay the boarding costs at vets and with fosters, anywhere they could stick a dog, and I'd acquire a property and get it up to their standards. This mine was up for sale, and I found a construction company willing to work around the clock to renovate it to make it acceptable for the dogs to live in while we try to find them homes. There are three hundred pups in residence, and every last one of them is now your problem. Well, mostly. This, honestly, was what I was working overtime to do. I needed to hire enough staff in the area to take care of the dogs, plus I needed to find a security team for the place. As other shelters have room, they'll be moved out to give them a higher chance of adoption, but our animals will take part of a lot of mobile adoption events."

My eyes widened. "A security team? For a pet shelter?"

Chase strode through the room full of barking dogs, stopping to stick his fingers in the cage of one with a graying nose and old, tired eyes. The beagle licked his hand, and my heart broke for the animal.

He'd probably spent all of his life in a cage waiting for someone to want him. Unable to tolerate it, I opened the cage door and picked him up, setting him down on the floor. He sniffed my hands, his ears pricking forward while he watched me with dark eyes.

Chase smiled, crouched, and petted the old dog. "I get the feeling we just adopted another dog, didn't we?"

"He's old. He shouldn't live the rest of his life in a cage."

"Yeah, he is. He gets scared in open spaces, so we have to put him in a carrier to take him outside. I'm just letting you know this so you're going in aware, but he's going to be a project. He's spent his entire life in a cage. That's where he's going to be most comfortable until he learns the house is his to explore. It's doubtful he'll be adopted with so many younger animals available. For now, none of them are up for adoption yet; they're being socialized to people, given treatments, and otherwise cared for until we're ready to start placing the animals. I've designated this as a no-kill shelter, and we'll keep animals as long as necessary. When the renovations are completed, we'll be able to board several hundred more dogs with multiple indoor playrooms. The mine pit itself will be converted to a dog park for them to play outside. There'll be a section of the shelter for cats, and we've already hired a few mousers to help keep the building clear of rodents. You probably won't see them. They're not used to people, but they're around."

"You got me a mine, you converted it to a dog shelter, and you rescued the beagles?" I whispered, and tears blurred my vision.

Chase leaned towards me and kissed my brow. "Your heart broke in that warehouse. I'm just putting it back together again. I have something to show you. A little justice was served, and while I can't claim credit for this Christmas present, well, I can't say I'm unhappy about that." Chase hopped to his feet, went back to the entry, and returned with a leash, which he handed to me. "His name is Cocoa because we agreed you like that even more than coffee."

"We?"

"Caleb is aware you are adopting a very elderly dog named Cocoa for Christmas. Honestly, I couldn't stand to leave him here, not after the vets told me it was probable he's lived his entire life in a cage. Caleb still has no idea he's getting a dog yet. It's cute. He's so jealous you're getting Cocoa, but when I told him Cocoa wasn't adoptable and would probably die in a cage otherwise, he became a pretty good sport about it. Gavin played along and suggested if he helped care for poor, elderly Cocoa, you might consider getting him a dog someday."

"That was clever, ruthless, and sneaky."

"And a temper tantrum was narrowly avoided. Good choice deciding on getting him a dog. Come on. I have one thing to show you before we get out of here. A few volunteers are coming by in a few hours to give the dogs their lunch and take them on their walks. That's been a bit of a disaster, as none of the dogs were trained to go outside, but we're bringing in trainers to help them get situated. I paid someone a disgusting amount of money to teach Cocoa this week. He mostly has the idea, but he's scared of going outside, so we'll have to deal with training pads for a while."

"Small price to pay. I cleaned up after a human infant. I think I can handle an elderly dog."

Chase grinned and led me through a maze of hallways to a small office. He sat at the computer, woke the machine up, and began playing a surveillance video. "This is why I am getting security. They let Timothy out of prison after he paid an absurd amount of bail, and well, he used his talent to get the location of the dogs. It looks like he wanted to take some of them and make a run for it." Chase pointed at the screen, which showed the mine from the outside. A chain-link fence surrounded the building, and more beagles than I could count ran around inside.

Timothy opened the gate, let himself in, and reached for the nearest dog.

Chase paused the video. "Before I continue, I should ask how you feel about extreme violence resulting in death."

"It depends?"

"There are three hundred and twenty-four dogs in that pen, and every last one of them decided they had a negative opinion about Timothy."

I grimaced. "All of them?"

"They knew who'd locked them in the cage and abused them. Honestly, the state wanted to put them all down for tearing the bastard apart, but I pointed out beagles are not dumb dogs. Timothy had tortured them. Only an idiot would expect any other result."

I thought about it. "Is it gruesome?"

"Well, the cleanup certainly was. Oddly, there's zero evidence any of the dogs actually ate any parts of Timothy, which worked in their favor. The dog that initiated the attack is in state custody, but he'll be put up for adoption as soon as it's confirmed he's not actually a risk to people. He doesn't last long, but it's definitely pretty nasty."

I shook my head. "I don't need to watch it."

Chase sighed. "That's a relief. Honestly, I've seen it a few times already, and I'd rather not watch it again. It's disgusting."

"Deserved, though."

"Definitely."

"Just how many pieces were there?"

"Well, they needed magic to get most of him off the ground. They were pretty thorough."

"Puppilante justice," I announced, lifting my chin. "Make your parents adopt the instigator. They're instigators. They should be able to handle a canine instigator."

"I'll suggest that to them. Oh, your guess about Gaithers Mutual Funds and Investments was spot on. Without his magic making a mess of things, we were able to get leads on the missing money. It all led back to his family's company. As you thought, they were taking the funds to cover up their various scams."

What an asshole. "And he came to take the dogs back?"

"We suppose, he could've been out for revenge, too. It seems I severely misjudged his character."

"It's over and done with. Let the bastard rot for all I care. Just make sure you give that first dog a lot of love. It sounds like he deserves it."

Chase chuckled. "That I can do. I'll go get a carrier for Cocoa, then we'll head to the country house for the actual festivities. I told my parents I wasn't waiting around all day to bust Cocoa out of this joint. His old, tired bones deserve a few bites of turkey with his dinner."

While I waited for Chase to get the carrier, I crouched beside Cocoa and petted him, trying my best not to cry over a man with more heart than he knew what to do with.

When he returned, I sniffled. "You need to give my heart back. You keep using it to do things that make me cry."

Chase laughed, knelt beside me, and wiped my tears away. "Believe it or not, I would've done the same even without watching you in that warehouse about to blow a fuse because you wanted to help all the dogs and couldn't. I could, so I did. The only thing I did differently was give the place to you rather than making other arrangements. There's a lot of paperwork to sign in a few weeks, but what I couldn't take care of directly, my parents did for me on my behalf."

I sniffled trying to stop my tears with minimal success. "First, you're pretty. Then you're nice. Then you're stupidly rich. Now you're being pretty, nice, and stupidly rich for me and these dogs. What did I do to deserve you?"

Chase graced me with his best smile. "You were yourself. No matter what shape you were in, you were smart, kind, and fascinating." His expression turned a little rueful. "Except that part where you bit the shit out of my hand for withholding chicken. I deserved that, but those little teeth of yours hurt. I promise I won't try to keep your chicken away from you again, just don't bite me."

I opened my mouth to suggest he should just give me the chicken without a fuss, transformed into a chameleon, and endured the excited licking of an old dog discovering a lizard for the first time.

My transformation resulted in a ride in Chase's coat, a win all things considered.

CHASE'S PARENTS lived in a large plantation house in the New York countryside, and I loved everything about the place. A bunch of cars promised we were the last arrivals, and Caleb bounded outside the instant we pulled in. I snuggled against Chase's chest, unwilling to leave his warmth to deal with my excited son expecting Christmas presents sooner rather than later.

"Where's Mom?" Caleb demanded.

"She's in my coat since she forgot the rule about not asking for chicken. Please get ready to open the front door for me so I can bring Cocoa inside."

"Does she like him?" my son asked as though he held the majority of the responsibility for my new dog.

"She cried and demanded she take him home, so yes. All I had to do was stick my fingers in his cage. She saw his old, graying muzzle and decided he wouldn't be staying in the shelter." Chase chuckled, got out of his car, and retrieved the dog from the back seat. "Is the crate ready inside?"

"It is!" Running to the front door, Caleb shifted his weight from foot to foot in his impatience to get inside. "Dad helped me pick up some last-minute supplies for him before Midnight Mass."

I loved my sneaky, generous, and sweet son—and I even grudgingly respected Gavin for enduring unnecessary Christmas Eve shopping, as we had enough dog supplies to outfit half the shelter.

"Thank you, Caleb." Chase grunted and hauled the carrier towards the house, nudging the back door of his car closed with his foot. "Did your grandparents show up?"

"They're inside helping with the cooking. Mr. Butler explained you were picking up Cocoa and told them all about the warehouse. And he had pictures of the place and your new shelter. They are dog people, and now you're their best friend for at least ten minutes. That's what Dad said."

"Ten minutes is a start. I'll take it." Chase spotted the crate in the living room near the pile of Christmas presents blocking the view of most of the tree, and set Cocoa down, opening the door. It took several minutes of coaxing to convince the old beagle to emerge, and when he did, the spacious room frightened him into the larger crate. "Poor old dude. It'll be all right. You just chill in there, and if you want to come out, you come out. You can watch us open presents."

Cocoa relaxed enough to investigate his new home. He discovered the dog bed, which seemed to puzzle him. Chase patted the soft material until the old dog climbed inside, turned in circles, and settled in for a nap.

My heart broke, and I wondered how many times it could keep shattering.

Gavin strolled into the living, laughed, and shook his head. "You're something else, Miriah. You can't even blame Mr. Butler for your current predicament. The fault is entirely on you. Set her down so she can change back, Chase. It'd be cruel to make her try to open Christmas presents while a karma chameleon."

Chase obeyed, and as soon as I skittered a safe distance from people and furniture, I popped back to human form. I shook my head to clear it. "That was my fault," I admitted.

"Not really. I did essentially goad you into it," Chase replied.

I rolled my shoulders to work out the kinks and glanced at the tree, still trapped in a prison of presents. "Caleb? Would you please bring everyone in here? If we're going to do this, we better get started or no one will be eating anything today. That's a lot of presents."

My son ran off, howling at the top of his lungs that it was time to open the presents. Within five minutes, everyone found a spot to sit in the living room. I opted to keep Cocoa company. "I vote Gavin gets to play Santa."

"I second the motion," Chase announced.

"Once again, wrong pantheon, but I'll humor you this once because I find infringing on the turf of other divines amusing."

Of course he did.

To keep Caleb from guessing too early what was in store for him, I cheated and gave Gavin directions without saying a word, and he grinned whenever I thanked him for being my lackey and being a good father despite being terrible husband material.

He wouldn't receive any physical presents from me. He didn't need them. The open invitation to visit Caleb and the chance to be part of our strange family was the best thing I could offer him. It cost me no money, it wouldn't even burden me much, but I thought it was priceless, a treasure only I could give.

Chase wouldn't mind sharing space with Caleb's father, and the knowledge I didn't even need to ask made all the difference in the world.

As expected, Caleb went straight into orbit when we unwrapped both of his new computers, and while he gushed over them, I peeked at mine before having them tucked into the corner to keep from overshadowing my son's enjoyment.

When the time came for Caleb to open the present Chase had wrapped, my son locked onto the horrific wrapping job, his eyes narrowing to a mere line. "That's just wrong."

"Made even more wrong as you're the one who gets to open it," Gavin announced, handing the booby-trapped gift over.

The realization Chase would hit multiple people with this prank sank in, and I relocated under the guise of sitting closer to Cocoa and petting him.

He licked my hand and wagged his tail.

"Is this the equivalent of coal for all the times I've been bad this year?" my son complained.

As I thought it was a brilliant idea, I did my parental duty of taking his idea and making it my own. "Yes, it is."

"Bummer. But I guess I wasn't too naughty. That was a lot of presents." Caleb eyed the tree, which still had a disturbing number of gifts piled beneath it. "Is a lot of presents."

I never thought I'd see the day my son could be overwhelmed with gifts. "Go ahead and open it."

He did, and glitter flew everywhere the instant he tore into the wrapper. My son sighed several times, which made it hard to avoid laughing. Chase's parents glared at their son.

His father pointed at Chase and muttered, "You're a bad child."

"Have fun getting that out of your house, Dad. Merry Christmas."

The string took Caleb a few minutes to unwind, but when he reached the leash and collar set inside, his brows furrowed together. He lifted it up, staring at the collar. "This is too small for Cocoa."

I did my best to appear puzzled rather than amused. "You give the weirdest gifts, Chase."

Chase rolled his eyes and kept quiet.

The next few presents, all various dog-care products, first confused Caleb, but then a mixture of annoyance and hope crept to the surface. He stared at me with open suspicion.

"You didn't even know you were getting Cocoa. Most of these are from you."

Chase's mother slipped out of the room, and moments later, she returned with Caleb's puppy, who wore a little red bow tied to his neck. She tiptoed behind my son and waited.

"That's so strange," I admitted, widening my eyes. "Why would I do something like that?"

"Mom!"

Before the temper tantrum could begin in earnest, Chase's mother placed the puppy on Caleb's lap.

While Caleb was a lot like his father in some ways, he'd inherited my inability to cope with too much good fortune without bursting into tears. Along with the tears came babbling, which I decided to ignore as it involved something about a puppy.

I waited for the worst of it to subside before I grinned. "You're still going to be partially responsible for helping with Cocoa."

Caleb resumed babbling, but I was fairly certain he swore he'd take good care of the little puppy for all eternity.

"My turn," Chase announced, and he left the room like his mother had, and when he returned, he held a purring Goliath, who ended up on my lap. Like Caleb's puppy, he wore a red ribbon around his neck. "I have reviewed your application to be a live-in cat sitter, effective immediately and for a permanent duration. To confirm your status as my live-in cat sitter, you must remove the ribbon from your cat."

I laughed and shook my head at the absurdity, but I did as told.

Tied to the ribbon was a golden ring featuring a solitaire ruby.

"I'm okay sharing you with your cat. He's devilishly cute, even when he's trying to use my face as his bed. While I'm hopeful, I'm prepared to wait until you're ready to say yes."

Some questions I didn't need to think about. From the first time I'd transformed into a chameleon when he'd walked into the room until today, one thing had become clear: I'd never meet another man like Chase Butler ever again.

Like my son, I sobbed, and once the sobbing started, I babbled. It didn't take long for my babbling to devolve into a gibbering mess. Unable to communicate an answer even if I wanted to, I held Goliath with one hand and waved the ribbon and ring with the other.

Gavin sighed, lifted his hand, and rubbed his temple. "Welcome to the rest of your life, Chase. She's trying to say yes, but it's not working very well."

While my tears blurred my vision, I couldn't have missed Chase's smile, which reflected in his eyes. "I wouldn't change her for the world."

Cheetahs Never Win is the next book in the Magical Romantic Comedy (with a body count) series. These stories, with the exception of Burn, Baby, Burn (sequel to Playing with Fire,) can be read in any order.

About R.J. Blain

RJ Blain suffers from a Moleskine journal obsession, a pen fixation, and a terrible tendency to pun without warning.

When she isn't playing pretend, she likes to think she's a cartographer and a sumi-e painter.

In her spare time, she daydreams about being a spy. Should that fail, her contingency plan involves tying her best of enemies to spinning wheels and quoting James Bond villains until she is satisfied.

RJ also writes as Susan Copperfield, Bernadette Franklin, Audrey Greene, G.P. Robbins, and Lilith Daniels. Visit RJ and her pets (the Management) at thesneakykittycritic.com.

Follow RJ & her alter egos on Bookbub:
RJ Blain
Susan Copperfield

BERNADETTE FRANKLIN
G.P. ROBBINS
AUDREY GREENE
LILITH DANIELS